Savage, grotesque, tragic . . . a[...]
Glasgow is seedier than ever. [...] [...] of John Niven,
you'll love *Bootleg Karma*.

Callum McSorley
author of *Squeaky Clean*, winner of the McIlvanney Prize for
Scottish Crime Novel of the Year, 2023

A tragicomic trawl through the hedonism and hubris of
Hollywood. In Charlie Donnelly, a failed Scottish film star
fuelled by revenge and drugs, Tinney has created the perfect
guide to America's seedy underbelly. His hallucinatory and
hilarious prose brilliantly captures the American Dream as it
turns into a coke-addled and drink-sodden nightmare.

Ewan Gault
author of *The Sound of Sirens*, longlisted for the McIlvanney
Prize for Scottish Crime Novel of the Year, 2021

Cleverly structured and maintaining an impressive intensity
throughout, John Tinney's *Bootleg Karma* gleefully extends the
thread of transgressive Scottish writing running from
James Hogg to Irvine Welsh.

Ricky Monahan Brown
author of *Stroke: A 5% Chance of Survival*

BOOTLEG KARMA

John Tinney

BOOKS

Bootleg Karma

Published by Razur Cuts Books (2024), a subsidiary of Nameless Town

Copyright © John Tinney (2024)

razurcuts.com
razurcuts@gmail.com

ISBN: 978-1-914400-75-9

Edited and typeset by Dickson Telfer
Proofread by Gillian Gardner

Author photograph courtesy of Hannah Davidson
Jacket design by John Tinney, Scott Steel and stonedart

Printed and bound by Martins the Printers, Berwick-upon-Tweed

BOOKS

nameless
town

For Erin

During the writing of *Bootleg Karma*, Elon Musk bought Twitter for a mere $44 billion, rebranding it in July 2023 as X. Given that 'X' and 'post' don't flow off the tongue as sweetly as 'Twitter' and 'tweet', John Tinney has opted to stick with the latter throughout, although the change is acknowledged towards the end of the book.

We hope this won't (and doubt it will) impact your enjoyment.

ONE YEAR AFTER EMBRACING AND MISUNDERSTANDING KARMA

I could merrily massacre all these cheese merchant hack Yank cunts in this constipation advert just to complete a solid shite again. I'd destroy their smug, fatuous grins with a semi-automatic weapon and cackle like a witch rubbing their fanny on a broomstick as the blood on the walls evoked Jackson Pollock. There'd be no more happy bastards shite-shaming me with their odds-on perfect, fuss-free toilet Maltesers and interrogating my dodgy life choices. It'd be righteous fucking carnage and a scene that could've turned that whacko cannibal Jeffrey Dahmer's stomach worse than a legless hamster in a maximum-spinning washing machine.

Fuck me, I fucking hate adverts. Even when I was in them, I wanted to sink to the bottom of the Atlantic Ocean and get chased by jellyfish with bad attitudes. Instead, I fell to the bottom of many glasses and inflamed my own bad attitude.

Those adverts were the beginning of my artistic delusions of grandeur dissolving. My fucking agent, Phil Casanova, always dangled the figures before me, and I still hadn't destroyed my brain enough to forget the tenements and crispy pancakes for dinner. So, I became a monumental whore. What else was I supposed to do in Hollywood? You're either a pimp or a whore about here. And I can drop my drawers pretty quickly when my bank balance threatens to give me dyscalculia every time I go to an ATM. Fucking Madison Avenue. Those cunts should've been sterilised before it got to this level of shite. Now it's gone too far, and we're all fucked beyond repair.

I'm trying to steer the Titanic from the giant ice cube, and this pish is my reward. American adverts are worse than any other. I'm aiming for good karma and getting served bad bullshit. Get the news back on so I can see the true face of humanity: the wars, the serial killers, the viruses, the illusion of choice, the pimps, the Wall Street whores, the swindling televangelist cunts. Make me feel better, philosophical that at least it's not me living with bombs for raindrops and a melted pop has-been with the personality of a syphilitic despot on my arm. Let me be happy. Let me keep on this karma road. Let me keep doing good things to feel better, or less of a piece of shit on a shoe getting trampled again and again without ever coming loose.

Maybe I'll get back on top or keep debt collectors off my back. Maybe my kids will give me the time of day. Maybe one day, I'll be nominated for an Oscar again. Maybe people will forget I fell so far that I appeared in adverts for douchebags and Bud Light.

I must keep a sliver of hope. This is an industry that welcomed back a cretin like Mel Gibson and kept shtum about all manner of reprehensible, bog-standard Hollywood behaviour. I only made some shite films, took a lot of drugs and was a danger to myself. Where's the harm in that?

'This just breaking in entertainment news . . .'

Great, the news comes back on after I sprint to Phil's cramped, windowless bathroom to carpet bomb the toilet. Fucking magic mushies. They're never magic on the way out, are they?

'Hey, Charlie!' Phil shouts. 'Get in here! Now! Hurry up!' Fucking pain in the bastardin hole. Phil doesn't appreciate that these magic mushrooms he pressured me into taking are running right through my system like my arsehole is an Olympic sprinter approaching the finish line. I return to the dank, fart-reeking, women-repellent living room of my lecherous agent, sit down on the sticky brown leather armchair and see myself on TV. 'The news says you're dead,' he says.

I take a moment to marvel at how young and handsome I was on that red carpet all those years ago. Then when my photo fades from the screen, I catch a glimpse of my reflection in the blackness of the segue. Who is this old, grey-haired, scruffy, bearded imposter with the Klingon forehead and a paunch? All that remains from those halcyon days is my light-blue eyes and even they're getting more bloodshot.

'Aye, it does resemble Hell in here,' I say, looking at the random bits of paper and takeaway trash strewn on the floor.

'Tributes are coming in for Charlie Donnelly on Twitter, Instagram and Facebook,' the newsreader reports.

'Shit,' Phil says, picking his beak and flicking something else to mingle with the floor debris. 'Your career died a long time ago. I suppose you were bound to catch up to it eventually.' He laughs, thinking he's a big hit for himself. 'Shit, man. You look so young there,' he goes on. 'What the fuck happened?'

Agents are only good for the ego when you need them the fucking least. Phil believes in denying the ageing process. That's why he has jet-black hair and the skin of a lizard, even though he's two years older than me at 61.

'Well, we don't aw stick Botox in oor faces and put shoe polish oan oor heids,' I say, not looking at him. Taking drugs with Phil is definite regression. I was trying to get my life back together, then I eat shrooms with a sociopath, and I'm dead. Karma comes to mind. I've spent a year helping the desperate and rescuing flea-ridden animals, trying to be good, and now I'm rewarded with gushing tributes. Who knew all I had to do was die? 'Ah'm no actually fuckin dead, though, am Ah?' I bark at the TV.

Phil guffaws like a fake laughter track. Every cunt's in their own fucking sitcom these days. That's the last thing you need when you're paranoid from hallucinogenic drugs. I get up and pace through rubbish. Corpses can't do this.

'Behind every genocidal dictator, there's a bad woman,' Phil says, looking at his fucking phone again. That thing needs launched into the sun post-haste.

'Whit the fuck you talking aboot?' I ask, taking a seat again.

'That's on your Twitter profile. I put it there as a direct quote.' He says this as if I had all the pertinent information drilled into my brain.

'Ah have a Twitter?' I say, confused, wondering if it's a terminal thing.

'Yeah, I set it up for you a week ago.' Fucking slippery, sleekit cunt. 'We put the publicity photos of you jogging and . . . all that other do-gooding and stuff. You have, like, nearly 49 thousand followers!'

'Right.' I scrunch my face, stroke my beard and look away from Phil's stupid grin to the scantily clad, Botox grannies on the TV arguing over who's the biggest cunt. These people are called Real Housewives, and I'm on social media against my will. And with 49 thousand people following me. What a fucking nightmare. 'Is 49 thousand good or bad?'

'You kidding me? It's good! It's all good, man. Instagram blew up when they saw you feeding soup to those hobos! Not bad, considering your career died around Bebo.'

I have no idea what he's talking about. I'm not sure I want to know. 'Whit does it say?' The dormant attention-seeking whore stirs.

'It's full of tributes already . . . People saying what a great actor you were.'

I keep myself from smiling, but my heart leapt for the first time in ages. I hope it's not a heart attack. These mushrooms have induced a bit of hysteria. 'Right. Well, they're no lying aboot that.'

'It was first reported last night,' Phil says, picking a slice of pizza from the floor. I'm pretty sure that's from yesterday. 'I love me some cold pizza!'

'What was first reported last night?'

'Your death,' he says, very matter of fact.

'Fuck me.'

'That would be necrophilia, Charlie.' He chuckles at his joke like he often does to avoid the sound of silence.

'Ah need tae tell people Ah'm alive.'

Phil looks at me in disbelief. 'Why would you want to do a stupid thing like that?'

'Eh?' Is it the mushrooms, or is his logic warped?

'You're in chronic debt; you can't get decent work; you're speaking in that heavy Glaswegian accent again, and you can't get . . .'

'Aye, awright, fir fuck's sake.' The last thing I need is too much reality. 'Take the glee at ma demise oot back and shoot it, then start behaving like you give a flying fuck.'

13

Phil pulls himself from the chair and stops mating with that dodgy slice of pizza. He adjusts his trousers and licks his fingers to fix some stray black hairs into a full Hitler side shed. I can sense he's about to pitch something to me, and I feel ill, yet excited. You get this feeling and accompanying sluttish anticipation after staying in Los Angeles for too long.

'You're a richer man dead,' he says, like this is the sanest idea in the world. 'Your kids will get money. Insurance money! Dead stars get a spike in sales! Your films, including that thing you wrote, will get people talking. Your kids might even love you again!'

He does have a point. He has several. There's just one major issue that's not computing.

'But Ah'm alive.'

'You call living in that crappy house in Arizona living?'

My heart sinks at the thought of returning to that ponderosa for the skint sad sack.

'You were stealing sunblock a year ago,' Phil continues, 'so your freckly Scotch Irish ass didn't spontaneously combust!' He's getting all animated now and standing within kick-to-the-balls territory. 'If this ain't hell already, it's doing a bang-up impersonation of it.'

'Remind me never tae take drugs wae you ever again,' I say, looking into eyes that remind me of black holes and mugshot photos of true crime superstars. 'You're the absolute worst person tae take drugs wae, and Ah did coke wae that action star cunt wae the turd hinging aff the back ae his heid. Fuckin cunt kept sticking digits in ma pressure points and nearly twisting ma heid aff.'

He steps over a pizza box and brings his phone to my face after sitting on my arm rest without an invitation.

'Read all these tributes and tell me you don't prefer death.'

I put on my reading glasses and look at this Twitter thing as Phil scrolls with a gormless smile.

@DumbFingerBang
Underrated actor.. shame he dead/

@sendhelpSatan
One of best of generation And Handsum!!!

@TrumpforPrez
saw him in Walmart. buying sausageswith his kid,tried to say hello. Sonofabitch woul'dnt even tak selfy wit me

'Whit the fuck?' I mumble, wondering why people would take time from the only, very finite life they get to concoct such utter pish.

'You always get some bad in with the good,' Phil mutters, as if this dangerous fiction is nothing.

'That never happened,' I say, jabbing at the screen.

Phil pulls his phone away from me as if I just hurt it. 'Yeah . . . don't be surprised if there's the occasional death threat too.'

'Death threat?' He's way too blasé about this.

'Yeah, it's just bullshitters venting.'

I rip some hairs from my chin and feel rigid and queasy. Phil's about as reassuring as finding out you're in a fallout zone. 'Why would Ah want tae read this toxic, incoherent crap?'

'Well, look at this one.'

@poetryisabitch
> Whatever happened to him? He was like Connery but less of a twat.

@angrybecauseofU
> He was robbed of that Oscar by that Spock-eared virgin spunk bubble.

@incelorgy00
> Did he no shag Monica Belluuciii? Lengend

'Ah never shagged her. Ah tried tae, but she looked at me like Ah was mentally challenged. No that Ah blame her.' I cringe at the hazy memory and wish for the ground to devour me.

'Stop getting bogged down in semantics. When the legend becomes a fact, print the legend. And leave it out there.'

'Or the len-gend.'

@GlesgaMegaJake
> Id have pumped him til the neighbours complained about the smell

@palinknowsbest
> He was a libtard Hollweirdo socialist fuckface.
> Hope he's down there with JFK and Betty White

'Whit kinda fuckin maniac didnae like Betty White? She was in *The Golden Girls*, fir fuck's sake.'

@enolagayforpay
> Good Riddance to that pro choice cunt. Chhoose life

@alwaysrightDICK

He was good in that Spielberg one, the one about the alien unionising that factory and starting a strike.

> **@spellingbeebitch**
> Spielborg? That wiz Farrelly Brothers film fucktard

@alwaysrightDICK
It's Speilberg bitch

'Ah was never in that film. And it wisnae the Farrelly cunts either. It was that German cunt wae the creepy pet meerkat.'

@anonymousperv
Who?

> **@cuntbecomeshim**
> His name is right above. Wanker

'Thank you.'

@Here4DaNips
Did he not get caught sucking his OWN dick in a McDonald's toilet???

> **@___whore**
> Think that was Gerald Cutler???

'No this shit again. It was a KFC! And Ah was shooting up smack! Ah've never been able tae suck ma ain dick.'

@steakpiesuppa9
RIP sweet prince

@stalinsbellend
He was republican

@KILSYTH90210
Yeah and now he's dead.

@FitbitLicker
Drugs always kill you in the end. They be poison!!!
Just say NO

@crack4life
Life kills you in the end. You might as well get high in the meantime.

@SirTweetsALot
Idiot

@brunchsissy
Moron

'Fuckin hell,' I say, forcing myself to look away and removing my glasses to wipe them. All this bile has created condensation. 'Dae people just fight oan here aw the time?'

'Pretty much,' Phil says, loving it and never taking his eyes away from the screen. 'It's brilliant. It's like a Pantera's box for assholes.'

'Pandora,' I say. I couldn't let that one go.

'What?' he asks me, without daring to look away from Twitter.

'It's Pandora's Box. Pantera's a heavy metal band.'

'Whatever,' he says, thrusting the phone at my face and invading my space again. His widening arse grazes my arm a bit.

'Gie's space,' I tell him, putting on my glasses and squinting at the screen.

@eatingoutllll
Needs a posthummus academy reward

'That would be nice. Ah dae like hummus, especially oan toast.'

@nosuchthingasTMI
I just shit myself!!!

@spellcheckprivy
Like Di Nero but nowhere near as good

@NotABotTotesReal
BUY CBD OIL LINK BELOW

'Whit the fuck is this CBD oil shit?' I ask the cheesing Phil, who just shrugs his shoulders.

'Never mind that,' he says, leaning over and touching my arm again with more than just his shadow. 'That's probably a bot.'

'A whit?' I say, pushing him upright and moving backwards in my chair. What is it with L.A. and all this touchy-feely hippie shite?

'A bot . . . A robot.'

'Robots can Twitter?' I gaze at two women on the telly trying to claw each other and a man crying over this staged scene. I already thought humanity was fucked, but we're in the final furlong if robots sell oil on Twitter. 'Is that no some *Terminator* shit? Should we no be unplugging them noo?'

'I think you've read enough,' Phil says, removing himself from the arm rest and hogging his phone.

'Wait a minute . . .' I pull him back and grab the phone. He sits back down and stares over my shoulder, breathing all over the top of me. I push him back a bit again.

@bythehammock
Scottish people always die young. They eat sheep intestines and fish suppers for breakfast.

@DarienScream
That cunt's no been Scottish since 1998

'Hated for being Scottish by Scottish people and non-Scottish people. Ah'm honoured.'

'Scottish people do like a fight on here, especially soccer fans,' Phil says, taking his phone from my hand like it's the Holy Grail.

'Dae Celtic have a page?'

'The Boston Celtics?'

'Naw, Glasgow Celtic. The fitba team. Ma fitba team. The team Ah always talk aboot.' Fucking knew that cunt never listened. Not that I bother to return the favour.

'Everybody has a page,' he says. I steal the phone out of his hand and he flails, spins and planks his arse down again. 'Even people like you who don't use social media have one.'

@armedbyJESUS
HEAL ROT IN HELL....HOLLYWEIRD!!!!!!!!

@LuxExterior708
Trump fscist

@armedbyJESUS
SUCK HILARY'S DICK….AFTER SHE
FUCKSS BILL IN THE ASSS!!!!

@laundrymatjunk
Did a lot of great films before he washed up. A lot
of shit ones too

@GhostofEbert
He was great in the Coen's film. I've never seen
someone so still and comfortable as a corpse. He
was a natural dead person.

Nostalgia. Sweet fucking nostalgia. All the glory
comes rushing back. The high times and the lays! The
boxers are back around the ankles, arse in the breeze,
and the vacant grin of the happy moron returns with a
vengeance. I am one of the happy advert cunts and all
because I'm dead.

Turn that frown upside down!

Accentuate the positive.

Pop philosophy comes easy when you're happy. It's
even easier when you're dead.

'See how good social media can be?' Phil says. 'It's a
great way to grow your brand and make money.'

He's always got to sully it. 'Aye, it's great if you don't
mind cunts telling ye tae dae yourself in or calling you aw
sorts ae names wae impunity.'

'Yeah, but just think about how many more followers
you'll get and how many people will buy your movies
again now that you're dead!'

I can practically see the dollar signs in Phil's mental eyes. 'Aye, there's always that,' I say.

What an age to be alive.

ONE DAY BEFORE EMBRACING AND MISUNDERSTANDING KARMA

With three hours to go before touching down on American soil, I offer my seat in first class to a pregnant woman sandwiched between a drunken prick and a twitching teen suffering from aerophobia. This minor act of charity makes me feel neutral for a few seconds before a black hole swallows me. My imagination takes me to the plane being brought down by a meteor and me drowning in the Atlantic after using all my energy to fend off molestation by a shark. That's a horrific thought, especially when I still have two full cans of shitey American beer.

Maybe I'm just bored. Maybe if I scream a Jihadi war cry, that will spruce things up a bit. No, this isn't the audience for it. You need to cater your material for your surroundings. I don't want another time like the one when I ran into A + E and shouted about my dick being too big. There were too many kids about for that. In fairness, I didn't see the kids until it was too late. It's not every day a chute collapses in a McDonald's crèche and several of the tiny victims get dotted around a hospital waiting area. That was a low point in my career, especially after the tabloids got the CCTV footage of it.

'Some people like you don't deserve something as great as an NHS,' Harry had said. That nurse kicking me out was the funniest thing in a long time. 'You've lost your way. Your maw was a nurse. You came fae panel beaters, trade unionists and unemployed people, and noo you're actor scum. Elitist. A silk stocking pretendy socialist who'd rather be caught deid in a mansion than alive in a chippie wae gherkins that look like pickled boabbies.'

'You're the one who fuckin dared me!' I pointed out to him.

'Only because Ah knew you would dae it.'

'Ah'm still in touch wae the common man,' I said, even though I knew it was bullshit.

'Just because you drink in the pub and bang wummin who speak in double negatives disnae make you Che Guevara.'

'Well, it disnae make me Mussolini either, ya prick.'

'Mussolini chewed less scenery than you, Charlie.' I remembered that really hurting at the time.

'Fuck you. You're the director, ya fuckin dick.' Always blame the direction.

'Aye, but Ah've no been able tae direct traffic since Ah lost the mojo.'

'You were bound tae lose your mojo if Ah was your muse.'

☆

I used to breeze through airports, but that was before I became a junkie. Now, a rubber digit invading my rectum occurs in cold, clinical surroundings by a probable neo-Nazi. I really should put up a fight. But if numerous pub brawls have taught me anything, it's when to accept you can't hook your way out, especially in a security-obsessed airport on the frontier between a vast empire and the subjugated.

The inside of my head burns like the most uninhabitable parts of Death Valley. It's all tumbleweed

24

and the occasional serial killer dumping a body. There's nothing else behind that big red blister of a face. How I want to pop my head between giant salad tongs until my children are orphans. I am filth. I am scum. But I'm still not scum like Shackler, the bigwig, pervert prick Hollywood producer. People like him who get to produce films because of inherited wealth, ego and arrogance will be the first against the wall if I ever become General Secretary. I'd even stick it on pay-per-view and trounce UFC and quaint porn channels into oblivion. You can kick people in the head and knock them out? That's nice. I'm crucifying hedge fund managers upside down. You can fit six Mars bars up your hole without it hitting the sides? That's cute. I'm firing Ronald McDonald out of a cannon right onto the window of my local McDonald's. That'll stop kids getting fat in that fluorescent hellhole, won't it? I'm finding all sorts of solutions to major societal issues.

Even without the probing, I rush to toilets like diarrhoea from a prolapsed shitepipe. Every fart is an ordeal, and every shite is a potential accident and emergency. I give it another year before my arsehole submits and gives me a death sentence. Poetic justice for all the curries, cocaine, meth, booze and digits from customs officials and companions. What happened to me? I used to be good. I used to be someone. I could've played Batman 15 years ago, but now? Now, I couldn't even get The Penguin to take a shite on me.

Fuck Hollywood. Fuck Hollywood up the shitter without lube and a reach around. In fact, scratch that. The old whore would probably enjoy all that. I know. I'm one to talk about whores. I'm an authority on it. My cock was glowing in the dark for nearly 20 years when I acted the goat, the maggot, and as if my life depended on it. That was before LSD made me hide in Paul Schrader's cupboard for eight hours after watching the washing machine for a full cotton intensive. That was before I tried to have a threesome with Nicola Sturgeon and Alexandra Ocasio-Cortex and got thrown out of that summit to save the whales, the world or whatever. That was before I got in a square-go with Donald Duck at Disney World. That was before Kiefer held that intervention for me, and I pissed in his fish tank after shooting up smack in his garden shed. That was before I took on that scumbag producer Shackler who liked to molest people. That was . . . well, now I'm just labouring a point. You know, and the world knows, that I'd need fucking Aquaman to locate my rock bottom.

Fuck me, how I hate those comic strip films. They're boring, derivative, artificial bullshit that could give a paracetamol a headache. Still, I'd drop my scants in a heartbeat if they would only throw me a line in one of those celluloid abortions. Fucking cunts. Everyone is a cunt. I miss Scotland, where I could toss cunt about freely. *He's a good cunt. His granny was a mad cunt.* Say cunt here, and people look at you like you're admitting to running a paedophile ring that funds ISIS. Fucking cunts.

Phil is pretending I don't exist. If you keep dodging rehab, eventually everybody declares you dead. *You need help, man. You can't keep doing this to yourself.* Sounds like a challenge to me. I can't do this to myself? Sit back and watch, ya pearl-clutching cunt. I'm going down quicker than your granny after someone lays a score in front of her. I'm already destroying guest spots on soap operas and contemplating reality TV with people who're famous for being famous or taking a cock up them in a 'stolen' video. If this is life, what fear does death hold?

I step out of the plane, and the sun is out like a parent on their first night out since their brat was born. That big yellowy-orange cunt must have a babysitter to combat the spirit-crushing hangover. I can never get used to this omnipresent, omnipotent sun. Fucking California and Arizona never stop with the light, the sun and the burning skin. It's like God's always watching, waiting for you to have a wank so he can show all his mates on HD while they piss themselves laughing. I understand vampires and goths when I feel sun like this on my skin. And I'll get melanoma soon enough if I don't hit the shade.

Arizona is to California what Paisley is to Glasgow. This is where you come to die when you don't have money. I once heard it's better to be dead in California than alive in Arizona, but whoever said that didn't know where all the best dealers are in Arizona. If you keep your imagination indulged, you can be anywhere. Why do you think some poor junkie looks ecstatic even when they're pissing themselves on the pavement outside a Tesco in Larkhall with only a tin of beans they can't open for company? Drugs, of course! Drugs aren't just good. They're the antidote to life's problems. They may also be a significant cause of said problems, but cause and effect are passé. Get yourself some decent drugs and stop taking life so seriously. Arizona should make that their motto. God knows everybody I see here is on something. Even the kids look sparkled. Maybe I just move in limited circles. My Venn diagram is narrowing. Soon it'll just be a circle with me and all the sainted wasters.

The good thing about falling so far and taking drugs for so long is that I'm fading into obscurity. Only the truly sober or the people I bore the tits off with my glory days recognise me. Even my Wisconsin fan club chapter made excuses to leave me alone. There were only three of them, but they scarpered a bit sharpish when I pulled out that crack pipe in Denny's. Those cheese merchants didn't find that cute or funny. They just looked at me like that dog no-one will ever rescue.

I stop at a McDonald's bang next to the airport and go to some speaker thing. 'Hello, you there? Give me a happy meal, please.'

'Sir, you need a car to do drive-thru!' She's said this twice to me now. The second time was even more cunty than the first.

'Well, Ah've misplaced ma car for the time being. Consider ma legs wheels,' I say this jokingly but get met with silence, then some theatrical exasperated sigh. She must think it's panto season.

'Sir. You. Need. A. Car. For. . .'

'Look, stop quoting me your daft rules, and just gie me a happy meal. You're no some android, are ye?'

'You need to come inside,' she huffs and mumbles something under her breath that sounds a bit like dick. 'This is for cars.'

'Fuckin hell. You'd think Ah was asking for ma jam roll.'

Is there any more damning proof that the human race is fucked than the inside of a fast food shitehole? Even smack can't make this place presentable. Kids overdosing on milkshakes and ice cream chasing each other into tables, chairs and walls make me think fondly of meteors, atom bombs and a Rapture where no good cunt survives. That's right, Jesus is coming back, but even the Bible-bashing cunts are getting macheted. And no before time either.

But I lived a good, Christian life!

That's it, cunt. You're the first to die for your insolence, ya Judas freak. Ah know whit you did last supper. Sound cunt is the Jesus. He was a carpenter and still managed to change the world forever. Then there's me: I've had the same boxers on for two days now and can't even be bothered to change a channel if the remote isn't within reach. But no-one's perfect. That's what I have to tell myself.

Smack doesn't always show me in my best light, but neither does the inside of a McDonald's. Too many fluorescent lights and awful shite on the menu to appeal to a reptilian has-been with no stake left in society. The guts need a salad, but the heart wants a coffee, burger, hit and a blowjob, not necessarily in that order. At least I can get a coffee and a burger without too much trouble. The smack and the blowjob can wait. And people have the cheek to say I don't have any self-control. What do those simpletons know?

'Bad things keep happening tae ye because you're loast. You're nuttin but bad decisions upon worse wans.' Why does this burger sound like my mother before she selfishly decided to die? Christ, why did she have to leave me? I was super famous then, and it's been all downhill since she died. 'It's time tae get a grip, son. Stoap biting aff mair than ye can chew. Ah didnae raise ye tae behave like this.'

'Stoap speaking tae me through a burger. Ah'm freaking out. People are beginning tae stare.'

'They're staring because you need tae sober up,' she says, calmly, to cut through all the crap. I'm guilt-tripped.

I once took peyote in a desert and ran away from a talking cactus even though I knew cacti don't speak. But this burger? This burger does seem genuinely sentient. What the fuck am I saying? Of course, this burger isn't sentient. It would never be able to stay still with these mingin gherkins writhing on it.

'You need tae dae good deeds and stoap eating this shite,' my maw says firmly. She's dead, and I'm still disappointing her with my antics. 'Stoap talking tae a burger in this shitehole, ya daft bastard.'

I need to go meet Karen, my fuck thingy, and get a drink – free drinks, preferably. Cash flow is a problem right now. Sewage flow is not. Maybe if Karen flashes enough of that cleavage and has a bartender whose mother didn't breastfeed him, we'll get a few free cocktails. Maybe the power of her cleavage is on the wane. It used to be force-sensitive.

Karen is ignoring me. She did tell me to jump in front of a train the last time I saw her. That's alright. She's just another person wishing death upon me. Social media is full of them, according to my children. But I'm informed these keyboard charmers wish death on anything with a pulse. You don't have to go on a deep dive on Twitter to find someone with a group or enough of a circle of like-minded fuckwits willing to invent new things to hate. Fuck knows how they have the energy to pull themselves off. Maybe that's the issue. Maybe if they pulled themselves off in the morning, they wouldn't fucking bring the black mushroom clouds with them. I only lasted five minutes reading the news before I got on Pornhub. People talking about saving the planet when they couldn't save a word document without calling it a chore. Fuck any more time engaging with that bullshit. I'd rather ram my piles with a fossilised donkey dick covered in sriracha.

I leave my talking burger mother and get the fuck out of McDonald's – far too many carbs and overweight children for this cowboy's liking. I stumble into a KFC across the road instead. I never understood all those junkies in bookies' toilets and railway stations hitting up until I started doing the same.

Bang!

Thud!

My skull gets smacked by a door, and it shoots up from my torso. 'You junkie fuck!' the cop says. 'Shooting heroin and trying to suck your own dick!' *Ah cannae suck ma ain dick! Ah'm no flexible enough!* This is what I want to say. Well, maybe in more understandable English to an American that can't filter accents, but I'm too busy drooling.

'Eh . . . diack . . . fex-ablita eno . . .' I am now bi-lingual, and all I needed was smack and my head getting battered by a micro-dicked cop to start speaking Latin.

☆

Jail cells are lonely places when you're in one yourself; how I'd kill for that right now. This chubby behemoth with the fire hazard beard, shaved napper and a swastika on his right hand looks a few sexual assaults short of satisfied. It doesn't help either that he's making bloodshot eyes at me like I'm Cleopatra in lingerie. I'm pretty sure I'm more a bin bag filled with farts, but hopeless Nazi romantics aren't always that discerning between gender, attractiveness and states of consciousness. I immediately get Jeff Dahmer and Himmler vibes from this leering cretin. He moves towards me like he's auditioning for George A. Romero.

'Ah know jujitsu,' I tell him. At least that's what I think I said. He backs away from me, looking haunted and confused. 'Ah had tae learn it for a John Woo film.'

'Guard!' the Nazi shouts, unhinged and way too overdramatic for me. The towering, brick-shithouse Latino guard is unimpressed when he saunters to the bars.

'What?' he asks the Nazi with contempt.

'Get me the fuck outta here!' the Nazi says, panic-stricken. 'This junkie is speaking in tongues!'

What junkie? I ask myself, looking around, expecting to see someone else.

'Fucking goddamn methhead Nazi,' the guard says, walking away.

Maybe there is a bottom. Maybe it's being able to scare off this tattooed racist tweeker with only my eyes and a mouth that has lost contact with my brain. I think of the burger, my dead mother. She was a good person, a nurse and a helper. At least she didn't get to see me become a full-blown junkie with a lousy work ethic. There's always that.

FIFTY-TWO HOURS AFTER DEATH

I've fallen down a Twitter rabbit hole, and it's taken over my life. Poor Gerry Cutler. I know how these scurrilous rumours can spread, but it's much more fun when some other poor cunt's head's in the noose.

@HWoodDailyStarz
Gerald Cutler denies sucking OWN Phallus

@LAdailyrecordo
Cutler the latest actor to deny AUTOFELLATIO

@TXSundaySport
Perversion and Hollywood: An Epidemic!

It's amazing how quickly stories take root here. A few mental comments and the gutter press are all over it.

@bolshoipigdog
He well sucked his own cock. The guy's in love with himself!

@CaptainHarlot
I bet he only cums to photos of himself or people that look exactly like him. I know the type

@yoghurtballs
HOLLYWEIRDO

@custerslastrant
All Scottish people can suck their own cocks.
FACT. The English took their backbones Lols

@KonkeyDong0
Why would he have to risk hurting his back
sucking his own dick? He's a celebrity. Plenty
of people to suck that piece of meat for him.
Yum.

@SiberianTits
It was the role he was born to play

@JUDGEDEAD8
LOCK HIM UP!!!!!!Throw AWAy KEYSS

@2411423SUM
Charlie Donnelly sucked his 2, Scotch pepil r
fucked UP bro

As you know, that was just a routine hit of skag in a
KFC toilet and GBH by a cop, but no-one wants just a
Hollywood has-been on smack. You need to throw in
some extra spice.

@GerbilOfGere
If I was Gerald Cutler Id suck me id suck me
all niggghhttt long

@KickOutTheBAMS
> Sucking your own dick isn't possible. It's just always out of reach like world peace.

I get more ice cream from the fridge. It's the low-calorie stuff that has the illusion of ice cream, but I have no intention of going back on crack, skag or Ben and Jerry's. I was the fattest junkie since that Mayor of that Canadian place looked like he'd been shooting smack with lard. And it's bad enough with the thinning grey nut and natural lines on the forehead that all the facelift junkies shoot second glances at.

@CNTNEWS
> Charlie Donnelly to be Cremated

> **@BandSubstance40**
> > RIP Charlie.

> **@anonymousalien**
> > Who da hell is that?

> **@iamharshreality**
> > Someone should tell them that shit doesn't burn

Bastard.

> **@MUTE2KILL**
> > HAVE RESPECT YOU FUCKING CUNT.

> **@iamharshreality**
> > Hey, fuck you asshole!!

@ThisIsSinema
Best actor of his generation. Also a decent writer. Tenement Porn was decent.

@crazysoup
He was so handsome back in the day the last time I saw him he looked like a wardrobe on legs.

That cunt obviously hasn't seen me since rehab and karma.

@PiginQuicksand
Charlie died doing what he loved Sucking his own dick

Lies. I never got the chance to love that because of my brittle shoulders and general inflexibility. I should've befriended a circus freak contortionist or got a few ribs removed. Nah, getting ribs removed feels like cheating. Maybe I just didn't want it enough. Maybe I don't love myself enough.

@fightfightfight
That was Gerald Cutler!!

@nocuntforoldmen
Cutler is still alive. And it's Gerrard fuckpig.

@PutinonthePres
Actually, it's Gerald. Twat.

The front door opens, and I scramble to hide the ice cream and protein bar wrappers. 'Jesus,' Phil says. 'Were you yanking your filthy chain again there?' Phil looms over me, leans in with his mixture of B.O. and aftershave, nearly choking me, and opens the laptop.

'Fuck off and don't touch that ever again,' I tell him, prying myself forward in my chair to shut the laptop again, but he picks it up from the table and stands looking at the screen.

'Twitter again? I almost wish you were on Pornhub . . . How long have you been on Twitter now?'

'Ah don't know. Ah'm Ah meant tae be timing it?'

He shakes his head like he's a disappointed parent. 'Have you even showered?'

I sniff under my left armpit, which seems ripe and needs a trim. 'Why?' Always feign ignorance. Smart people with too much information always get hassled.

'Why? Because . . . no offence, Charlie, but you smell like a mackerel's asshole.' A small part of me wishes that hurt and was a wake-up call, but I'm past caring, and Phil's opinion about standards doesn't carry much weight.

I'm staying here at Phil's in L.A. for the foreseeable after my landlord put my Arizona home on the market. That's what happens when you fake your death.

'Come on, Charlie. I know you're dead and all, but you need to keep up standards if we're going to capitalise on this whole scenario.' He picks up an empty protein bar wrapper and drops it right at his feet again. 'We can't be sitting here eating this shit and scrolling Twitter and Instagram all day.'

'You're the cunt who put me on to it,' I say, taking the laptop from the table and sitting it on my knees, waiting for the cunt to take the hint. Phil sits down in his chair, pulls a little hash pipe from his pocket and loads it with some pungent grass.

'That's what you said when you got addicted to crystal and started sticking your arms with needles,' he says before lighting the pipe at his mouth and coughing like he had stage three throat cancer. 'I told you not to do it if you couldn't handle it.'

'Sage advice fae the world's best agent,' I say, while looking at photos of myself on Twitter before I committed the cardinal sin of growing old naturally. 'Whit did Ah ever dae tae deserve you?'

'Hey, I got you reads with the Coens, Spielberg, Scorsese, Cronenberg, Bigelow and Woody Allen!' Phil puts on that Real Housewives shite again. He's definitely got another problem to add to his list.

'Aye, thanks very much for aw that, especially Woody Allen. You goat me tae read wae Woody Allen after he was persona non grata. Ah had tae take a shitstorm ae abuse for working wae him just for the production tae get pulled. Ah was never even intae Woody Allen apart fae *The Purple Rose of Cairo* and *Crimes and Misdemeanours*. Ah didnae even know aw the ins and outs of whit he was getting accused ae.' Phil looks at me as if I have a bolt through my neck and lobotomy scarring.

'Well, you should've known. He's one of the most renowned directors about. I did warn you about the hot climate.'

'Did you fuck warn me,' I say, looking at a photo of me with dark hair, a chiselled face and one chin. I momentarily lament the halcyon days, then remember I was still a bit of a miserable cunt even then. 'And whit climate? Ah was an actor without the internet, whacked oot ma skull most days. Ah might as well been living in outer fuckin space.'

'That reminds me . . . Polanski was looking for actors,' Phil says, laughing and sneering.

'Fuck off,' I say, giving him the finger and looking again at a bunch of plastic people shouting at each other on the screen.

'Yeah, you're better off dead,' he says, casually. Something tells me he's pulled this scheme before, even if he's denying it. 'Much easier to make money that way.'

'You sound like ma life was an inconvenience,' I say, skipping another article about this autofellatio garbage I supposedly did.

'Well, a lot of people live long enough for their life to become an inconvenience. Why do you think nursing homes are a booming industry?' He offers me a hit of his pipe, but I show some restraint. The smoke engulfing me will probably be enough anyway.

'How long are we gonnae spin this death shit?' I ask him while I read another half-arsed obituary that calls me an English actor.

'Spin?' Is he actually going to pretend he had nothing to do with this? Phil lies as he breathes, but I've known him long enough to make the bullshit transparent.

'Aye, spin. Ah assume it was you who put oot the news that Ah'm dead. Who else would sink that low?' Phil gives me his wounded puppy routine. An actor he is not.

'That's very cynical, Charlie,' he says, shaking his head. 'All those protein bars and exercise don't agree with you.'

'And neither dae the magic mushies you practically forced me tae take.'

'Oh, come on, Charlie!' He pulls more grass from his pocket. 'You always said hallucinogens were important for creativity and good for the soul.'

'You should be locked up in jail wae Weinstein, Shackler and the rest ae the creeps, ya fuckin bampot.'

'Okay, I know Harvey Weinstein was a monster,' he says, flippantly. 'But I'm just an agent! Pushing middling hallucinogens on creative types to get the juices flowing is part of the MO.'

'Ah don't think it is,' I say, looking at these fucking harpies screaming about their life of luxury while cunts starve and shoot each other on the news channels. 'And turn this fuckin crap off.'

'Relax, Charlie. You'll live longer.' He pulls out a tobacco tin from the leopard print man bag at his feet and throws me a joint.

'Get that away fae me,' I say, throwing it back and hitting him on the chin.

'Fuck's sake, it's only a joint of medicinal, low-grade stuff. I'm not throwing you a dildo covered in shit.'

'Ah'm an addict,' I remind the insensitive bastard.

'Addict schmadict. Weed is medicinal. One smoke won't have you sucking a smelly cock for crack . . . I don't think.'

'Aye, you really don't think. And Ah never sucked cock for crack.' I did lick that old . . . er woman's pussy for smack, though. He stands and brings that leopard print abomination over for a close-up. He reaches in and produces a slick-looking box.

'There's the smartphone you wanted me to get. I suppose that's safer than a needle.'

☆

What do you do when you're dead? Well, you find ways of wasting days just like when you were alive. Twitter, Instagram, Facebook and Reddit help with that.

@Memory_Pain
Charlie Donnelly: A Life in Pictures

Fuck me. I was a handsome bastard. I still am for a dead cunt. Liked by **@PaulaBancroft**, **@cumquat666**, **@penisreceptacle** and **@Fluidmonster**.

@cumquat66
KFC bathrooms are for sucking your own cock.

'Pry yourself away from that laptop and phone,' Phil says without looking up from his phone. He really is the first among equals when it comes to hypocrites.

'Why?' I say, not looking away from a video of a man face-planting into a rose bush. That should've been funny, but I felt nothing.

'There's the small matter of your cremation,' Phil says, grinning. He's a spoilt brat on Christmas morning, and I'm a Jehovah's Witness.

'Ah'm no goan tae ma cremation.'

'You're the guest of honour.'

'Stoap smiling like a fuckin simpleton,' I tell him. 'Ah thought you wanted me tae stay dead anyway.'

'Ain't you curious to see what your funeral will be like?' I suppose it would be interesting to see who bothered their arse to make an appearance. That way, when I really die, I can haunt the cunts who were a no show. But I am comfy in this chair and armed with a world of entertainment in my hand.

'Aye, but Ah'm meant tae be a corpse. Me suddenly being seen walking aboot outside the coffin may shatter the illusion.' I type my name into Twitter again.

'We're not gonna announce our arrival and start a song and dance number. We go casual. In disguise. Incognito!' I think fondly of Phil going missing for a while. Not necessarily death, but just abducted by the government and taken to Guantanamo for a sabbatical.

'You seriously need tae get off the drugs.'

@itsallfakenews
Charlie Donnelly was still alive????

'Need I remind you my car has tinted windows . . .'

@STATEtheFacts
He was hot. WTF happened!!!!

'And? Whit's your point?'

'My point is we go along and watch, see who arrives.' He sits at the edge of his leather chair and rubs his hands with excitement. 'Then we can go to this massage parlour I know and get our dicks greased!'

'Fir fuck's sake,' I say, feeling defeated and depressed.

'They're all Asian!'

I look at his expectant, happy face, which still carries a distinct sinister vibe. 'Ah'm no goan tae some hellhole and listening tae you pumping some poor victim fleeing poverty. Ah'm meant tae be dead!'

@hardcoremourn
DIDN'T HE SUCK OFF A SHEEP OR SUMPIN?

'Right. Well, come to the funeral, and then you can decide if you wanna do the brothel or not.' He says this like I'm the dumbest cunt going if I don't take him up on a trip to a manky brothel.

'Ah'm trying tae be good.'

'Don't start talking about karma again or lecturing me about drugs or people trafficking. Can't even get a blowjob or snort a line without thinking about the planet ending.' He sighs and sinks further into the arse indentation on his chair. 'Even Prozac gets depressed with all that talk.'

'Ma heart bleeds.'

'Yeah, that's the problem.'

> **@ManGetOut**
> WHY DO ACTORS THINK THEY
> KNOW ANYHTING BOUT ANYTHING?
> THEY DON'T KNOW NOTHING BOUT
> NOTHING,, THEY TRIP MAN.
> FUCKING DOUCHE1

'Face the facts, Charlie. Being good doesn't suit you.'
I must be on the right track.

> **@weegiebored0**
> SUCK IT, BITCH. Charlie's cock's last words
> to him ROFL!!

'Eh?'

'I said being good doesn't suit you.' He's moved forward in his seat, ready for pitch mode again. 'You're an actor, a wild-man, a reprobate!'

'Trying to be good is the only reason you're still ma agent. Ah'd rather you saw the light than cut you loose.'

'You really need to stop thinking all this hocus-pocus, voodoo shit. Good things don't happen to good people. It's all a random freakshow spinning in space.'

I suspect he might be right, but there's no way I'm agreeing with him. Fuck that.

LONG BEFORE KARMA AND DEATH

Charlie Donnelly was born the same day Queen Elizabeth II first tried a sausage supper, and the Pope first heard the Velvet Underground and didn't much care for them. At the same time, a flying saucer was spotted in the Gorbals after it was launched along with the teacup from Charlie's da, Big Charlie, at an orange order march passing under his window.

There was no phone in Big Charlie's house, and he didn't know his wife was in labour three weeks before her due date. It was a simpler time for feckless men with alcoholism like Big Charlie, who thought the telephone was the first step towards enslavement. If a broken clock can be right twice a day, then Big Charlie could be right twice in his entire adulthood.

☆

Charlie's mum, Leanne, was both the prime breadwinner and the person responsible for ensuring the house wasn't a pigsty. She had immense patience and resolve, but it didn't feel like it in the delivery room when wee Charlie was ready to slash his head through her vagina and rip her perineum in two like tissue paper.

'FFFUUUUUCK!' Leanne shouted again. It was the word of the day.

The doctor's hairy monkey knuckles were disconcerting, but not as much as his flippant attitude to her agony. 'Use your gas and air,' he repeated. Leanne couldn't reach to kick him, but she had a fertile enough imagination to picture sticking a fork in his scrotum and telling him to use the gas and air instead.

Charlie had no conception of time and no idea he'd caught everyone unaware by his imminent arrival. It was one of the many stresses he'd inflict upon his mother before she could eventually go to a cinema and see his handsome face on a giant screen. But that was still a long way off.

☆

The hospital wasn't even on Big Charlie's radar. He was still busy at home defecating in a bucket and yelling 'IRA' as he threw it over the orange hangers-on, singing their chants of religious intolerance. He was no fan of shitting anywhere except a toilet, but sometimes the end justified the means. Fortunately for some of the people below, they heard the IRA shout and dived away from the flying shite like extras in *Apocalypse Now*. A few of the more heavyset marchers were not so lucky. Shouting matches ensued between local born-again Fenians and their orange, unionist enemies. People launched bricks at Charlie's window, but the advantage of living three up was evident to everyone except paralytic Orangemen hosting an impromptu try-out for Olympic discus throwing. It wasn't long before those on the pavement who objected to Orange marches got dragged into the carnage, and newspapers got to fill some pages with reports of 'skirmishes' and 'disorder' the next day.

☆

Charlie was blasting the rebel music when Mrs Kinsella chapped on his door. 'Charlie!' she shouted through the letterbox.

'Aw, fuck off,' Charlie said. He wasn't the neighbourly type, but Leanne was, which often sucked him into the community orbit against his will. True to form, it hadn't even dawned on Charlie that Leanne might currently have her legs in the air and have a student midwife passed out on the floor beside her.

☆

'Ah don't think she's gonnae make it,' said the head midwife to another after Leanne's screams alerted them to their stricken colleague.

'Ahhhhh!' Leanne said, wanting to die ten minutes ago.

'Vasovagal syncope is whit Ah heard,' said another midwife, casually.

'Ahhhhh!'

'Whit's that again?' The midwives continued to lounge about at the foot of the bed while Leanne tried to kick the nearest one to return them to earth and focus on fixing her torture.

'Sensitivity tae blood and that. It makes you faint.'

'Ahhhh!' Leanne tried to shimmy down the bed.

'How can she be a midwife if she cannae stand the sight of blood and that?'

'FFFUUUCK!' Leanne screamed at them this time.

'Poor lassie. She'll need tae get another joab.'

'Fuckin help me, no her!' Leanne said.

The midwives shared a glance like Leanne was a killjoy. 'You get her intae a chair, and Ah'll get Lisa.'

'It's Leanne,' Leanne said, just stopping herself from adding 'fuck you'.

☆

Charlie answered the door only because it wasn't the polis or debt collectors. 'Awright, Agnes . . .' he said, barely giving Mrs Kinsella the time of day.

'Terrible aw that fighting, in't it? Ah don't know whit the world's coming tae.'

'Aye,' Charlie said, looking at his wrist where his watch had been before he pawned it last week to help make rent. 'Times were better during the wars wae the Luftwaffe drappin bombs,' he added, sarcastically.

'They shouldnae be drinking aw that drink and behaving like that,' Mrs Kinsella said, fixing her glasses while Charlie checked his bare wrist again. 'They gie orange marches a bad name that lot.'

'Right . . .' Charlie said, remembering he had chips in the oven.

'Some horrible person even threw their business fae a windae – a number two!'

'Did they?' *Fucking shoot me*, Charlie thought, as he tried not to look at Mrs Kinsella's wrinkled face.

'Aye, it's revolting whit the world's coming tae,' Mrs Kinsella said, shaking her head. 'Ah'm just glad Ah'm no growing up noo.'

'Aye, the great depression and the second world war were the times tae grow up, win't they?'

Mrs Kinsella nodded her head and took a moment for quiet reflection while her brain rekindled the actual reason for chapping Charlie's door. 'But people dumping excrement fae windaes is no whit Ah came doon here fir. It's Leanne . . .'

'Aye?' Charlie said, trying to keep his head upright to listen.

'She's in labour wae the wean,' Mrs Kinsella said, calmly.

'Whit?'

'She's hiving the wean right noo. Ah wis tae tell ye that.'

'Fuckin hell,' Charlie said, resenting the imposition. 'Ah've just opened a can and put some chips oan.'

Charlie waited for his chips, reasoning that another hour would hardly make a bit of difference, but one can of lager became three and a plate of chips became two plates of chips and a pie.

☆

Leanne cursed her husband and found solace in thoughts of a quickfire divorce. The doctor returned reeking of Golden Virginia tobacco.

'Gas and air,' he said, almost bored and jaded while looking up into the eye of the needle. 'You're still not in active labour, I'd say. Just be patient, Mrs Connelly. It'll happen in good time,' he mumbled, glancing at his watch and noting it was time for a cup of coffee.

'Donnelly!' Leanne screamed. 'It's! Donnelly!'

'Yes, that's right. Of course. I'll be back soon. Don't go anywhere,' he said with a forced smile. Leanne looked for something to throw, but she had nothing within reach. She made a mental note to pish and shite all over the bastard if the chance presented itself.

'Whit a dickhead he is,' said one midwife to another, thinking she was whispering.

'Thinks he's God's gift tae wummin.'

'Ah still would, though.'

'Aye, me tae.' They laughed and pushed each other on the shoulder.

'He is a dick, though.' Leanne felt invisible and fell deeper into Hell.

'He's a doacter. Maist ae them are dicks. It's the God complex in them. They aw think they can walk oan water even when they're slipping oan linoleum.'

'Help, fir fuck's sake!' Leanne said, pleading and wiping tears and snot from her face.

'Gas and air, darling. Gas and air.'

'EPI-FUCKIN-DUUURAL!' Leanne screamed before bawling.

'She wants an epidural noo,' one midwife said to another and rolled her eyes again. 'You sure you want an epidural, darling? Dae you need tae read the leaflet again?' Leanne moved to her knees on the bed, and her red face twisted into unambiguous, murderous contempt as she got closer to the midwives.

'Know whit, bring me some Jane Austen and Ah'll read that instead!'

'Eh?'

'Get. Me. The. Fuckin! Epidural! NOW!' Leanne shouted, throwing an oxygen mask at the midwives.

☆

By the time Big Charlie dragged his arse to the hospital, Charlie had emerged via an almighty struggle with a brutal and unforgiving pair of forceps. Big Charlie looked down at a kind of purple, misshapen potato, and knew right away that he wasn't cut out for fatherhood, or at least fatherhood that wouldn't completely fuck up his son.

☆

Wee Charlie grew into his head, and his hair arrived to hide the trauma of his birth. He was a happy infant with his mother, and he went from strength to strength until his da took to building up his character and presenting him with a lifetime of psychological problems. But what doesn't kill you only makes you stronger, except for, you know, lots of things.

THIRTEEN DAYS AFTER DEATH: FUNERAL FOR ME

'This is a safe enough distance away,' Phil says as he parks his car in the cemetery. I shuffle nervously and feel I should be anywhere else. The coffin might be more comfortable than sitting here with Phil in his god-awful Hawaiian shirt, cargo shorts and gel sandals. What a prick. He even makes me seem overdressed, and I'm in black jeans and a grey T-shirt that has a fresh ice cream stain on it. 'Relax, Charlie. No-one can see through these windows, baby!'

'We should be a bit further back,' I say. 'Ah don't like it. And where the fuck is everybody?'

It's majorly depressing when you live to see the pitiful turnout at your own funeral. Lots of people think they're popular and worth at least a few hours to say goodbye to, but I imagine not a lot will ever get to see just how many bastards gave their funeral a body swerve.

'At least your kids and your ex-wife showed,' Phil says, pointing at my rake-thin, vampiric daughter, Lilly, staring at her phone and my long-haired, chubby son, David, doing the same thing. For all they're bad, it's my ex-wife, Carly, who takes the fucking biscuit. She yawns like my death is an inconvenience on her day and glances at her watch. But she has put weight on. That's a plus. I guess I can get a bit of satisfaction from that.

'Aye, they showed. But they're no even wearing black. Lilly has a blue dress oan, and David's wearing a grey suit. And where the fuck's his tie?'

'What are you, the colour police?' Phil says, reaching around the side of his seat and pulling out a bong. That'll be the source of the overpowering stench.

'It's a funeral. You usually wear black or dark clothing.'

'Your daughter's dress is navy.' Phil unscrews his mineral water and pours it in the bong. I look at my emaciated daughter and worry that she has an eating disorder, a serious drug problem, IBS, or a terminal disease. Phil nudges my shoulder and smiles. 'And your son's suit is grey! Grey is death.'

'Black's death.'

'Grey too.'

'Fuck off. David's been a goth for over ten years, since he was a teenager, and noo he's in grey wae a white shirt. A goth wearing grey at a funeral, fir fuck's sake.' Phil lights his bong and practically blows the thing for rent money. He coughs, and I cover his mouth. 'Keep it doon. How are you still coughing like that after aw the shit you've smoked?'

'You need to chill, Charlie.'

'Carly's in red. Whit's that all about?'

'Burgundy.' I ignore Phil and his usual pedantry.

'Where's the respect? There's hardly any cunt here.'

'Well, what did you expect? You burned a lot of bridges, then pissed on the dying embers.' Phil takes another bong hit and coughs again. 'Your sister's in black and looks unhappy.' He points at my wee sister Paula in her habit, looking thin, morose and plain, which is pretty much standard.

'She's a nun. And she was auld and miserable before she became a nun.'

'Yeah . . . she weirded me out, man, even for a nun.' He dangles the bong in front of me. 'You want some?'

'Ah'm trying tae stay oan the straight and narrow, remember?'

'I'd rather not remember that,' Phil says, rolling his eyes and putting the bong between his legs on the car seat.

'Dae you think they look sad?' I say, pointing at my ungrateful children.

'Your kids?'

'Aye.' David is straight-faced, looking at his phone, and Lilly's doing the same.

'Yeah . . . your daughter looks sad and skinny. Your son looks sad and fat.' I punch him on his arm. He winces and rubs at it. 'There was no need for that.'

'They're just glued tae their phones.'

'And? Everybody uses phones to distract them from feeling. They're probably hurting inside.' I stare over at them and beg for tears, pain, laughter, something, fucking anything other than this shite.

'It disnae fuckin look like it. It looks like they'd rather be anywhere else even if anywhere else was a fuckin jail cell.' I fight back the tears. 'Fuck it, gies a hit ae that bong.'

'FUCK YEAH!'

'Keep your voice doon, ya fuckin tit . . .' I take the bong and give it a thorough wipe. I see my gut escaping my T-shirt and inhale hard and long.

'Jesus, Charlie,' Phil says, smiling and dancing in his seat. 'Stop sucking that big, phallic bong like it's a big-time Hollywood producer. It's obscene.'

'Fuck you,' I cough out. 'Ah don't suck for parts. Maybe that's ma problem. Maybe if Ah sucked dick, Ah could stoap waiting for you tae fail tae get me any decent auditions.'

Phil pretends he's hurt. Fucking amateur porn actor cunt. 'I don't think you could suck yourself to the middle, never mind the top,' he says, laughing. He's so slapable when he cracks himself up and nobody else.

'Aye, well Ah'll just stay at the bottom wae you then, will Ah?'

'Safest place for you these days, especially now you're dead and all.' He chuckles again like a moron, but I'm too distracted by a rush of serenity and acceptance.

'Fuck me. This weed is good. It's no that strong stuff that's some introspective nightmare right away.'

'Botox Manson . . .' Phil says as if I know what he's talking about.

'What?'

'Botox Manson does all the best pills, weed, coke, mushrooms . . . He's my new number one dealer.'

'Botox Manson?'

'You never met Botox Manson?' Phil says, loading the bong again. He definitely has a problem. 'I forgot you're doing this whole clean thing. You were so wasted for so long that I need to remind myself that we're contracting . . . No, not contracting . . . Yeah, contracting . . .'

'Please be quiet,' I tell him. Thankfully, he's got his mouth around that bong again. 'Ah'm trying tae watch ma funeral in peace here.' Phil lets out a cough and splutters. 'You sure you've no got a lung condition?' He waves my suggestion away.

'Botox Manson looks like Charlie Manson if he never went to jail and if Charlie Manson stuck Botox in his head instead of scraping a swastika on it. He talks in sixties jive too. He's a total throwback!'

I see my kids laughing with each other. My kids laughing at my funeral. Fuck me. That's just what a parent wants to see. I wasn't the greatest dad what with being a kinda functioning junkie who eventually couldn't get a part in a DIY shop, but I gave them the best start in life and a life that didn't involve bolting from one area to another to avoid a doing.

'You know he never killed anyone, don't you?' says Phil, staring out the windshield at my excuse for a funeral.

'Whit are you talking aboot?'

'Charlie Manson.'

'Whit aboot him?' I ask, shaking my head at David, giggling at something on his phone and showing it to Lilly.

'He's not even a murderer. He gets lumped in with Ted Bundy, Dahmer, Kemper, John Wayne Gacy and Ridgeway, but Charlie didn't kill anyone.'

'Whit's your point, man?'

Phil is silent and probably stopping to consider if he has or needs a point. 'Well, I'd be a bit pissed off if I were a serial killer who'd put in all the hard yards – all that killing, and this little midget shit is more famous and notorious than me. That would sting big time.'

Is that Carly crying? I'm hopeful until I realise she's just trying to get something out of her lazy left eye.

'They're serial killers, Phil. Who gives a shit whit any ae they lowlife cunts think or dae aboot anything? It's like getting aw misty-eyed aboot your favourite STD.'

'Netflix, Amazon Prime, HBO, Showtime, MGM, Warner, every book publisher. Never underestimate the American public's obsession with fear and the macabre. Guns don't just sell themselves outside the old reddish states with the John Wayne wannabes. We need fear, and lots of it.'

'How reassuring,' I say, feeling hungry and depressed. Like a bucket of fried chicken and a large dose of Prozac depressed. I pull out my phone and get on Twitter to stop the emotions from taking over.

'You know I fucked a girl who was in the Manson family, right?' Phil says with a creepy smile. He knows I know. Even though I try not to listen to him, he's told me that enough for it to stay locked in my memory.

'Aye, you've told me several times,' I say, scrolling through people fighting with each other over midterm US elections.

'It was great at the time. But, you know, you have to draw a line somewhere.'

You can never take Phil seriously when he's trying to dispense moral wisdom. 'Well, at least you drew it after you had your dick in there,' I say, 'especially after you fucked that other serial killer's daughter.'

Phil lights up, slaps the steering wheel and smiles at his remembrance of things shagged. I feel I've said too much and asked for it. 'Yeah, she was really fucked up! Talk about daddy issues. Fucked like there was no tomorrow, though. Every time I swore it was over, she pulled me back in . . . literally.' Please make it stop. This weed is too good for my imagination, and I'm picturing his fat bare arse in the air. 'But talk about crazy! She made you seem normal!' Phil enjoys another laugh with himself.

'Her da did kill multiple women, and her ma married the psycho while he was oan death row.' I see my kids look over at the car. 'Fuck!' I duck, peek and sweat.

'Tinted windows, Charlie. Tinted windows.'

'Let's get the fuck oot ae here,' I say, looking around, paranoia pulsing through me. 'We shouldnae have come here tae begin wae. Whit kind of fuckin idiot goes tae his own fake funeral?'

57

'Relax, Charlie,' Phil says, loading that bong again. He's such a greedy bastard. 'Fucking Predator couldn't see you in this baby.'

'Fuck that,' I say, still ducking behind the tinted windows. 'They'll smell this weed a mile away. It's like a Snoop Dogg gig in here.'

'Jesus, Charlie,' Phil says, disappointedly. 'A little bit of weed, and you're CIA fucking MKUltra paranoid. What the fuck happened to you?'

'Shut the fuck up and take me tae a KFC,' I say, sitting up again and looking in the mirror. I look old, done in and very stoned. Even my attempts at clean living and exercising have not stopped the goose-step march to wrinkled, grey-pubed oblivion. At least I bothered to shave off that grey and white beard that wasn't adequately hiding my double chin. Phil got a great laugh that I made a bit of an effort for my funeral, unlike him.

'Botox Manson's sent me a WhatsApp. He says he's . . .'

'Fuck Botox Manson.'

LONG BEFORE KARMA AND DEATH:
GROWING UP IN PICTURES

I'm 14, hiding up a tree with my da pishing below on the trunk. How has it come to this? A chill hits me as I see my wee sister Paula wailing from the pram just behind my da's half-arsed parenting. The brake isn't even on the pram and it's clearly on a slight incline. I should at least go down and stick the brake on, but I don't want that cunt to see me. He's supposed to be indoors with Paula, waiting on a phone call for a possible job, but he's half-canned and pishing in public. Pishing outside where I thought I was safe. Outside where I thought I could smoke a joint and get away with it. These kinds of jobby touching cloth moments are now par for the course. I must've been Hitler in a past life or one of the cows that pished on that weirdo Nazi cunt.

I can see Jimmy and Paul laughing away in the bushes and pointing at me. There's no honour among friends like these. I can only hope their maws walk in on them wanking, or they catch their maws getting pumped off that Pontius perv, the postman who caused a crabs outbreak in most of Glasgow's south side. What a guy Pontius is. Nearly half the boys in my class think delivering letters is guaranteed to get you your hole now. What they fail to realise is Pontius is actually handsome and nicknamed The Tripod. That's before you get to the novelty, blasphemous name. Only Judas Iscariot could do better about here.

How long can one person pish for? Fucking dick could keep Armitage Shanks in business all by himself. Jimmy and Paul start chucking stones over. One hits the trunk above my da's head. I'll kill them if any hit that pram. I might not be able to fight sleep according to my da, but maybe I just need a good reason to assault people. We can't all be like him or lots of the other cardboard gangsters hanging about here.

My da's swaying head looks up, and they duck behind the bush. He suspects, but he doesn't know. It could be the wind or his overactive, shellshocky imagination.

'Fuckin cunts,' he says to the tree.

I'm practically breathing through my arse now, trying not to make any noise. Dead bodies aren't this quiet. I really should be an actor, even if my da says they're all bent, skint or perverts. Like he would know anything about actors. He knows fuck all about anything.

'It wis a fuckin miracle you goat intae Holyrood Secondary School, never mind Hollywood.'

'Whit dae you know about acting, ya daft prick ye? Acting weird is aw you're good at.'

'Aye, Burt Lancaster will be shitein bricks and building mansions at you trying tae take his parts.'

'Take techie or sumfin normal. Even Home Economics is mair useful than drama, fir fuck's sake.'

He starts squeezing the last few drops and grunting. Kill me now. I'm 14-year-old and hugging a tree like a demented hippie shouting about greenhome gases or whatever the fuck they're called. Stuck up a tree, still dreaming about getting a blowjob and another stinky index finger. What a life.

I see a squirrel staring like I'm breaking and entering. Up this close, the wee cunt is nothing but a rat with a nicer tail. I try to scare it with my best silent war face. It keeps staring. Another stone smacks the squirrel on the arse. The thing has a shitfit and runs up my legs all the way to my face.

'Whit the fuck?' my da says, looking up after a nut hits him on his empty shell of a head. I see a quick flash of a memory of my gorgeous French teacher's knickers before I hit the pishy grass below me. My da drags me to my feet as I hear laughter, then scurrying away from the bushes. Pair of absolute wankers.

'Ma leg,' I say, looking down at it, hoping it's broken for the street cred and to spare me a doing from this bastard.

'There's fuck aw wrang wae your leg! Staun up so Ah can kick you doon again!' I get up, run and keep going until I'm far away from him.

Jimmy and Paul have vanished. Fuck them. They say the best revenge is living well, but I'll punch them both in the face in the meantime just to be sure. I don't think I'll be living well for a wee while yet, not unless I find a suitcase with a million quid in it, or my ma finally sees sense and stops letting him impregnate her. Fuck knows what she ever saw in him, except for a chance to mother a broken bastard with a booze problem.

☆

In times of great stress, it's here I come to hide. I don't have enough for a ticket, but the usher who's always distracted by anything in a skirt is on today, and thanks to his creepy eyes, I get to see another film for free.

Ah, Sean Connery. He'd kick fuck out my da and seduce an international ride all before breakfast. That's what I need to do. There's no way I'll get respect or my hole if I'm not assertive and borderline homicidal. That's what lassies and guys want here. No cunt cares if all that bravado is disguising an emotional cripple in dire need of proper therapy.

Therapy isn't on the menu about here. We do drink, drugs and people instead. Therapy is for Hollywood films and people from Milngavie. Maybe it's more nature than nurture. My nature isn't to automatically start kicking the shite out of any cunt for any perceived slight. Aye, I need to be realistic. Take acting classes in the toon and meet some lassies that way. Maybe I could stay a virgin until university or try to meet a nice lassie.

The cardboard gangsters are getting all sorts of crabs, even if they're ugly cunts with massive spots all over their pasty bodies. In what world is that shovel-chinned psycho Nuts and Bolts more attractive than a sophisticated cunt like me. His name is Nuts and Bolts! The cunt is nuts and spends his time bolting away from the polis for various crimes.

I saw him with his manky snake tongue down Yvonne McAdam's throat a few days ago. Yvonne McAdam! She's probably the nicest lassie in a mile radius, and that revolting jailbait psycho cunt is pumping her. Maybe it's the name. Maybe I need some ridiculous nickname like Nuts and Bolts, Smasher or Stabber.

Like I have the energy and enterprise for all that exhausting criminal shite. I'm only on the outskirts of all the casual destruction of public property and gang fighting. Fuck worrying about ambushes every time I'm stoned and want a buttered roll and chips. That's the last thing my stress levels need. I'm already dicing with fights inside and outside the home on a daily basis.

TWENTY-FOUR DAYS AFTER DEATH

I'm yesterday's news. Things do move quickly on this social media. I semi-trended for an hour and bobbed about for a few days as a mild curiosity before a small spike during my cremation.

#RIPCharlie
#shitedontburn
#legned
#HOLLYWEIRDPERV
#bawbag

I've only been on these sites for days, and I can scarcely remember life without them. Is it healthy? Probably not. But define healthy. Doing smack and hanging about Hollywood wasn't healthy. Pretending you're dead and googling yourself while going relatively drug-free seems a bit better from my perspective, at least. I guess it's all about the little victories. It's just a shame my body is atrophying. I could exercise indoors, but that's where my laptop and phone are, and outside is where I'm dead.

'You're totally addicted,' Phil tells me. 'Like, totally 110 per cent addicted.' I cringe and feel like throwing something at him, but all I have at hand is my phone, and that's way too important.

'Fuck off. Ah'm just checking the fitba scores. And don't say 110 per cent. You sound like a fuckin dickhead.'

'Addicted,' he says with an air of smug self-satisfaction.

'Gies peace, ya mad hypocrite.' Man United really are shite since Ferguson left.

'You've not been off that phone or laptop since you died. How the high and mighty have fallen.'

'Fuck off. Ah'm no addicted.' I really am. I know enough about that subject matter to detect the tell-tale signs.

'Gooble gobble, one of us! One of us!'

I lose it for a second, launch my iPhone at him and rescue it as if it's my new-born baby. So what if I'm spending too much time on this? It's not like the old days of crystal meth, smack, Burger King, KFC and McDonald's. At least I'm on here debating and taking people down. This is productive.

'Are you trolling people?' Phil says, looking at my hairy stomach, which keeps escaping all my T-shirts. Death has made me fatter, to the point I might need a new wardrobe.

'Trolling?' Ignorance is where it's at.

'Yeah, you've just called Chris Christie a cunt and said Karl Marx was the second coming of Jesus on a Christian Conservative Twitter page. That's textbook trolling.'

'Stop looking at ma screens and gieing me yer pop terminology. Ah'm a righteous crusader.'

'You'll get suspended or banned altogether.'

I already have before a reprieve, but fuck telling Phil that and giving him a punty onto that high horse. Someone as dodgy as Phil doesn't get to seize moral superiority. I'm not Trump, Polanski or Ellen DeGeneres. I've always treated cunts with respect regardless of how fucked up I was. I was only a danger to myself and toilet bowls.

But Phil? Phil is a felonious, unscrupulous drug fiend with a distinct lack of morals. He forgets we're currently making money off my death, and it's me taking risks to execute this harebrained scheme. Don't get me wrong, it's worked so far: my landlord is no longer hounding me, credit card companies have ceased chasing me, and we're making some decent coin. Of course, I asked him for a more long-term strategy, and he just trailed off. But I understand it's better to live in the moment. A lot of my misery came from idealising the past or thinking about everything I wanted to achieve as I sat with a crack pipe between my legs. That wasn't exactly healthy.

Give me a break and allow me to philosophise. People get sanctimonious once they've climbed down after partying like MDMA at the end of the world. Now, I live day to day and distract myself from my fake death and approaching real death with life on a screen. I am no different from anyone else. I am not exceptional. I'm just another one of the herd bashing at buttons until the end. So what if people think I'm dead? I only existed to a few anyway and they seldom answered my calls – not that I blame them. The future and the logistics of being a dead man in America can wait for the time being.

Who's to say if creating multiple social media accounts and winding people up is healthy? All I can say is here we are.

@DeadNLovinIt
@SamLRidgelyMP Suck a cheesy bellend and stop pumpin the NHS up the arse, ya chinless Etonian

wanker. Chairman Mao would know what to do with you, ya hamshank.

@DeadNLovinIt

@GeraldCutler Hang in there. There's fuck all wrong with sucking your own dick anyway. It's only natural #lovethyself #hollywoody

@DeadNLovinIt

@savethepandas Stop interfering and worrying about pandas fucking and get your own hole, ya bunch of freaks. #leavethepandas

@DeadNLovinIt

@KingFarage We all know you wank it to immigrants and can't admit it. That's when you're not fiddling sheep, sheep fiddler.
#wereallimmigrants #muttonmolestor #fiddleronthehoof

@DeadNLovinIt

@OrangeOrder4all It's nice to know there's Twitter in the 17th century, ya bunch of inbred, incestuous sister and cousin shagging mutant bastards #saynotohatred #spreadzegenepool

Well, that feels just splendid.

LONG BEFORE KARMA AND DEATH: DADZILLA

Charlie had heard the stories about his father's absence at his and his sister's birth and decided not to be the same. It was just a shame that his overexuberance was way too much for his wife, Carly. It was way too much for any person. Carly was not particularly violent, but after a night of Charlie telling her what foods would help her back pain and him reading his lines and *The New York Times* to a bump, she often had dreams about killing him. That she didn't wake up horrified, but horny and reaching for the sex toys in her drawer, tells you that Charlie was even more intense than the strongest setting on her favourite vibrator.

Carly didn't want to hear about guerrilla fighting in Nicaragua, never mind the bump. Nor did she want to hear Charlie running lines about his imminent gang-molesting courtesy of three Aryans in San Quentin. The only saving grace was that the rape scene, like many male rapes in movies, was shown off-screen and didn't require Charlie to really test Carly's ability to remain a pacifist.

Charlie ploughed into all the scans and the midwife appointments cracking jokes and wearing a broad smile that came off as desperate and indicative of a person with deep psychological wounds. At least that's how it seemed to Carly. She'd never seen Charlie smile so much, and it freaked her out. To see his transformation from a young Gene Hackman into a *Blue Peter* presenter was a major turn-off. She tried dropping hints by putting on headphones a lot and turning the telly up louder and louder, but Charlie was still the biggest pain in her arse since that mortifying dose of haemorrhoids she got when she was 22.

As most things did at the time between couples, it all came to a head in Mothercare. 'Stop it, Charlie!' Carly shouted at him. 'Enough! I can't fucking take it anymore! You're like fucking Dadzilla!'

Charlie was hurt. 'Ah'm just trying tae help, Carly,' he said, sheepishly, but Carly was done tiptoeing around his mania.

'What, by asking the cashier if I can try on breast pumps and by interrogating that postman because he accidentally bumped into me a tiny bit?'

Charlie didn't see the issue. 'He banged intae you,' he said, simply.

'It was an accident, and you threatened to put him in a post-box and mail him to his family members!'

Charlie smiled uncomfortably at another couple with their kids, who quickened their pace. 'It was only an empty threat.'

'What kind of empty threat is that?' Carly said with manic eyes and her fists clenched. Charlie nearly took a step back. 'It's so fucking specific and weird. And fucking mental!'

'It got the job done. He apologised.'

'He apologised, but he would've apologised anyway,' Carly said, dismissing Charlie with her hand. Charlie scoffed. He knew people didn't just say sorry because they hit a pregnant woman with a door. If the world was that simple, people like Augusto Pinochet wouldn't be considered paragons of virtue.

'People don't just apologise,' Charlie said, like Carly was naïve and stupid. 'Cunts like Pinochet and Maggie

68

Thatcher widnae have been running things in the 80s if that was true, would they?'

Carly threw open the door to Mothercare, then stopped after Charlie followed her out. For a second, Charlie thought he was getting a haymaker, but Carly took a deep breath.

'I don't even know what that fucking means,' she said. 'And I doubt you do either.'

☆

Charlie sank into depression without talking to the bump and left for Prague to film scenes for a movie featuring a secret sect of ninjas solving crimes and performing surgery amidst political turmoil and casual female nudity. Prague was the type of city he'd usually love exploring and getting drunk in, but rehearsing lines written by a dullard for a cynical cash-in wasn't exactly what he needed to keep him ticking over.

'That was a strange sound,' Kevin Lasso said after Charlie took off his ninja mask and emitted a strange sigh that morphed into a dying foghorn. Kevin was the elder statesman on set and a once in-demand character actor, but those days were long gone.

'That was ma dick talking through ma mouth,' Charlie said. That sounded better and more macho than admitting he missed his pregnant missus and was worried about his unborn child.

'I hear you,' Kevin said, taking off his peculiar, transparently bogus sensei moustache that screamed cultural appropriation. 'My goddamn dick stopped working years ago. Fucking useless piece of shit.'

'Ah'm sorry to hear that,' Charlie said, loosening the button on his shirt and removing the tie that was choking him. For some reason, the ninjas dressed formally when interrogating potential suspects while Kevin Lasso got to vegetate on set and on film with a glorified bath robe that barely covered the y-fronts that struggled to keep in his genitals.

'Don't be. That sonofabitch only lived to get me into trouble. Four marriages and goddamn how knows many relationships that thing ruined. Now, look at me,' Kevin said, opening his legs and flashing his pants before crossing his legs again. Charlie pretended it didn't happen, but they both knew. 'I'm decrepit, alone, and in some low-budget piece of shit halfway around the goddamn world.'

'This piece of shit might no see the light of day at this rate.'

'Who gives a fuck?' Kevin said, drinking from a flask reeking of whisky. 'It's all about getting paid in this game. You do your job, get paid, and you can hold your head high . . . unlike my goddamn pecker.'

'Ah usually pick ma parts and only do things that excite me.'

Kevin offered the flask to Charlie, but he declined, and Kevin gulped the rest down like a man who had a problem for every solution. 'And this European softcore shit with ninjas and a goddamn Martian trying to control the weather didn't do it for you?'

'Once your wife is pregnant and you're struggling tae make rent, every part you're offered becomes like the lead in *Citizen Kane* and *One Flew Over the Cuckoo's Nest*.'

'Orson Welles?' Kevin said, spitting towards the ground but hitting his robe. 'Now that was a goddamn asshole.'

'You knew Orson Welles?' Charlie said, smiling.

70

'Sure! I had a small part in *Chimes at Midnight* – bastard stole a chocolate doughnut from me one time and wouldn't admit it. I could see the chocolate on his goddamn teeth. Lying son of a bitch.'

'Good filmmaker, though.'

'Yeah, I suppose so. Everybody looks competent compared to this cocaine cowboy who thinks he's the goddamn second coming.'

☆

Charlie tempered his excitement and went full method. He supported Carly but set limits. Those tactics lasted for a while until the day arrived a month before the due date. This sent Charlie flapping and Carly apoplectic. She couldn't deal with the return of Dadzilla when her vagina was the subject of viewings, prods and speculation.

Charlie asked questions for questions' sake and questioned the answers. 'Will you please shut the fuck up!' Carly said after another contraction. 'Just. Shut. The. Fuck. Up!' The room was already too small, and now it was suffocating. Charlie knew he was getting on everyone's nerves, but acute social discomfort kept his verbal dysentery relentless.

'She doesn't know what she's saying,' Charlie said, making a massive mistake. A plastic cup of water narrowly missed his head, and he saw Carly looking around for more things to throw. The midwife rubbed her hand across her forehead and looked like she was about to blow a gasket.

'Maybe you should go get a coffee,' the midwife said through gritted teeth.

'But . . .'

'Go get a fucking coffee!' Carly suggested.

Charlie turned corner after corner looking for the cafe and stared out a window having his 14ᵗʰ existential crisis since he'd heard the baby was coming. He saw two doctors speaking to each other about banging a nurse in the gynie ward. Charlie was horrified and listened more intently until he forgot he was there to get a coffee and watch his kid entering the world.

'See you later, masturbator,' one doctor said to another.

'In a while, necrophile,' said his mate, laughing.

'That's not funny.'

Charlie rushed back to find his wife, who was still not pleased to see him. 'Don't just fucking stand there like a statue,' she said. 'I need fucking drugs!' Charlie hugged Carly and kissed her head, but the positive vibes and oxytocin didn't register. She was too far gone with pain and Charlie's bullshit.

'The epidural's coming,' the midwife said.

'You're having an epidural?' Charlie asked. Carly had an expression on her face that suggested she wasn't just thinking about a routine murder but one that was prolonged and as violently chaotic as possible. 'You do whit you need to, darling.'

☆

The next 17 hours was a blur of different scrubs and swearing. Then there was an issue with the baby's heartbeat, and Carly was wheeled away for a caesarean. Charlie sat there feeling more helpless than usual after putting on scrubs and a mask again. 'This is the ninth time Ah've put scrubs on this month,' he said to the doctor. 'It's never-ending.'

'Yeah?' the doctor said, not caring to even humour Charlie. Charlie was undeterred. Even with Carly doped up, there was a look on her face telling Charlie to stop speaking, but Charlie made a conscious effort to stay out of her eyeline and only engage with the crowd of masked hospital staff scurrying around.

'Ah just played a doctor-detective wae a background in martial arts. We filmed some of it in Prague. Beautiful city, by the way.'

'Really?' The doctor said, still unimpressed and focused on the important task at hand.

'Aye, but it probably won't see the light of day. It's a real piece of crap.'

'My Sharona' came on from a radio in the corner. 'Turn that up,' the doctor said as what looked like a teenager beside him studied and anticipated his every move. Charlie felt a presence behind him and a hand on his shoulder. Charlie looked up at a man who could've doubled as a heavyweight boxer.

'I'm Bert, the anaesthetist,' he said. 'If you need to faint, just faint. But tell us if you're feeling that way or overwhelmed, and we can help you.'

'Right,' Charlie said, completely ignorant of why he would have to do something as dramatic as faint to get attention.

'You wouldn't believe the number of men who faint in here,' Bert said. 'We had a middleweight champion keel over one time.'

Charlie could tell from Bert's bright, happy eyes that he was smiling, and he didn't much care for it. 'No bother.' he said. 'Ah'll be sure tae let you know.'

'We have plenty of tissues, so don't be afraid to cry too.'

'Right.'

'Plenty of people cry as well. Big hardy men break down like little boys when they see their child for the first time, particularly if it's a girl. There's something about dads and daughters.'

Charlie held Carly's hand and waited for the 50 pence to run out on the anaesthetist's monologue function. 'My Sharona' had thankfully ended, and 'Bad Medicine' arrived like a train crashing through the operating room. The doctor nodded and was all thumbs up and steely eyes. It occurred to Charlie that this man looked badly medicated himself, but he supposed cocaine might make him more focused.

The student behind him copied the nods and broke out a bit of air guitar before he nipped it in the bud after catching Charlie's best serial killer stare. 'You were in that movie with Chuck Norris, were you not?' Bert asked Charlie.

'Eh?'

'That one about the guy living out in the woods in solitude, who comes back to the city to avenge his sensei's disembowelling . . .'

'Aye, Ah was. That was a while ago . . .' Charlie said, wondering why he kept getting parts in movies with a sensei in them.

'He's an actor?' the student asked the master. These doctors were not adept at whispering.

'Supposedly. I didn't recognise him.' One of the midwives sidled up.

'He was in that one where the wife killed her husband,' she said. 'And she got haunted by him until she killed herself.'

'That stupid comedy?' the student asked.

'That's the one!'

'He's the husband?'

'No, he's the . . . I don't know.'

'That was Ciarán Hinds,' Charlie said. 'And he's Irish. And much older than me . . . Ah think.'

'What's happening?' Carly said. 'Is the baby coming out or what?'

'You're doing great!' Charlie said, wincing and vomiting a bit in his mouth after a sight of blood. 'Excellent!' He'd starred in a few horror movies with gratuitous gore and unspeakable acts of depravity, but this was way too real. Now he could see why fainting was optional.

'So, what was Chuck Norris like?' asked Bert.

'Ah don't know. Ah was only in one scene wae him, and Ah never really spoke tae him. He did kinda nod at me, but people said tae me that he does that fae time tae time – one too many blows tae the head.'

'I heard he's an asshole.'

'Definitely,' the doctor said as he yanked somewhere below him to produce a crying baby covered in cheesy vernix, reddish-purple blood and amniotic fluid. Charlie did not see the miracle of birth, but something that put him off Italian food, his favourite food, for a couple of days.

'Fuck me,' Charlie said, spewing into his mask.

'Are you okay?' asked Bert. Charlie shook his head and swallowed the rest of his sick.

SEVENTY-THREE DAYS
INTO EMBRACING AND
MISUNDERSTANDING KARMA

I was picking up rubbish by the side of this road and hoping no-one from my immediate past would recognise me, but you can't always get what you want, especially in somewhere as God-forsaken as L.A. I fake a half-hearted smile at Marie, who counterfeits one right back at me. I'm a better actor, but I'd wager her smile was more convincing. Marie, pronounced the French way, recently dropped her surname to create more mystique. I suppose she had a lot to live up to after being named Marie Curie.

'Is this community service?' Marie asks me with her phosphorescent teeth framed with red lipstick and her fake tits bursting from her short pink dress. I suppose that hood-down black Porsche convertible must put a smile like that on your face – that and 30k worth of dental bills.

Marie lived downstairs from me for a while and tried to make it as a singer, but she'd got bored with waitressing and was now making decent cash blowing guys and licking pussy on camera. As you do. She was still on drugs, as her career moves hinted at, but she was driving a much fancier car and had one of those dead-eyed fake smiles plastered across a face caked in more expensive makeup. Her hair looked blacker and shinier too. It seems getting far away from me has really made her thrive.

'Just doing a good deed,' I say, trying to suck in my gut. Thank fuck for this stupid bright-red, loose-fitting high-vis I'm wearing that obscures it a bit. I've been hitting the gym, but the ravages of time and fast food have done a number. Well, at least I'm wearing a ridiculous fisherman's hat to hide the grey hair. There's always that. 'Ah was due.'

'But you're picking up garbage at the side of the road. Is this for the, you know, whole sucking your own cock in Burger King thing?'

'No. And that never happened. Ah was taking smack in a KFC. There was no sucking ma dick, or anyone else's for that matter. Don't believe all you read. It's bullshit.'

'There's nothing to be ashamed of. It was, is, your dick. Hell, I'd lick my clit if I could. Maybe in another life I'll be flexible enough. Ain't got the back for it now.' That's right: Marie believes in reincarnation. Looks like she has designs on coming back an even bigger slut. No, not slut. That's slut shaming. And you can't just shame her for being a slut. Let's just say . . . even more amorous for pay. 'You okay? You seem a bit spacey.'

'Aye, of course. Thanks for the support.'

'Don't mention it. How many hours did you get?'

'Hours?'

'Yeah, your community service!' She didn't have to raise her voice so excitedly there.

'Ah'm no doing community service. At least no court ordained.'

'Why the fuck are you picking up trash then?'

'Ah'm trying to . . . be better.'

'Come again?' She's used to saying that. No, stop it. You're better than that or at least pretending to be. No, not pretending. You are better. You're a new man.

'It's for good karma,' I say, ashamed of myself for trying not to be a cretin.

'But what's the angle?'

'There is no angle. It's karma. You do know whit karma is, don't you?' Her face suggests between her ears is spare ground.

'Not really. I've heard of it. But I've never known anyone who was on it.'

'On it? It's no cocaine.'

'Yeah, I can see that. It looks more like a Debbie Downer.' She laughs and snorts. I forgot about that honky chuckle she has. She might be beautiful, pretending she's her version of high class, but that laugh is permanent and a dead giveaway.

'Right.'

'Oh, come on, Charlie! Get a grip, and get your balls reattached!'

Mist, red fucking mist! 'Aw, piss off, eh?'

'Excuse me?'

'Ah'm trying tae better myself here, and you're denigrating it.'

'Den-a-what?' She's genuinely offended by vocabulary.

'If you do good deeds and that, good things can happen tae you.'

'So, you're picking up trash to . . . what?'

'Ah'm helping clean the environment.'

'This ain't no environment, Charlie.' She takes a sip from a coffee. 'This is L.A.' She did have a point. People keep chucking stuff from their cars and ignoring my existence. She's the only one who's stopped, and that's because we smoked some crystal together and fucked a couple of times. I did get the distinct impression they were pity fucks, and ignorance on her part that I still had a career – and that by fucking me, she was networking. Little did she know that my career was deader than genuine artistic merit in the Hollywood studio system. Still, we had fun while it lasted. Well, I did. I'm not sure my cunnilingus game was up to much after all that meth, but like a true future porn star, she hammed it up like it was panto season and met every thrust with histrionics that would've made Neymar proud. Faking orgasms was the part she was born to play. Me? Hitting rock bottom is just me going method before my triumphant return to the top. Doing good things and getting sober will be my redemption.

'Good karma,' I repeat, trying not to show she's riling me. I look at a bin and imagine putting her in it headfirst.

'I knew you were a bit of a method actor, but all this do-gooding is just weird!'

'It's not method acting. This is me. This is who Ah am now.'

'C'mon, Charlie, you put the meth in method actor.' She thinks that's funny. She knows how moreish meth is and how hard it is to kick. Just because she's probably still sucking on pipes after speed-dating cocks doesn't mean she can taunt us cunts trying to do a one-eighty and delude themselves into self-denial. No, not delude. This is who you are now. You used to be good decades ago. You used to be altruistic. My mum always said I shared in nursery. It was when I went to primary school I started to go downhill. And by the dying embers of secondary school, I was a lost cause. No, not lost cause. This is your arc of redemption now. People can change. Don't let this slu– . . . person bring you down.

'Ah need tae get back tae work,' I say, turning away in the fervent hope she gets to fuck.

'Jesus,' she says, chortling. 'The red carpet to the trashman! Hero to zero, winner to loser!'

I see the red mist again, turn to face her, and it leaves my mouth before I can bite my tongue. 'Aw go suck syphilis, ya fuckin moron.'

And here comes her skinny latte over my face. Now I can make the leap to how she feels when she gets her face painted with cum. At least my money shot wasn't filmed for posterity and didn't have a multitude of witnesses. And it's only lukewarm. That's a plus, even if it is Starbucks.

I deserved that. That's karma for getting down in the gutter and trading insults with a porn star. I need to be better, right after I throw this empty beer can at her stupid Porsche. She gives me two fingers and speeds out of my life. There goes another woman who hates me. You can add her to my ex-wife, that *New York Post* critic I banged, and my aunt who hated anything with a dick.

I pick up the empty Coke cans, McDonald's wrappers, coffee cups and cigarettes off the street and think fondly of Glasgow. "Good things happen to good people," my mum used to say with no sense of irony. She was dealt a lousy hand her entire life and continued with this demented philosophy – though she did get to see my Oscar nomination, so I suppose it wasn't total bullshit. Then death spared her my fall from grace after she died with a vibrator in her hand. I couldn't begrudge her that. That seemed a good way to go. I just didn't understand why my auntie, who found her dead, had to tell my sister that and spread it everywhere. Aunt Paula always took feminism too far. I'm all for equal rights and pay and abortions for all, but Aunt Paula wanted to destroy every man in the world and become some unfuckable, detestable overlord. It was only by the grace of God that she was too hideously ugly to even become a popular politician. Thank fuck.

Politics may be showbusiness for ugly people, but Aunt Paula was near enough a laxative for the uninitiated. One look and you were no longer constipated. Kids down her street called her Sasquatch and used to tell folkloric legends about her. Finally, she had to up sticks from Glasgow and live in relative isolation somewhere past Perth. But, even there, where they were short on pageant winners, a farmer with bad eyesight mistook her for some cryptid creature and opened fire. Poor Aunt Paula. Underneath it all, she was still a horrible person, but at least she believed in something and had a few progressive big bones in her massive, hulking body.

I've always said there are way too many nihilists and fundamentalists about these days. We need more people who give a shit, but not too much of a shit that a whole bunch of people end up dead or waiting for the end of the world like it's a bus to a brothel full of Italian models. We can all do with less of those cunts.

LONG BEFORE KARMA AND DEATH: HOW TO SPLIT UP WITH YOUR WIFE

Charlie's granny used to tell him you can only push a man so far unless you pushed him down the stairs, and you could only push a woman so far before she pushed *you* down the stairs. He surmised wisdom was in there, but he often needed paracetamol after listening to her. She would've given him a belt around the ear for his recent behaviour if she was still breathing. Unfortunately, she had a fatal heart attack after a bad line of coke and being 68 when she snorted said line.

Despite her predilection for booze and drugs, Granny Frances was strict about monogamy and self-denial, at least in the sexual sphere. She advocated perseverance and communication and, when that failed, violence. She wouldn't leave his Granda Kev, but she'd punch, kick and put him in hospital if it merited it. Violence as a solution was less frowned upon then. It was the days when violence was just diplomacy by other, often more effective means.

Carly hadn't appreciated how much Charlie was self-destructive and not the brightest. She'd seen him perform him on stage, Shakespeare no less, and assumed this was a deeply thoughtful, intelligent person. But that wasn't the full picture. Charlie had his moments, but shining bright is hard when, after drinking too much, you lock yourself in a toilet cubicle with a dodgy door and then attempt to squeeze under it, over the pishy floor, only to get stuck and need a couple of bouncers to help you out. That was a particularly shameful Tuesday afternoon.

Turning a blind eye to Charlie's philandering was a depressing routine for Carly. Charlie was a star, especially in his own mind, despite his protestations that it was all about the work and being an artist. The word artist was getting thrown about far too much for Carly's liking, and it became his hypocrisy, and not the fucking around that really infuriated her. Of course, her dalliances cushioned the cheating blows, but listening to Charlie talk about creative peaks and studying Stanislavski to star in a film with a talking dog and a wisecracking pigeon made her want to annihilate him with her Dr Martens.

The only thing that stopped her was her history of never hitting anyone. Well, that and he was the father of their children. No matter what, he was still that, and he was always much better at that than he was at being a husband. But after watching him getting interviewed on TV with that conceited smile on his face as he did the press work he alleged he loathed, she resolved to excommunicate herself from him. That he'd fucked one of her pals was incidental now. Rhiannon Smith's legs had always been goalposts, and she did not doubt Charlie had been on her much-fabled suck it list. Sex was like shaking hands to her, and friends were often just waiting in line to become enemies. Most of the time, the wait wasn't too long. But Rhiannon and Carly went back a long way, and Carly naively thought she might be due a bit of loyalty.

Carly finished taking a shit inside that hideous vase trophy Charlie got for Best Supporting Actor from the Sunderland Movie Critic Association. It went against her nature to resort to this kind of revolting retribution, but her descent to join Charlie in the gutter was long overdue. He'd pushed her to shit in that ridiculous award, and if he wanted to salvage that accolade, he'd have to get *his* hands dirty for a change.

Carly had planned to piss all over his clothes and stick the nut on the bridge of his nose, but the wine was wearing off and giving her a sore head and early onset recriminations. It was always up to Carly to take the high road and be the mature, sensible one. She resented Charlie turning her responsible. They'd had the kids on the premise they'd share duties, and he'd left her to set the boundaries and stay sober-ish. He was the fun one to the kids, and she became the shrew. Every time the kids stepped out of line, she had to badger Charlie into being a disciplinarian, and by that point the kids knew she was twisting his arm.

You think you couldn't possibly defecate on anything else or cut up any more clothes, but then you see Charlie on your TV and you get a surge of righteous indignation to destroy more of his stuff and slap him as he steps into the house.

'Whit the fuck!'

'Rhiannon fucking Smith! Rhiannon fucking fucking Smith!'

'Aw, that,' Charlie said. Flailing limbs connected with Charlie's shins, balls, arms and face. He'd neglected to get his legs up to guard his balls and bent over double with the dry heaves. He would've had something to spew if he wasn't coming down from a binge where eating food didn't matter. His stomach was already in knots and he felt all he could do was retreat to bed for a day or two. There was no such luck. The cheating and hypocrisy were coming home to roost all over his fleshiest and boniest body parts. Carly smacked, slapped and punched everywhere he didn't want to get hit. He cowered and retreated to the floor, lost in pitiful stasis and pathetic apologies that rang hollow.

'I'm gonna fuck all your friends now!' Carly shouted. 'Not just some of them!'

'Eh?'

Smack!

Slap!

Punch!

Boot!

Boot!

Boot!

Slap!

Slap!

Boot!

Charlie wondered who had commandeered his wife's mind. Somehow all the beatings he'd taken from his father, bullies and bouncers seemed insignificant. Those people were cunts who didn't need coerced to commit GBH – it was their raison d'etre. But knowing that he'd pushed Carly to this hurt nearly as much as the kick to the balls.

Once Charlie had finished taking his beating like a man well used to it, he knew it was over. Cheating on and needling each other had created a toxic environment, and Charlie wasn't Jack Nicholson enough to act like everything was utopian. The kids were young but not stupid and knew their parents were only staying together for them when all they wanted was for them to divorce and do it yesterday.

'We tried tae stay together for youse,' Charlie said years later.

'Well, I really wished you wouldn't have,' Lilly said, as Charlie noticed cocaine between her nose and lips.

LONG BEFORE KARMA AND DEATH: GWENETH / MARY SUE

Charlie Donnelly was riding the crest of a wave and a supermodel. For a Glaswegian accustomed to a grey council estate, he felt like someone had granted him a wish. Everywhere he looked was tinged with beautiful sunlight and bright colours. And as if life couldn't get any better, he was now in a relationship with a supermodel/aspiring actress who turned people's heads wherever she walked. Gweneth Lancome, real name Mary Sue Hickenbottom, had come a long way from a trailer in a depressed Appalachian mill town. She'd come so far that she now spoke with a voice infected with delusions of being a platinum member of a non-descript and soulless transatlantic upper-class elite.

Charlie knew this one wouldn't last, but he was addicted and loved it when Gweneth would revert to Mary Sue in bed and around the house. Of course, he didn't much care for Gweneth. Gweneth was pretentious and career-obsessed and would stick a knife in the family cat to get a speaking part in anything.

Charlie took off his shirt and threw it on the four-poster bed with the Alaskan king-size mattress in his spacious L.A. apartment bedroom. He hoped Gweneth would collapse to her knees and worship the new toned body he'd punished himself for, for a part in an action movie, but she was too busy staring at a script that wasn't one of his.

'Can you run lines with me?' Gweneth asked Charlie. 'I really need to get this part.'

Charlie was now a surrogate acting coach – a position his selfishness abhorred. He'd been happy to help at first, but felt Gweneth was taking liberties with his free time, especially as he had little of it. Plus, she'd stopped giving him blowjobs, except for special occasions. Charlie had never been one for that Fourth of July bullshit, but it couldn't come quickly enough this year.

'Sure,' he said. 'It's no like Ah'm busy or anything.' He could kill Phil. It was him who'd managed to get Gweneth an audition with Shackler, who was always open to auditioning supermodels and anything he thought he could fuck.

Charlie watched Gweneth morph into Mary Sue to deliver the lines of trailer trash stripper number four. He actually found it endearing, albeit worrying, how the accents became muddled between her two identities.

'More Mary Sue and less Gweneth,' he said.

'What the fuck's that meant to mean?'

It started another argument. The relationship was now at the point where arguments were routine, and the make-up sex was fading to a distant memory. Call him an old-fashioned dreamer but Charlie preferred to get along in a relationship and resolve tension with conversation instead of hurling insults at each other about their respective genitals. He was hardly an agony aunt doling out relationship advice, but he knew that saying your girlfriend had a wide pussy after she gave him the pinky in the air treatment wasn't healthy. It certainly wasn't happily ever after.

'Ma dick is six fuckin inches! That's above-average, okay!'

'Yeah, just like you're six-foot!'

'Go get the measuring tape then! Ah'll fuckin prove it! You're the one wae the fuckin manhole!'

'What did you say?'

'Ah said even a porn star couldnae touch the sides!' Charlie was lying. The truth was Charlie was Goldilocks on the third attempt every time he was inside Mary Sue. It was Gweneth that didn't feel right, but he suspected this was less to do with the actual dimensions of her vagina and more psychosomatic on his part. One thing was for sure, Gweneth vanished as the fight escalated, and Mary Sue was back channelling her rustic roots. If Charlie could only see her, he'd be proposing marriage, but he'd already stormed away to the kitchen drawer with all the junk in it to locate the measuring tape. For some reason best known to competent therapists, he already had a semi. He heard Mary Sue shouting in that wonderful cornbread accent, which made him go full cup final. He came out of the kitchen with the measuring tape, saw Mary Sue in the living room about to chuck another one of his awards and showed he did indeed scrape the billed six inches.

'See!' he said. 'Ah told you!' Mary Sue stopped hurling Charlie's obscure indie awards around and burst out laughing. 'See! Six inches!' Charlie said with a smile. Charlie picked up his Arkansas Movie Critics Award for Best Supporting Actor and laughed too. Before he knew it, Mary Sue was doing a modest line of coke off his hard-on and they were both exploring sex positions that would aggravate Charlie's sciatica.

The next day, Charlie rehearsed Mary Sue's lines and went all-in to the point he felt like he was doing some countrified rube version of *My Fair Lady*. But he was fine with that. It was now his mission to change this

Gweneth character back to who she really was, the one he actually liked.

'You've got a good chance of getting this part,' he said, and he meant it.

☆

Charlie watched Mary Sue leave his house in character as her real self and felt a warm glow. He was getting back in touch with a fictionalised past life of helping others who weren't just his kids – kids he saw less of as his career reached a zenith he thought was only the middle in a rise to leading man.

Becoming the greatest and most successful Scottish actor in history was in Charlie's sights, especially after Sean Connery's interviews from another era resurfaced. Eventually, everyone lives long enough to become a villain, especially if they could sometimes be a bit of a tadger to begin with. We can't all be Jesus of Nazareth or Betty White. That's just way too unrealistic in this world.

'He'd been untouchable in his day, but noo he's in trouble,' Charlie said, laughing to himself. He often laughed at his own jokes now. Along with using excessive moisturiser and dying his hair, it was a tell-tale sign his ego and vanity were spiralling out of control. He could picture his da calling him a jessie and a fanny every time he hit the Grecian and Oil of Olay. In his da's bigoted world, you didn't have to suck a dick to get called bent. You just had to care enough about your appearance or wiggle your arse to a song with an up-tempo rhythm. God forbid if you hit a dancefloor, even if you were doing borderline foreplay with a woman at the same time. As soon as you danced, you were for the watching.

89

Gweneth came home to the apartment shaken and traumatised. Charlie pretended he wasn't just about to have a wank, and played the attentive boyfriend.

'He tried to touch me,' Gweneth said, sitting on the couch beside Charlie, who'd hidden a lingerie catalogue under the cushion that featured Gweneth but, most importantly, other women.

'Eh?' Charlie said.

'Shackler,' Gweneth said, putting her head in her hands. Charlie grasped the gravity of what she was saying and felt enraged. 'He was trying to corner me in his room with his disgusting cock out.'

Charlie pictured Harry Shackler in that robe, in that grubby hotel room full of fast food and empty bottles of booze. He wanted to kill him. 'You did the right thing getting out quickly,' he said, with a vision of eviscerating Shackler.

'No shit, Sherlock. He's not the first scumbag I've met like him. That fucking asshole!'

'Has he tried tae contact you since?'

'Of course not. I ain't getting the part now. I should've kicked the fucking creep in the goddamn nutsack!'

Charlie could feel nothing but fury and humiliation – and just as Gweneth needed him most, he decided to take matters into his own hands.

LONG BEFORE KARMA AND DEATH: A FRIGHT AT THE OSCARS

I step out into the chaos of paparazzi, lights and noise on the red carpet at the Oscars. The massive lines of coke were a mistake, in hindsight. I feel the Valium and wee hipflask in my suit trouser pocket and touch the eccie and banana I meant to eat on the way in the other. Left for upper, right for downer. Mary Sue is firmly Gweneth for the evening. More's the pity. We tried to put that Shackler cunt behind us, but the odious bastard is trying to fuck up my career just because I punched him and called him a scumbag who needs shooting.

I've had a part in some comic book crap pulled, and a story about me arguing with a bouncer – a KKK redneck cunt no less – has appeared in the press courtesy of that colossal prick William Smith. The net result is that I've gone from second favourite for the Best Supporting Actor to rank outsider in the space of a month.

Gweneth will soon be looking for an upgrade, and I'll be after someone more age-appropriate. I can't be dealing with her going on about Facebook any longer. Our relationship is now nothing but a business arrangement for another few weeks. This way, I get an attractive Oscar date, and she gets to be seen at the Oscars and keep herself relevant while that reprobate Harry Shackler tries to ruin another career.

Gweneth stops me and wipes coke from my beard. 'Fuck's sake,' she says, going all Mary Sue. Even Mary Sue is a pain the arse now. Sure, she's great in bed, but I'm not as shallow as you think. I enjoy conversation and bonding now and again. It can't all be blowjobs, anal and rimjobs in a relationship. Once you've ploughed through all the lofty heights, there must be a foundation that isn't just toxic, sludgy quicksand. I know you may not think it, but I have standards. Fuck up and don't laugh.

The sunglasses help a bit with the sensory overload. I know only wankers and legends like Jack Nicholson and D.B. Cooper get away with this, but I'm hiding a black eye I got after falling over in the bathroom – incidentally, never mix Jack Daniel's, eccies, half an ounce of purple haze and flip-flops. It's a fucking disaster waiting to happen.

I asked my mother to come to the Oscars instead of Gweneth. It didn't go down well. Just because Gweneth's family are swivel-eyed God and sheep bothering rednecks doesn't mean every cunt excommunicates their family members. My mum couldn't come anyway, what with her bad lungs and herpes flaring up more than usual. More presents from my da before he shuffled off this mortal coil and into Hell's ashtray. I hope he's down there now looking up at my success, wishing he was nicer to me and every cunt else he ever met. Fucking cunt. I don't really know why I'm thinking about him as this face of Botox and desperate, unnatural smiling interviews me about what I'm wearing. Maybe it's because I think I can see myself and how phoney I look in the phosphorus teeth of this freakshow celebrity shagger.

The Valium goes into my mouth, and I drink it down with the vodka in the water bottle. Gweneth is a natural on the red carpet, but I look like a man transplanted there from a 15th century tavern in Sligo. The interviewers naturally gravitate towards Gweneth despite her lack of acting credits. She's the real celebrity here. I'm just a character actor who turned in a good performance and can't play the game without alienating all these people pretending they're normal (or Hollywood normal). This is not the place to be different or take the piss. This is this town's midnight mass, and woe betide if you don't pay homage to it.

I realise as I avoid another shouting boyband member lookalike with a mic that I've swallowed the eccie instead of the Valium. Brilliant. How much more manufactured euphoria can I take? I'll need to find the most wasted people here and stay close, so I don't stand out too much. For all this glamour, beautiful people cutting about and the oncoming rush of ecstasy, I have the strong feeling I'll be wiping my feet on the way out of this awards show and taking a dip in a bath filled with antiseptic gel. It has the same vibe as a sewage plant, albeit one with many more fuckable people.

I avoid that evangelical atheist actor with the double-digit IQ and his born-again Christian uncle, who snorted, fucked and cornholed everything with a pulse until he became a tedious, sober, hectoring prick. It's amazing how many people smile and say hi to you here, and how you can still feel like an interloper.

A tall, dark, handsome, wide-grinned guy with a well-trimmed goatee beard comes right up to my face with his hand gripping mine, shaking it. I have no fucking clue who he is or what he wants.

'Hi!' he says. I quickly shake his hand. He doesn't say anything else.

'Right,' I say, feeling very uncomfortable. 'Hi?' You fucking shit-grinning, moronic arsehole.

I can feel myself coming up and coming down. A few people, much more famous than me, walk right towards me. I try that L.A. thing of smiling at strangers now that I'm a nominee, but they give me awkward grins in return. Apparently, their acting skills don't extend to giving a cunt the time of day.

'Couldn't even wait till the after-party,' Sandra says to Meryl.

Oh, shit. I feel a burst of love and joy. This is not good. It's a sweaty nightmare.

'He's an embarrassment,' I think I hear a woman's voice say.

Gweneth has disappeared behind a sea of sycophantic bores and whores. I take refuge in the bathroom and drink from my hipflask on the toilet as I eccie poo, shitting my brains out and possibly parts of my colon. This is not a diet conducive to a decent life expectancy. You can take the boy out of the Gorbals, but you can't make him eat tofu and do yoga when there's an abundance of booze and drugs about. I hear someone leave the cubicle two down from me and cough. I thought I was alone and allowed my arse carte blanche to go to town on the toilet bowl like it was the Luftwaffe, and my hole was a Supermarine shitfire. Even though the person probably couldn't pick me out of a poo-lice lineup, I put my head in my hands and cringe.

Just when I think things can't get any worse, I raise a hand, reaching for the toilet roll in a large, silver, circular dispenser that's like medieval armour, and touch nothing. I try again, expecting a different result, but I can only look on in horror at the missing bog roll and listen as a couple of guys come in the toilet, talking and heading to the urinals. What kind of major Hollywood awards event doesn't have toilet roll in the bogs? This is fucking

94

amateur hour. I feel around in my jacket and pull out my speech. Fucking thing looks longer than one of Fidel Castro's speeches. That's what happens when you don't want to leave any cunt out, lest you hear about it for the rest of your life. The Gettysburg address was only 272 words, and that was actually important.

I suppose a pilled-up, steaming actor lecturing people from a stage is the modern-day equivalent. Like I'm going to win anyway after that grotesque waste of skin Shackler's smeared my name just because I punched the fat bastard in a restaurant bathroom. Fuck it. I reach behind me and wipe my arse with my Oscar-winning speech. It feels like my arse has ripped in two. Of course it fucking does. It's not a quilted Oscar speech, is it? If the worst comes to worst and I win the Oscar, I'll just say thanks and get the fuck out of there. If it's good enough for Joe Pesci, it's good enough for me. Fuck sticking about to thank every cunt who's ever met me and slabbering on about ending poverty and how war is icky. I'd never live that down.

I wash my hands, marvel at the size of my pupils and then return to the orgy of sycophancy filled with some of the most renowned faces to ever have existed. I know I should make the most of this plastic, excessive nonsense, but I start to drift in and out of my life and observe myself from above, occasionally tutting while having fun below. This place is not sacrosanct, and I have no compunction about telling every cunt that it's all meaningless and utter bullshit designed to inflate and fellate the egos of the last people in the world who need it. I think I'm being tactful and cool with my whole schtick, but Tom and Steven's looks tell me I'm a pain in the Nat King.

I'm accosted by some officious gimp and ushered into the hall towards my seat. I see a man missing imperfections who gives me a reassuring smile. We met before at a party, and he was pretty sound for a guy you would expect to radiate cunt.

'How are you?' Brad says. 'You okay?' I feel words won't come without something in my hand, so I grab the banana I meant to eat in the limo and pull it out like a gun. Brad flinches for a second before laughing.

'Have you ever been poked by the scratchy side ae the banana?' I ask him. He's still smiling, but not in a genial way.

'You alright, man?' he says in that calm, measured way that kind of makes me hate him.

'Aye, you trying tae say Ah'm no?' That came out more Glaswegian and confrontational than I intended.

'Come again?' he says, no longer showing me those perfect teeth.

'Aye, you'd like that, wouldn't ye?'

He looks confused and a bit shocked. The tall, curvaceous black woman with striking brown eyes and a perfect smile he's with stops talking to some old guy and comes over to get him away from me.

'Hey, man,' Brad says, regaining his composure. 'Take it easy. I have a smoke here if you . . .'

'Aw, piss off, ya perfectly proportioned, handsome, talented cunt.'

He moves away like everyone else. Never mind, I can alienate dozens of famous people with my patter. I walk, stumble and nearly trip with my banana pointed in front of me. I see that English actress whose cleavage has a member of parliament.

'Hey, Judy! Have you ever been poked by the scratchy side ae a banana?'

'Excuse me?' she says. She's another one bamboozled by a wasted guy holding a banana.

'Ah'm a republican, by the way. No the American Republican Party. Ah mean, like a proper republican who disnae have time for the monarchy.'

'That's nice . . . Well, enjoy the evening.'

Every cunt is just so nice and polite. It would make you sick. Where have they hidden all the cunts? Where are all the big-time producers? Where are all the deviant criminals? Stick them in their best clobber, dangle some awards, and they all become different people.

I see another two guys hogging the aisle and interrupt their conversation about Pilates. 'Where's that Polanski cunt tae Ah stick the nut oan him?' I ask them.

'Polanski?' says that cunt from that shitey war film . . . *Pearl Harbour*? I think it might be that one. Fuck knows. If I see another shitey war film, I'll be the cunt with PTSD.

'Aye, Polanski . . .'

'He doesn't come here in case he gets arrested,'

'Aye, he still gets nominations, though . . .'

These guys are giving me a body swerve as well now. They're not as good as Gweneth, but they walked down that row to their supposed seats quite expertly. Kudos. I think I just passed my seat, but who's caring?

'Here, Jerry!' I shout at the guy I met at the *Showgirl Death Match 2* audition. He turns around and actually rolls his eyes. I knew that cunt never liked me. 'Have you ever been tickled by the scratchy end?' He glances at me and quickly turns away. I'm noticing a pattern.

'What's wrong with your jaw?' the next bampot asks me. It's another actor I bumped into at some awful Beverly Hills shindig for the eternally damned. I don't appreciate his informal tone, especially when I barely know him. His big pal, who never leaves his side, is staring down at me, trying to figure me out.

'What's right wae it?'

'Excuse me?' He looks affronted.

'Aye, you can understand the Martians in that film wae ye, but you cannae understand a cunt speaking the same fuckin language as ye fae the same fuckin bastardin planet.'

'I need to go. I'll see you later. Good luck with the nomination.'

You'd think I was walking about releasing farts that could end a bond between mother and child the way these cunts are acting. Some people just don't want to give time to even a fucking scintilla of reality . . .

☆

More scenes missing due to another Charlie Donnelly blackout.

☆

I wake up in a bathroom big enough for a sniper to have a target practice exercise. There's a shite in the sink. One thing is for sure, this isn't my bathroom, and I don't think it's my shite. At least, I hope it's not my shite. I don't eat sweetcorn for a start, and my latest shites are more of a messy network series than one big movie.

This bathroom belongs to a far richer person than me. Fuck's sake, I've rented smaller flats. Not that I'm jealous. I'm meant to be a socialist. At least that's what the McCarthyite interviewers cast up whenever they see me dining out or wearing designer clothes. Like I'm

98

supposed to be a tramp and slum it just because I came from 'nothing' and have a social conscience. Fuck them.

I hear a party somewhere below me. In a Hollywood place like this, it usually has more bathrooms than two Irish Catholic families would ever need. That doesn't change the fact that I need to get out of here before I become the prime suspect in jobbygate. Some people are the worst, and the others aren't far behind them, including me. I used to have such morals too, but nothing lasts forever. Even the sun will explode one day.

The first time I heard the sun would explode, I thought a chance would be a fine thing. I'd barely seen the sun for six months anyway. But then paranoia hit me, and it was up there with the worst acid trip I've ever had. The sun will explode one day, and there's a huge shite in this sink. I don't think the two are related, but why take the chance? I'm already heading for pariah status with Shackler ruining my name and me behaving like me.

I leave the toilet and walk quickly down a hallway to anywhere else. I see that guy who used to be a hotshot sitcom actor snorting coke off a mirror while three girls from that country-pop band cheer him on like he's delivering the baby Jesus. Don't get me wrong, I'm not judging. I'd kick fuck out of Bambi for a line too, but I'm well aware there's a trail from me to that shite. And you never outstay your welcome, particularly when you may have shat in your host's sink. That's just asking for trouble. And I've enough trouble in my life.

ONE HUNDRED AND NINETY-ONE DAYS INTO EMBRACING AND MISUNDERSTANDING KARMA

Phil has an exaggerated, visceral reaction on his face as he sits his bong on the floor. It's the first he's really moved much in that chair since I arrived ten minutes ago.

'Your son got circumcised?' he says. 'You know they make clones out of the discarded foreskins, don't you?'

'Can you no see how disconcerting it is that ma agent believes in aw this Illuminati bullshit?' I check my watch and remember I said I'd help at the soup kitchen again. A falling feeling in my gut makes me sit back and sigh.

'Don't be so naive, Charlie,' Phil says, picking his bong from the floor. 'How do you think I got you so many big auditions in Hollywood?' He lights and coughs and reminds me I don't miss it. At least not in this moment when I'm looking around his messy apartment that looks like a grenade could improve it.

'You're in the Illuminati now?' I say, kicking a pizza box away from my feet.

'No, but I have the connections – the right connections.'

'Had.'

'Well, you do burn some bridges when your drug habit gets out of hand. You've not exactly helped yourself, Charlie.' Phil and his usual transference of blame, but that's okay. I must own my actions too.

'Ma son's a man now,' I say, wondering where the time's gone. 'A man goth. If he wants tae marry a Jewish goth woman and convert tae Judaism, then fair play tae him.'

'Well, it wouldn't be me,' Phil says, loading his bong again. I suspect they're not exactly queuing up for an overweight agent who's failing to look in his thirties despite the miracles of hair dye and Botox. 'They could guarantee me heaven, and I still wouldn't be mutilating my cock.' It's just everything else that's on the table.

'Yet you get sex workers tae drip candle wax oan your arsehole and your balls.'

'Be quiet, Charlie,' he says, panicking. 'I told you that shit in confidence, for Christ's sake.'

'Even the seagulls know you're a dirty wee whore, Phil,' I say, standing up for fear of getting stuck in that armchair like Phil. 'It's fuckin ancient news at this point.'

'They don't call me Phil Casanova for no reason.' Man, that big, sleazy smile he does can make my skin crawl.

'They call you that cos you changed your name fae Bates tae Casanova,' I remind him.

'It helped get me clients.'

'Ah found it off-putting tae be honest. Ah only went wae you cos Gary Busey recommended you.' I was beyond high that night, even by my standards. 'It turns out listening tae Gary Busey at a party wisnae exactly the smartest thing Ah've ever done.'

'Gary might seem crazy, but he's one the sanest people in this whole town.' Phil lights and coughs and reminds me there's snooker I was going to watch later. I feel very deflated for some reason. 'Helluva actor too.'

'Well, the sanity bar is set lower here than anywhere else. It doesn't pay tae be too normal aboot here. In that respect, Busey's a visionary.'

I shouldn't trivialise mental health, even in L.A.; especially in L.A. This is where nutters come to roam free and rummage. I need to empathise as I used to do before I became so consumed with using public toilets to snort, shoot and toot. I do still miss it. Sometimes I feel I could kill every cunt at a meeting just for one line off a nice, warm tit. Right now, I'd even maim for a line made of 90 per cent baby laxative off a manky, skanky cistern that's inches above a decimated, shite-reeking toilet bowl.

My last hour-long stint at the soup kitchen felt longer than the final part of the *Lord of the Rings* trilogy. How many endings did that film have? Fuck me. It was a good film, but they really do rip the cunt out of it. I could barely feel my arse cheeks for two days afterwards. I didn't even get to see this Sauron bastard either. Still, David loved it and was obsessed with all that fantasy stuff for what seemed like most of my life. You can't imagine my disappointment when all I found were J.R.R. Tolkein's books and wrestling figures under his bed. Not one porno, football magazine or a bit of hash to make me feel better. That I was scavenging for weed at the time is neither here nor there. But, I suppose, somewhere, deep down, I was proud of David for not being a carbon copy of me.

I still wish I'd got a part in one of those *Lord of the Rings* films, but I didn't lift my skirt high enough, and I was too handsome, threatening and 'junkie chic' to play a hobbit, apparently. And by the time I landed myself two scenes in *The Hobbit*, David was getting his hole and was knee-deep in *Game of Thrones*. Here was me trying to be a movie actor, and every cunt was defecting to telly. I did try to get on *The Sopranos* once, but I wasn't Italian enough, what with me having no Italians in my family tree and a surplus of Irish and Scottish alcoholics.

'Ah wish Ah could give David a big wedge of money tae help wae the wedding and the honeymoon.' I wish I could turn back time too.

'Yeah, well, all we need is one opportunity,' Phil says. 'Maybe if you get on social media and stop living like a caveman, we might get somewhere above nowhere.'

Social media, women and drugs is about all he talks about these days.

'And be like every other person mindlessly caressing their phone like it's fuckin them?'

'C'mon, presidents use it now.'

'Is that meant tae sell it? Donald Trump was president, fir fuck's sake.'

'What's wrong with Donald Trump?'

I get a good look at Phil to see if he's taking the piss, but it seems a sincere question. 'Whit the fuck's right wae him? He's a classless, disgusting skidmark oan civilisation.'

Phil locks eyes with me for a few seconds, then nods until I see the salesman in him arrive. 'Yeah, I don't exactly like him, but he did pretty well for himself . . . in business, I mean. You have to admit that, at least.'

I have to admit fuck all. 'Aye, if you ignore the bankruptcies and aw the inherited wealth . . . Did you actually vote for that tangerine cunt? You fuckin better no hiv. You said you didn't.'

'No . . .' I think he's lying, but agents lie for a living anyway, so I don't think he even knows what the truth is anymore. 'I don't vote. I haven't for a long time now.'

'Aye, why risk it, eh?' I say, throwing his *National Enquirer* off the spare armchair and sitting down again.

'This country was sold off a long time ago. That's why you cannae even get healthcare.'

'I've got healthcare,' Phil says, tapping the side of his head like it requires a devious scheme to get an ambulance to arrive.

'Ah mean wider society. You know, free at the point of contact healthcare. No this mad casino shitshow.'

'Yeah . . .' Phil says, turning the channel from an irate chef shouting at a vacant busboy to the cute puppet calling the scruffy puppet who lives in a bin a grouch. 'I'm not sure I really believe in society.'

'Whit?' I want to slap him, but that doesn't seem very karma.

'Society is a load of bullshit.'

I don't know why I expected better. 'You're a Tory cunt.'

'I don't really know what that means.'

'It means you're a self-centred, probably inbred, cunt.'

'Hey, man. I've voted Democrat in the past.' The grin on his face makes me think there's another in-joke I'm not getting. 'I give to charities . . . a charity . . . occasionally.'

'Ah don't believe in relying oan charity. Philanthropy and the need for it is a failure ae society. It never goes tae the root causes.' I look over at Phil, who's busy scanning his phone and probably blocking me out.

'What?'

'We should aw have a good welfare system . . . robust . . . a more egalitarian society that negates the need for greed fucked pricks like Musk and Bezos tae put up the veneer of philanthropy.'

'Yeah, like that's gonna work,' he says, laughing at something on his phone. 'Human beings are assholes. You've said so yourself.' He's right. I have said that. For all my bleeding-heart spiel, I am misanthropic. 'Besides, you were living in a big house and eating in expensive restaurants before your career went kaput.'

'Fuck you.'

Phil looks at me with a hurt expression. No, not fuck you. Enter reasoned debate and resist the urge to lay him out with a punch. He is still your agent, even if he's as useful as lipstick on a piranha fish.

'Don't get touchy just because you're a hypocrite,' Phil dismisses, looking at that phone again. 'We're all hypocrites from time to time. We're all full of shit.'

'You been reading Socrates?

'I don't read much . . . you know that.'

'Aye, Ah know.' I feel guilt, crushing guilt. I want to help my son. It's just a pity the bank is charging for me being skint, and I have more red letters than a strip of Amsterdam filled with sex workers. 'Fuckin money. It's the worst. Sometimes Ah think Ah'd be better off six feet under.'

'Don't talk like that . . . That's dark . . . Besides, cremations are cheaper. And I know a good loan shark. She charges reasonable interest for a loan shark too!'

'That's just whit Ah need,' I say, standing and pulling the jeans from my arse. I might have lost a bit of weight, but all my clothes still leave flesh wounds.

'No, seriously. She offers a competitive rate. It's not much worse than your average crooked bank! I don't even think she's murdered anyone either!' I've heard enough. I never thought I'd look forward to going to a soup kitchen, but Phil's helped with that. I must be due some good fortune soon. Surely to fuck.

'Aye, that's very reassuring. Maybe it's the fairer sex thing, eh?'

ONE HUNDRED AND ONE
DAYS AFTER DEATH

'Jesus,' Phil says, as I let my gut show its true self after another takeaway and numerous protein bars. 'You know you can't just keep eating protein bar after protein bar because they're meant to be healthy. You'll still gain weight.'

'Ah'm dead,' I say, looking at my pale, grey-haired gut. 'Ah don't exactly have a lot tae live for now, dae Ah?'

'This is grim, Charlie,' he says, sitting down in his chair with his fat stomach relaxing and spreading over his trousers. 'I mean, I saw you taking crack and shitting your pants, but this chain-eating protein bars and social media shit is worse.'

'Leave me alone, fir fuck's sake,' I say, reading people arguing about Clash albums on Reddit.

'This is my home,' Phil says, cracking a beer.

'Naw, it's no. This is your secret apartment away fae your soon tae be ex-wife.'

'Exactly,' he says, tanning the can. 'It's meant to be a sanctuary.'

'Fuck your sanctuary. Did you bring the whey shakes?'

'Yeah,' he says, kicking the bag at his feet, 'but I don't think you need them. I think you might have a problem.'

'Whit the fuck would you know about whit Ah need?'

'I've been your agent for decades.'

'Aye, decades too long.'

'You're mean when you've had . . .' – he looks at all the protein bar wrappers – 'however many protein bars. I don't think they agree with you. I don't think all this Twitter, football forums and Facebook shit agrees with you.'

'Social media is a fuckin cesspit,' I say after reading some cunt say Green Day are better than The Clash.

'Why are you glued to it then like it's your conjoined twin?'

He's got me there. I'm becoming the thing I used to moan about. 'Whit the fuck else Ah'm Ah meant tae dae aw fuckin day?'

'I don't know, man . . . Go a walk, get liposuction.'

'Fuck off. You're no exactly a whippet yourself, ya fat cunt.'

'A what?'

'A wee greyhound.'

'Yeah, maybe not. But you must've put on about two kilos since you died and discovered Twitter. It ain't healthy, Charlie. You need a purpose. Trolling doesn't suit you.'

'In case you didnae notice, Ah died. It might arouse suspicion if Ah start cutting about the streets.'

'Shave your beard off, wear a disguise, become a walking tattoo. Just get some vitamin D and spend 20 minutes without your eyes melting in front of a screen. It ain't healthy.'

Maybe Phil does have a point. I have so much hate inside me that 280 characters in an echo chamber isn't exactly a fulfilling outlet for it. There are only so many times you can call a person a dick on Twitter without it getting a bit boring.

Phil looks at the TV screen and another Netflix special I've put on about a psycho whose idea of romance ends with leaving dead bodies around isolated parts of America. They're mostly American, aren't they?

And the documentaries usually begin with the whole "Nothing ever happened around here" shite. You just don't think your neighbour with the midnight gardening hobby and the job at the abattoir will kill 22 women because his TV broke, and his momma used to dress him up as a girl and cattle prod his special area. I mean, that's no reason to go on a murdering rampage that's essentially him killing his mother over and over. Absent and cuckolded father and a domineering, sadist mother. It's textbook. The inverse can also be applied many times over, but my favourite irredeemable, horrible psychos tend to have the wee Heinrich Himmler mother.

'Have you not had enough of all this true crime shit?' Phil asks me.

'Aye, maybe.' Maybe I need to make a list too. People think I'm dead anyway. But murder is a moral minefield, isn't it, even if you're just killing cunts who deserve it, like televangelists? Christ knows some people do deserve it, and I say that as more of a New Testament man who vehemently opposes capital punishment.

There is one guy, though, who definitely deserves it. One towering bawbag above all others. One of the biggest scumbag cunts in Hollywood, which pretty much puts him in the running for the world champion of scumbags. Anytime a woman threatens to go public, he's there with intimidation, with a payoff, with his political contacts. That cunt doesn't deserve to live. I suppose nature might take him soon, what with his age and arse size, but that's not soon enough. This town is full of vulnerable people and desperate dreamers who will fall into his trap in the meantime.

'Do you want me to get you a peloton?' Phil asks me with a big slapable grin on his coupon. 'I think we can swing a couple with the money you've made since the death thing.'

'Whit the fuck is a peloton?'

'It's a fancy exercise bike.'

'Get tae fuck, man.'

Where's the sociopathic Shackler's karma? He exploits everything he touches. He sexually assaults, bullies and is now helping fund a Republican candidate and promote another *Star Wars* film. Is there no level this monster will stoop to in his quest for power? Shackler should be getting a sentence imposed on him from the almighty. Since the almighty is absent, it'll need to be the next best thing.

LONG BEFORE KARMA AND DEATH:
A MUMMY'S BOY

Big Charlie sat in his armchair and exhaled a puff of smoke towards his son's face. 'Drama?' he said, looking at Charlie like he'd just shat on a church pew and thrown it at the altar. 'You chose tae dae fuckin drama at school?' Charlie stood there silent, paralysed. 'Are ye fuckin bent or sumfin?'

'Naw,' Charlie mumbled, avoiding eye contact.

'Well, whit's wrang wae ye then?' Big Charlie said with a scowl whilst tipping his cigarette in the ashtray on the armrest.

'Nuttin . . . Ah just like acting.'

'Acting!' For someone who spent many hours extolling John Wayne chewing scenery and cutting about with a broken arse, Big Charlie couldn't grasp how anyone would want to act. 'First, you leave school, don't get an apprenticeship and noo you want tae be a fuckin actor! You're sumfin else, in't ye? You must've been swapped by gypsies, ya daft cunt ye!'

'It's ma dream.'

'Dream? Who taught you tae dream, fir fuck's sake? You dream when you're asleep, ya stupid prick ye! Noo, piss off before Ah slap ye intae next month!'

Being told no by his da made Charlie want to be an actor even more. It was part of the reason he told his father. He needed justification and an excess of defiance and determination. It was petty to want to do something just to get it up people who didn't believe in him, but that fuel would help Charlie with nagging doubts and handling rejection. It made him learn how to do the craft better until it was a job that could provide a good life for him.

Charlie's mother, Leanne, took a different view from his father and quietly encouraged him to make his dreams a reality. She was taught not to dream by her parents and wasn't going to let her husband do the same to their kid. Just because Big Charlie was bitter, cantankerous and lost didn't mean everybody else had to be. Leanne had only stayed with him out of misguided loyalty and notions he might change, but he never did, and the odds on him doing a 180 now seemed non-existent without lobotomising him.

Leanne was happy to see her son becoming a man, but she missed when he would come home dirty like a mendicant and still try to avoid a bath. Now all Charlie did was fuss over his appearance and make sure his clothes looked immaculate before trying to impress women. He was no longer her wee boy kicking a ball, building dens and setting fires. It made Leanne feel old, and the thought of living with a broken husband in this drab, utilitarian flat was enough for her to consider Citalopram or throwing Big Charlie in the Clyde.

Big Charlie staggered home reeking of booze and a fish supper – half of which he threw at a car that beeped at him while he was in the middle of the road. Everything was someone else's fault. That was his mantra. He'd like to blame himself, but that would just be textbook masochism and patently untrue. He prided himself on his own brand of honesty which required mental contortions to pretend he wasn't lying to himself.

When Big Charlie got home to his confined, modest, if well-kept two-bedroom flat, he immediately wanted a confrontation. Wee Charlie was the focus of his wrath, but he knew he'd get blowback from Leanne. It was inevitable those two would stick together. *Charlie's a mummy's boy* is what he'd tell everybody. *A wee fuckin mummy's boy.* Like he was supposed to be a daddy's boy when all his father did was beat and humiliate him.

Big Charlie walked into the living room and saw them both sitting watching TV. 'A fuckin actor, eh? A fuckin actor!' This was how he greeted his son; a son who was stressed and getting ready to go to bed. Charlie said nothing. It was better to keep silent when confronted by a paralytic mess. 'A fuckin actor. You really are a stupid wee cunt. The village fuckin idiot.' Charlie switched off and let it wash over him. This was nothing, only temporary. He was leaving this flat and never returning. Charlie saw his da looming over him, baiting him, but he didn't rise to it.

'Leave him alone,' Leanne said, standing up in front of her sitting son. 'And stoap shouting. Paula's sleeping.' Big Charlie didn't care that his 4-year-old daughter was sleeping and looked past Leanne at Charlie. Leanne tried to find her voice, be firm and stare Big Charlie in the eye. 'So help me if you touch him.'

Big Charlie scoffed. 'Whit the fuck you gonnae dae, eh?' He turned his attention to Leanne and got in her face. She pushed him away. 'Eh? Ya stupid fuckin boot.'

'That's it,' Leanne said. 'Leave and don't come back!'

'This is ma hoose, ya bitch!'

Charlie snapped back into life at the sight of his mum taking another slap from his da. He'd vowed never to let it happen again, and now he dashed to the adjoining kitchen, opened the cutlery drawer and returned brandishing a steak knife at his father. Big Charlie laughed it off and goaded his son until he collapsed onto the carpet and looked up at Charlie standing over him, a knife dripping with blood in his hand. It was the last thing he'd ever see.

Leanne sprang into action as Charlie entered a zombified state. She took the knife from him and wiped it with a dishtowel. 'Everything will be fine,' she said to him, sounding like she wasn't really believing it herself. Charlie was 16 and couldn't go to jail; he wasn't built for it and would never make it, especially with the considerable stigma of being handsome and a murderer who'd killed his own father. She couldn't have a sensitive boy like him, a bag of bones, still more boy than man, trying to survive in a ruthless hellscape with real murderers, psychos and rapists.

☆

Leanne assumed responsibility. She took the sentence and got a lenient one, given she'd allegedly committed murder and had a judge who was also hamstrung by having a dick and balls. The grubby right-wing tabloids whose readers still wanted to reinstate hanging called the three-year sentence generous. One particular tabloid journalist, William Smith, speculated why this was and rubbished the psychiatrist who was damning in their assessment of Big Charlie's violent tendencies.

During and after the trial, William Smith harassed Charlie and his family, all in the pursuit of salacious details for the lowest common denominator. William Smith was a man without scruples, an obsessive, dangerous man who thought it was better to print bullshit if it would sell more than the truth. It was all about profit for William, so it was no surprise when he found himself writing for a trashy gossip rag in the US.

An article about Charlie's mother murdering his father appeared courtesy of William Smith in *The National Exposure*. The omission of the domestic abuse and painting of Big Charlie as a salt-of-the-earth type is what really drove Charlie insane. He threatened to sue, and William Smith backed off for a while, only to return with glee when Charlie graduated to smack and crack.

'Charlie Donnelly was found with his head drooping and a needle in his arm in a fast food bathroom!'

William looked at his underling and smiled. 'Excellent,' he said. 'Was there anything else?'

'Not really. The cop busted the door down, and Charlie was allegedly out of it with his head on his lap . . .'

'On his lap?'

'Yeah, on his lap.'

'So, he was trying to suck himself off as well?'

'I don't know if . . .'

'Yeah, he was. He was trying to suck his own cock while high on smack. Get typing.'

AFTER DEATH: AN AGENT OF KARMA, PART 1

Shackler does a lot of his disgusting acts in hotels where a rich, powerful man has little business being caught dead in with his trousers around his ankles. For years, he's got away with parading his dick in front of young men and women and taking advantage of his power. There's a culture of omertà around this cunt, but everybody knows he's a bully and definitely dodgy. He tried to corner Mary Sue, and I have it on good authority that he's groped, coerced blowjobs and raped. In short, the cunt's a dirty fucking beast and is long overdue his comeuppance.

Phil stated casually that Shackler is a rapist, but Phil's an agent, and you can't expect moral currency from that cunt. Me? I have to be better. I must make amends. Punching Shackler and threatening to castrate him was not enough. Instead of exposing that cunt, he smeared me and made me a pariah. So what if I didn't help myself with all my incidental felonious behaviour? This town is full of fannies on drugs and drink who think they're the second coming of Humphrey Bogart and Audrey Hepburn. I'm not the exceptional cunt here.

The Hotel Percy is particularly seedy for Shackler. It's three-star and barely a cut above two. But that's the thing about Shackler. He knows people dream about making it big since childhood, and he knows he's one of a select few who can make or break a career that's heading nowhere or hasn't even begun. It's too much power concentrated in the bloated hands of one reprobate, and it's about time some cunt gave him a dose of karma. Fuck knows karma has been sleeping when it comes to this dickhead.

It's a perfect crime. Dead men can't kill. As long as I can push down my conscience for the rest of my life, I'll be fine. If I can't and doing good things other than murdering this cunt doesn't help, there's always drugs to help me out. Good old drugs. Where would I be without them? Probably still alive, for one. Terrifying.

I put on this joke cowboy hat and check my weird little stick-on goatee in the mirror of the new second-hand blue Prius I bought off Craigslist whilst in another disguise. I hate looking like this hipster fanny, but going chameleon to avoid becoming a murder suspect or people speculating whether you're alive requires a degree of fashion catastrophe. It's not like the paparazzi or any cunt is watching me now. Death makes you invisible in this town, and so does being a nearly 60-year-old man with a gut and bad dress sense. You become older here quicker in the eyes of others than in most places. That's why people spend thousands injecting their faces with poison and walk around looking three-quarters lizard. Growing old is for the Midwest or parts of the world that don't have major fashion shows.

I've had to stake this place out and stalk my mark for days. Fuck knows how assassins do it. I have a whole new level of respect for anyone who has to watch a grotesque blot on the landscape eat his way to a heart attack before the opportunity arises to corner them in a secluded spot and hand them over to Satan for processing. I was tempted to walk into McDonald's and shoot the bastard point-blank in front of witnesses, but that seemed dim, even for me.

116

Shackler steps inside this basic room. He's on his phone again, salivating at whatever he's looking at. Don't worry, I'm not going to let him get his tadger out before I open the closet. He puts the phone to his ear. That looks like a novelty these days. How quaint it is to see someone with a phone at their ear in the era of FaceTime, earbuds and Snapchat. I still remember landlines, the Phone Book and the Yellow Pages. But that's enough nostalgia. Life is about moving forward, especially when you're planning a murder. I can't go back now or stand still like a fucking statue in this closet until this cunt comes in for his tools.

I hold the Ruger American pistol in my jacket pocket – bought in cash, in person via the Craigslist of guns ARMS4US while I was wearing a MAGA hat and T-shirt, which I immediately binned.

'Come up in, say, 25 minutes, room 78; we can talk about the role and if you're a good fit for the part.'

You slimy, revolting fuck. I see him lying on the bed with his head propped on the pillow, eating fried chicken straight from the bucket and washing it down with a warhead of Coke. He grips at his chest, and a burp rips from him. It's time I came out of the closet, yet I'm still inside it, sweating and about to sneeze. Oh, fuck me. Fuck off. Fuck.

Choo.

The muffled sneeze gives the game away.

'What the fuck?' Shackler says, gripping his chest again. I burst out and lose the hat and sunglasses. Shackler tries to pull himself up on the bed and slouches to the side. 'Charlie Donnelly? But you're dead. You're a gh–ost!' He falls off the bed face-first onto the carpet. I roll him over with my boot and see his face looks a wee bit on the dead side.

'Shit,' I say. It's one thing to think about murder in the abstract, but it's another to haunt a man, albeit a monstrous man, to death with the help of a bargain bucket of chicken and too much Coca-Cola. I'm able to induce a cardiac arrest by virtue of being a ghost. I'm like one of those comic book villains, but a more realistic one.

I check his pulse just to make sure, then check mine to confirm I'm still alive. Aye, I'm definitely still here, alive and kicking Bob Shackler's fat gut. Well, this is a worrying development. Kicking a corpse, eh? If only my mother could see me now, she'd be really disappointed. At least my da would probably be proud. He was a sick cunt too. What a shame I had to kill him.

I pull myself together by remembering the deterrent of American prisons and convince myself that kicking him is overkill. I had a job to do, and it's more than done. All I'm doing now is hurting my foot. I don't want to become a majorly demented cunt and start enjoying this kinda shit. Before I know it, I could be keeping pickled dicks in fridges and chasing the postman bare-arsed down the street. If I've learned one thing from too much true crime shite, it's that serial killing is a slippery slope all the way to lethal injection.

The good news is that I kinda feel bad and euphoric at the same time. Maybe I need a line of coke to even me out. Nah, I can't start taking drugs and becoming a vigilante. That's like mixing public speaking and ether; someone is bound to notice. Besides, getting clean-ish was the right thing to do. It was the boring thing to do, but the right thing. Since I got sober, I've died, wiped out my debts, took solid shites regularly and helped rid Hollywood of one of its biggest bogeymen. All things considered, it was the correct decision – for now.

LONG BEFORE KARMA AND DEATH: SISTER PAULA MORPHINE

Charlie could still recall the first time his little sister Paula told him she wanted to join the convent in Kirkintilloch and how hard he laughed before he remembered his sister needed a humour transplant and couldn't possibly play this for laughs. His mother gave him a stern look to get him to show decorum – something that was difficult for a cynical, decadent actor who was already drunk for the evening and heading towards pished.

'Why would you want tae be a nun, fir fuck's sake? You're no even auld enough yet. You're only 16 wae your whole life ahead ae you,' Charlie said after hearing Paula talking about the convent again and heaving his washing into his mum's kitchen. 'It's 1993, society's becoming mair and mair secular and it defies every biological urge in . . .' Charlie looked at his sister's eerily perfect posture and expressionless, psycho face sitting at the small kitchen table with a cup of tea. 'Well, maybe no in your case.'

'Charlie!' Leanne yelled, chastising him again and turning in her seat at the table to give him her serious face. Charlie was the apple of Leanne's eye, but Paula couldn't know that for certain, even if she suspected it. 'Have you thought long and hard aboot it, Paula?'

'Aye, Ah've thought about it,' Paula said, holding her cup of tea. 'Of course Ah've thought about it. Ah want tae do good in this world, do something substantial, make a difference.' She aimed the last few comments at

Charlie, and her face was a picture of uncut condescension. Charlie waited until his mother turned away, then gave his teenage sister a middle digit. At 28, maturity wasn't yet troubling Charlie, and any sign of it faded with each passing drink. He was riding high on the back of theatre appearances and numerous minor roles on TV and film, and he wasn't going to let Paula make out like he wasn't reinventing the wheel or doing something great for humanity.

'So, whit, Ah'm no daein anything important?' Leanne got up and left for the living room to get the paper and distract herself from the bickering. 'Is that whit you're inferring here? Ah've been on *Taggart*, had lines in a Mike Leigh film, a Ken Loach film . . . Ah've been in numerous . . .' Paula snorted derision while Charlie pulled out a block of cheddar cheese from the fridge and broke a bit off with his hands.

'Are you just gonnae start rhyming off your CV and expect us tae bow before you like you're king of all creation? You're so pathetic. And get a knife to cut the cheese, ya minger.'

'Ah'm a republican socialist. Ah don't believe in any ae that monarchy and elitist pish.' Paula guffawed and dunked her Rich Tea biscuit into her tea. 'Whit?'

'You'd be a millionaire autocrat if only the world would let you,' Paula said.

Charlie looked with disgust at Paula sucking on a soddened Rich Tea. 'Who the fuck eats Rich Tea when there's chocolate biscuits in there? Rich Tea is a last resort biscuit. They're fuckin disgusting.'

Leanne walked back in, sat down with the *Daily Record* at the crossword page, and ignored Charlie gnawing on a bit of cheddar cheese.

'Stop swearin,' she said. 'It isnae a Ken Loach production in here.'

'Ah like Rich Tea,' Paula muttered.

'They're fuckin prison biscuits.' Charlie realised what he'd said after he caught his mother looking away.

'You could be daein wae getting used tae them then,' Paula said with a smirk.

'Right,' Leanne said. 'That's enough. Nae mair prison talk or fighting aboot biscuits or else Ah won't buy any biscuits at aw.'

'Well, don't buy Rich Tea,' Charlie mumbled.

'You're no even meant tae live here anymair,' Paula said, giving her Rich Tea an extra-long dunk.

'It isnae your house.' Leanne left the kitchen again to sit on the toilet and pull strands of her hair out – a habit she'd developed in a prison cell.

'Aye, but you have a flat, yet you're here aw the time getting ma mum tae dae your washings and cook dinners for you and tae massage your ego aboot your three scenes in *Take the High Road*.'

'It wisnae three scenes. Try three *episodes* of *Take the High Road*.' Paula looked momentarily flustered.

'*Take the High Road* is utter rubbish anyway.'

'So? It's a paying gig. You need tae dae these things if you want tae get recognised as an artist.'

'As an artist? So, whit, you're Van Gogh now?'

'He'd have cut aff both his ears if you were his sister.'

'You actually think you're an artist?' she said, laughing. 'That's cute.'

'And you think you're in tune wae the Almighty . . . That's delusional.'

'Naw, it's no.'

'Aye, it is.'

'How is it?'

'Because there's nae God for a start,' Charlie said. He wasn't sure if there was, and he usually wouldn't be so emphatic in anything ecclesiastical, but he wasn't just going to let her slag him with impunity.

'Aye, because you're the foremost authority oan the meaning of life.' Paula looked down at Charlie's trainers and shook her head. 'You're nearly 30 and you cannae even tie your laces properly.'

'Away tae the convent and gie us aw peace,' Charlie said. 'Ya fuckin boring bastard.'

'You don't even live here!' Paula yelled.

'Ah'm daein ma washing, awright? Ah don't have a machine.'

'Go tae a laundrette then.'

Charlie scoffed. 'Aye, everything's so simple tae you.'

'Everything is simple when you're no a simpleton.'

Charlie looked at Paula's neutral expression, her folded arms and rigid, upright posture in her chair. 'Aye, you'll fit right in wae they nuns. Quite a few ae them are sadistic psychos as well.'

Paula just stared, not a flicker of emotion. 'And you'll end up dead soon wae aw the drugs and drink you take,' she said with a clenched jaw. Charlie's eyes widened and he looked away from his sister to the rain running down the window behind her. He let out a chuckle, focused on Paula's face and narrowed his eyes.

'Ah'd rather be a drug-addled actor and dead than a teetotal, fire in brimstone pain in the arse.'

'Aye, and then you'll be in Hell.'

Charlie shook his head and sighed. 'Jesus, man,' he murmured. 'You're warped. Ah bet you know everything aboot Hell and fuck all aboot Heaven.'

'Stop swearing in front ae me.' Paula frowned. 'Ah don't like it.'

Charlie could see the worst traits of his father present in his sister – all that was missing was the copious amount of booze and a chip on the shoulder about an inability to hold down a job. Maybe his da should've been a nun. 'You don't like swearing, but you'll wish Hell upon people,' he said, finishing his cheese and leaning against the kitchen counter. 'You're a weirdo. You must've been swapped at birth.'

'Druggie.'

'Ah smoke hash and take a bit of speed. Ah'm hardly Iggy fuckin Pop. Although if Ah stayed here wae you, Ah'd need fuckin morphine. It's nae surprise Ma is oan they downers listening tae your pish. Ah'd be oan smack if Ah lived here 24/7.'

Paula shot up from her seat. She threw half a soggy biscuit, which slapped off Charlie's cheek and landed broken on the kitchen linoleum. But that wasn't enough. She launched the *World's Greatest Mum* mug next, smacking Charlie square in the forehead, stunning him slightly and causing him to fall against the fridge.

Charlie pulled an Oban magnet off the door, to launch a retaliation, but he dropped it, much to Paula's amusement. 'Ya fuckin psycho ye!' he shouted. 'Ah'm oan set the morra.' He could already feel the lump forming, and his current skinhead haircut for the part of racist number two in a Channel 4 drama wasn't going to hide it.

Still smiling, Paula fetched another mug and made another cup of tea for dunking her biscuit.

'Where's ma mum?' Charlie asked.

They both walked down the hall to the bathroom. Charlie chapped on the door and heard nothing.

'She's definitely in there,' Paula said.

'It's locked,' Charlie stressed. 'Mum!' He tried to shoulder it open and tried again.

'Out the way,' Paula said, before kicking the door near the lock to break it and get in the bathroom. It looked worse than it was, and Charlie, already stoned, hungover and half-pished, panicked and entered the realms of a meltdown that made him useless in a crisis. Leanne was sitting on the closed toilet pan with a knife at her feet. She'd only nicked a trickle of blood from her wrist before the hemophobia, which developed from a brutal fight she'd witnessed in prison, made her unconscious.

'Shit,' Charlie blurted, staying rooted to the spot. Paula pushed past him and fell to her knees in front of Leanne, taking her pulse. Leanne groaned a bit, and Paula breathed a sigh of relief.

'She's fine,' Paula said, exhaling. 'She's just fainted.' Charlie glanced again at the slight cut on Leanne's wrist, felt drenched in sweat and watched the walls of the already narrow bathroom come to meet him. Then everything went darker than lights out in jail, and he promptly hit the linoleum.

LONG BEFORE KARMA AND DEATH: HUNTING WITH EUGENE HARRISON

Mary Sue/Gweneth was adamant that Charlie had to meet her father. Despite her name, accent change and memories of her mother dying in that exploding trailer, Mary Sue could not resist the pull of home. She still loved her daddy as she called him in that infantilised way that made Charlie occasionally scream into his fish tank.

Mary Sue was aware Charlie and her father, Eugene Harrison, were quite different people. Eugene had been a cop until he hooked up a Mexican's balls to a car battery and forgot about the CCTV. The Mexican's only crime was being in the wrong place at the wrong time after someone robbed two pigs from Tom Janetty's farm. Tom, a militant racist, blamed the only Mexican in town, so Eugene went to work on finding out what had happened to these prize-winning pigs he was sure Tom was banging on the sly. Bestiality didn't concern Eugene as much as immigrants coming into their peaceful, sleepy, redneck town that had only seen two active serial killers (they did work together) and one minor school shooting in a ten-year period – only two fatalities.

Eugene didn't discriminate much when it came to his police brutality. He had tortured Hispanics, Asians (both the ones he liked to masturbate to and the ones he didn't), Irish Catholics, middle easterners, African Americans, Russians (both actual Russians and people he thought were Russian) and the occasional white with an Arkansas accent (some of them even Republicans). But

Eugene was relieved of his duties after one stray CCTV camera in a garage, and a changing climate towards torture from liberal types.

'Liberal hippie bullshit,' he'd often tell people at bars. 'Sensitivity training and pillow biters in the army.'

'Ah, you said it, Eugene,' said Peter Dewsbury, deputy grand wizard of the OKKK (the Original KKK). 'Ain't no morals no more in this country, that's for goddamn sure. That's why we need to recruit for the original Klan. Get back to our roots.'

'What, and dress up in a white sheet like half a ghost and half a cum tadpole?'

'The Klan is more than just the white uniform.'

'I ain't joining no clubs. Them days are done. I'm living off the land, hunting, drinking. Like a real man should. Burning crosses and putting on them dresses is goddamn child's play.'

Given Eugene's surly, homicidal disposition, there was no doubt Charlie had his work cut out. That Charlie was a lefty pinko to Eugene, and famous and successful with it, only made the task near impossible. But Charlie didn't care. This was just a formality for him so he could keep banging Mary Sue and have a beautiful woman more than a decade younger on his arm. Charlie suspected that once what sex was left had gone, the relationship with Mary Sue would soon follow. Still, he reasoned if he could play the role of noble gentleman, getting to know the wizened father of his supposed one true love, it would make his life easier and stop Mary Sue harping on about her daft old daddy. Of course, Charlie had only heard the abridged version of Eugene Harrison. He had no idea the man was a disgraced former cop with a far-right-wing take on just about everything.

Mary Sue neglected to mention her daddy's vocation for killing animals, distaste for Miranda rights and his lack of tact when discussing politics or anything else. She was just happy she had a father in her life after her mother told her 'goddamn gipsies' left her on the trailer step, then how she was immaculately conceived when the questions became too much. It was only later that Mary Sue found out her momma had been a local sex worker, and the odds on immaculate conception were pretty long, like Cowdenbeath beating Real Madrid over two legs. After her mother exploded in a trailer along with those three guys, Mary Sue searched deeper for her father and found it was none other than a cop with standing in the community.

Eugene hadn't known Mary Sue was his daughter and thought he could never father a kid given his one regular and one peanut ball situation. But there was no denying biology in this instance, even if 'liberal agendas' often twisted biology to promote its wanton evils. Eugene, for all his unrepentant hatred, was an attentive father, but he suspected Mary Sue's mother did considerable damage that he couldn't reverse. He accepted Mary Sue's descent into Hollywood immorality was inevitable given the lack of God in her life and the presence of too much Tom Cruise and Nicole Kidman. Tom Cruise was no substitute for God, despite what Tom Cruise thought. But Eugene saw enough of himself in Mary Sue to cut her a break, even if changing her name was a kick to the gut. The next time she visited, he intended to deprogram her by any means necessary. Hollyweird was just another cult to Eugene and deserved the same treatment.

Charlie put on his bravest face and went method again. He couldn't show Mary Sue that wilderness and a lack of concrete freaked him out, much less tell her. He had to go all the way to preserve this particular valuable piece of his mid-life crisis.

'Beautiful country,' he said, looking around for sheep shagging and gangs of rednecks using pitchforks as makeshift dildos. The whole place reminded him of that trip to Girvan when he was eight. 'Ah can see why you still talk about it. It really is stunning.' Mary Sue only reminisced to laugh at some of the backward ways or talked about a childhood that sounded straight out of the *Texas Chainsaw* canon.

'Yeah, it's just the people who ruin it,' she said. 'But ma daddy's different.' There was more than a tinge of myth about the last statement, and Charlie's bullshit sense was tingling.

'Must be a lotta good people here tae,' Charlie said. 'This is the heartland.'

'This place ain't the heart,' Mary Sue said. 'It's more like the asshole.'

'An arsehole that could use a trim,' Charlie said, looking at all the hideous trees and vegetation. 'Where's an amoral logging company when you need them? The Amazon, probably.'

Charlie drank Jack Daniel's from a flask and offered some to Mary Sue.

'Not while I'm driving,' she said.

'Of course,' Charlie said. 'It was a reflex.' Charlie had a reflex bump of coke and tried to settle down, but it wasn't happening in these troubling, yet tranquil surroundings.

☆

After watching an ultraviolent yarn made by some hippie sympathiser called Stanley Kubrick, Eugene decided he'd like to emulate certain brainwashing scenes. With the basement ready with a chair fitted with arm and leg restraints and select viewing for the TV, he polished and loaded his rifles for the trip. Betsy and Anna were his preferred options. Betsy for himself and Anna for this Eurotrash actor.

Anna's sight was more Mr Magoo than Superman, and she had a troublesome knack for jamming. That made it perfect for his adversary just in case Charlie had learned how to use a rifle in that uber-fake Sodom called Los Angeles.

Home of America's Best Turnips *and worst hookers*

You are now entering God's Country *asshole*

Knockemstiff, Arkansas Population 4832 *stupid*

Abandon **hope for all who enter** *ME*

America love it or leave it *or just accept it*

Trespassers will be shot! *with cum*

The *inbred* **People Rule**

Honk if you're horny, die if you're Canadian

Freedom isn't free. *But Blowjobs are and blowjobs are better*

In God we Trust *in Satan we jizz*

Build walls not bridges. *Build Lego asshole*

Never give up! *Never fucking try to begin with*

Charlie took in all the signs by the side of the road and bumper stickers and longed to shake the hand of the graffiti artist who'd done a number on some of them.

'Home of Paul Gherkin and Larry Vickers,' Charlie read off a bit of cardboard. 'Did they not kill like 20 people?'

'22, I think,' Mary Sue said casually. 'They lived down the trailer park from us.'

'That's grim,' Charlie said, thinking town pride was obviously at a low ebb.

'I suppose, but most of the park went to their barbecues . . .' Mary Sue seemed way too casual about this, Charlie thought, and he hadn't exactly grown up in an idyllic suburb in Connecticut. 'No-one had any idea they were murderers.'

'Ah would hope no,' Charlie said, looking out the window for any *Hills Have Eyes* mutant types. 'They were cannibals, were they no?'

'Yeah,' Mary Sue said, getting bored with the fascination with these two pedestrian killers. 'They had a couple of trailers side by side at the back of the park behind the bush. They loved cooking day and night. Apart from that, they just seemed normal. Dull.'

'Did you ever eat at their barbecues?' Charlie asked, morbidly fascinated.

'Oh, no. Me and momma were vegetarian at the time. We were the freaks in town.'

'Sounds it.'

'What's that supposed to mean?' Mary Sue said, taking it the wrong way. She was always sensitive when discussing her childhood.

Charlie opened a can of beer. 'Well, there were cannibal serial killers aboot,' he said, taking a swig. 'Their weirdness supersedes yours.'

'Supersedes?' Mary Sue said, turning away from the road to give Charlie a contemptuous look. 'Don't use words like that round Daddy.'

'What? Does he no like a vocabulary?' Charlie smiled, but Mary Sue didn't.

'He's meat and potatoes,' she said, cutting the air with her right hand. 'Words like that won't endear you none.'

Charlie took a drink from his beer and gazed out the window again. 'You better no use the transatlantic accent then,' he said, not resisting the urge to reciprocate with snideness.

'Yeah, thanks for the wisdom. I won't once we're there.' What a relief, Charlie thought. He'd grown sick of Gweneth and was starting to see the end with Mary Sue too. Another few months was what he was looking for; another few months of using each other to try and revive their ailing public profiles after the Shackler treatment. Gweneth might cut him loose before that, given his star was plummeting. He knew she was sizing him up and waiting to see if his Oscar buzz would carry through to more offers or if Shackler had ended him as a going concern.

As he grew closer to Eugene's cabin, Charlie knew he'd made a mistake and should've postponed this trip indefinitely until the inevitable split from Gweneth ended the possibility forever. 'Ah can see why you miss the place,' Charlie said, shuddering at some of the scenery.

'Who says I miss it? I didn't say that.'

'You talk about it when you're drunk.'

131

'And? That doesn't mean I miss it. I talk about beatings when I'm drunk. I don't miss that, do I?' Charlie must've been gone too far on drink and drugs to remember the beatings seminar. It was curious how often and how long two people could speak to each other and retain nothing of it. The narcotics didn't help with that, but Charlie knew that with receding respect and tolerance for each other's bullshit came deaf ears.

'There it is,' Mary Sue said, going native in preparation for Eugene. It was a welcome relief as Gweneth began conjuring up images of Tory cabinet members. The more she got in the papers, the more Oxbridge she became. It was strange how many people transformed into a fanny as soon as too many cameras focused their attention on them. Charlie liked to think he kept it real by retaining his accent and bits of dialogue, but he was learning way too much about alternative lifestyles and quinoa not to be considered a sell-out by people back home. He even heard them calling him a pretentious prick whenever he ordered an imported beer or ate a salad. People where he was from were happy to see you do well to a point. If you're nominated for an Oscar and living in L.A. with a model with a plastic accent, you're at least a bit of a show-off cunt.

Charlie saw the cabin during another one of his existential crises – this was not a good state to meet a sociopath. It didn't help that something in the air suggested this sociopath had nefarious plans for the man presumably manipulating his daughter into prancing about catwalks with her arse chewing lingerie.

Eugene needed to direct his anger somewhere. That his daughter had become Gweneth before she met Charlie didn't matter. Eugene wasn't interested in history. He was all about the here and now and reclaiming his daughter.

Eugene was waiting at the door, standing in a boiler suit with thinning, slicked-back hair like Hannibal Lecter in a cell with no reassuring bars. This was him cultivating an atmosphere and doing everything intentionally to turn Charlie's stomach into a washing machine filled with liquid shit. 'Fuck me,' Charlie said. 'Is he a Hannibal Lecter impersonator?'

'That's just daddy,' Mary Sue said. 'He looks a bit weird, but he's harmless.' Charlie didn't know about all the police brutality, but he seriously doubted a former cop in a place where cannibals were staples of the community was harmless.

Eugene enjoyed seeing fear in Charlie's eyes and savoured his monosyllabic answers to Charlie's awkward questions. 'Be nice,' Mary Sue said again.

'When am I not nice?' Eugene said, spitting on his floor. Charlie had lived in a few slum landlord places in his time, but he never went about grogging on the floor as if he'd stepped into the lair of a mortal enemy.

'Lovely place you have here,' Charlie said, looking at all the wood panels, pictures of Jesus and the stuffed animal heads on the wall. He'd never wanted to campaign for animal rights more, and spruce a place up with some sacrilegious artwork.

'What's *love*-ly about it?'

'Daddy . . .' Charlie's brain flailed about in the dark until even the stuffed bear and deer heads on the walls looked uncomfortable.

'Ah like the pictures of Jesus! They remind me of home!' Eugene's photos of Jesus had worked a trick. The truth was he was playing up his Christian zeal and had only just bought the pictures for this visit.

'You Christian?' Eugene asked, poker-faced. Charlie knew lying to a cop was risky, but he was Oscar-nominated.

'Yes,' Charlie said, nodding and deploying his serious face. '. . . of course . . .' His voice got deeper as he kept staring into Eugene's eyes, willing him to blink or look away first, but Charlie caved and made eye contact with a dead deer on the wall that had more life in its eyes than Eugene's. 'Ah love Jesus.' Charlie saw Jesus on the wall, doubling as a ripped Robert Redford. 'Absolutely love him!'

'What do you love about him?' Eugene asked, still staring.

'You know . . .' Charlie had nothing. He needed this interrogation to end.

'No, I don't. That's why I'm asking.'

'Daddy . . .' Mary Sue said, after her enjoyment at Charlie sweating lost its lustre.

'Relax, baby girl. I'm just asking.' Charlie grimaced at baby girl.

'You know, the whole dying for our sins . . .' Charlie said, willing his struggling brain to improvise. Eugene wanted more. 'And how . . . he was able tae turn the other cheek and that . . . We could all take a lesson from that!'

'I don't really believe in turning the other cheek,' Eugene said sardonically. 'You Catholic?' Charlie was getting serious Grandmaster of the Orange Order vibes, but he didn't know enough about Luther or Calvin to bullshit otherwise.

'Yes,' he said.

'Practising Catholic?'

'Ah like to say Ah don't need to practise anymore because Ah mastered it years ago.' Charlie smiled, and

134

Mary Sue's face suggested a turd had fallen from his mouth.

'Right,' Eugene mumbled. 'He has a sense of humour then?' He rolled his eyes and sighed. 'Well, at least you're Christian, even if it's of the Roman popery variety. I was half expecting some crackpot Buddhist bullshit or you to come out with that goddamn pussy-ass agnostic crap.'

'Aw, no,' Charlie said. 'Jesus all the way for me.'

'What's that mean? Jesus all the way?'

'You know . . .'

'Like you wanna fuck Jesus?' Eugene quizzed with his eyes fixed on Charlie's.

'Okay, Daddy,' Mary Sue said. 'That's enough of the interrogating. You ain't a cop no more.'

Charlie needed a line and a time machine to take him back a few hours and forward a century. He wasn't holding his own here or endearing himself. He suddenly felt he couldn't act his way into an audition for a campaign advertising hard-on pills.

'Who all wants a drink?' Eugene asked. Charlie hesitated, unsure if this was another test and potential grilling in the works. He waited until Mary Sue took one, and Eugene asked him again before he took a whisky neat, reasoning that Eugene might respect him if he could drink a whisky with no dilution.

'We'll have a few drinks, then do a bit of hunting,' Eugene said to Charlie. 'Get to know each other a bit better . . . You ever hunted?'

'Just for some good deals in the shops,' Charlie said. The words were out before he realised he should've just killed himself instead.

'You against hunting?' *Fuck yes.*

'Not at all,' Charlie bluffed like an experienced senator. *Who doesn't want to spend their spare time traipsing off*

135

*into the heart of darkness, firing deadly weapons at fast-moving,
potentially dangerous animals you won't even have the good grace to
eat?*

'You get a lot of hypocrites who have no regrets bout eating animals but don't wanna know when it comes to the crunch. Whole country's been pussified. No offence.'

Eh? 'None taken.' *Ya sadistic redneck cunt.* 'Aye, Ah don't mind hunting,' Charlie lied again. He might play a villain on film from time to time, but it's called acting for a reason.

Eugene threw a rifle at Charlie, who dropped it. 'Careful. That thing's loaded.'

'Sorry,' Charlie said, not sure why he was apologising for not displaying Lev Yashin reflexes to catch a heavy instrument of death.

'Don't worry,' Eugene said, forcing an unnerving smile on his face. 'I take it you know how to use one of them things from your pictures.'

'Yeah.' Charlie held it as far away from himself as possible.

Mary Sue explored her old bedroom and decided to plunder heirlooms and childhood possessions that had taken on increased sentimentality after she attempted to become a socialite. The old dolls found their way into a suitcase along with the diaries – diaries she thought other people would be interested in once she reached true superstardom. That the diaries were about as interesting as varieties of excrement didn't register to an egomaniac like Mary Sue.

The basement, where the old Harrison generational quilt was, was locked, and if there was one thing Mary Sue abhorred, it was a locked door. She was naturally too inquisitive, a nosey bastard if you will, to let this slide. The only problem was Eugene saw to it that only an ardent criminal or an experienced head with gunpowder could breach that door. Fortunately, Mary Sue had spent considerable time around criminals and gunpowder.

☆

Charlie couldn't see the deer Eugene claimed he was tracking because it didn't exist, but he followed Eugene and showed the right level of gullible deference to play into Eugene's plan. After hearing numerous annoying birds, almost falling into a ditch/open grave and shiteing it at the possible dying call of a hyena, Charlie was ready to call it a day. He didn't belong here, just like Eugene didn't belong on a catwalk in Milan with hot pants riding up his crack. Charlie didn't belong on a catwalk either, but he would've felt much more at home there than in this desolate forest, presumably replete with mass graves and perverts.

Deliverance kept filtering in and out of Charlie's mind, especially a few choice scenes. He began to feel like he was nearing the end, and no-one would ever find his corpse except for wild animals and determined necrophiliacs.

'Should we not head back now?' Charlie said, quivering. 'It's getting a bit dark.'

'Quiet,' Eugene said, looking every inch a murderer missing remorse. He pointed at some majestic animal not too far ahead. Charlie couldn't place it, but he was sure it wasn't a bear or a lion, which was a decent enough start. 'Go for it.'

'Eh?'

'Shoot.' The hearing-impaired white-tailed stag was happily munching and pondering what happened to his hearing after it narrowly missed dying at the hands of the last hunter he encountered. Charlie raised the rifle and prayed for the stag to scatter, but it was doing nothing of the sort. This was the stag's time to stand and have lunch in peace while thinking about when his hearing would return.

'Well,' Eugene said.

Charlie looked through the scope at his target and aimed off to the right at a tree way behind it. He squeezed the trigger, and just like that, he was in despair.

'Good shot!' Eugene boomed. 'Excellent! Who would've thought it?'

'What the fuck,' Charlie said in disbelief.

'You even made up for that lousy sight!' Eugene was a pig in shit, while Charlie walked over in a daze, heart pounding and gawked into the lifeless eyes of his victim.

'Ah'm sorry,' he said to a dead deer before turning around to see Eugene had disappeared. 'Eugene?'

☆

Eugene's basement blew open, revealing the interrogation/brainwashing room he'd set up for his daughter. Mary Sue knew her dad wasn't perfect, but this was the kind of room the CIA would fly a person to with a bag over their head until they confessed to all manner of crimes. She saw pictures from her childhood on the wall and clicked on a projector that conjured quotes from the Bible. It chilled her to the marrow and made her quickly flee the premises. Whatever her dad had planned, it wasn't good, and as much as she thought she should save Charlie, she also thought it was a lost cause. There was no time for Scout's honour or romance novel bullshit. This was reality. This was America. And reality and America don't run on charity. They run on money, fame and staying free from manacles.

☆

Charlie didn't know he was about to become the hunted, but he was already unravelling. Valour was quite a distance behind staying alive and having orgasms. Charlie was no expert on death except to say he was sure your days of cumming were over once a chainsaw-wielding serial killer chops it off and puts it in his mummified granda's stewpot. He could hear nothing, which freaked him out worse than anything he'd ever experienced. Surround him with roaming gangs, carjacking and constant sirens, and he thrives, but give him nature, and he's ready to surrender and die. And that was before getting tracked by a psycho with a gun.

Deliverance was there again, and Charlie failed to reassure himself he was just being hysterical. *Not hysterical enough*, said the voice at the front of the queue. He really wanted that shitebag gone, but he usually was the loudest, especially before casting auditions.

Charlie heard rustling behind him. Sweating, he quickened his pace, looking around and muttering to himself, heart thumping in his chest.

'I am the angel of death!' Eugene shouted while watching Charlie swivel his head around like he was trying to get it off his neck. 'The day of reckoning is here!' Eugene loved a bit of psychological bombardment before turning the cold war hot. He wasn't just a wham bam, thank you mam torturer. Any sadist can let loose on a person's face and scrotum. What Eugene did was much more sophisticated than that. He sang to them off-key, let taps drip by their head, waterboarded, tickled their feet, and danced naked in front of them while tucking his uncircumcised cock between his legs. Everything was on the table except for a decent, nutritious meal.

'Why you daein this?' Charlie beseeched the trees and the bushes. 'This stopped being funny ages ago!'

'Ain't no joke,' Eugene said, emerging from behind the greenery into the light with his rifle pointed at Charlie's chest. The man had clearly done this before. There were no second thoughts or even a whiff of apprehension. Eugene cocked a half-smile and his eyes widened.

'You're a fuckin psycho!' Charlie yelled, hoping someone would hear him. The heroes were missing.

'I'm just a father.'

'Ah'm a father, and Ah don't go about pointing guns at people for fuck all!'

'Well, maybe I am a bit of a psycho if you go by conventional morality,' Eugene conceded. 'But I ain't got time for none of that bullshit.' Charlie felt sweat meander down his face and his legs become warm and wet with piss.

'Are you actually gonnae shoot me?' he asked, desperately, looking around for the best direction to sprint. It was all just trees and green oblivion.

'That's the plan, asshole,' Eugene said, caustically, spitting on the ground.

'Why?' Charlie squeaked, tears beginning to snake down his cheeks.

'Gotta shoot somebody,' Eugene said flippantly.

'You really don't!' Charlie fell to his knees and clasped his hands in something resembling a praying position he recalled before lapsed Catholicism.

'I'm doing it for my baby girl.' Eugene said, lowering the rifle to point at Charlie's chest again.

'Why?' Charlie asked, looking up, tears impeding his vision.

'Because she's not goddamn Gweneth or this junkie model she's trying to be,' Eugene spat, face twisted. 'She's Mary Sue!'

'Ah agree! Ah prefer when she's herself!'

'Is that right?' Eugene looked at the piss stain on Charlie's khaki trousers and scrunched his nose with revulsion.

'Aye, it is!' Charlie creased his brow through tears to gaze up into Eugene's eerily neutral face.

'Well, it's too late now,' Eugene said coldly. 'You can't save a pig after it's already been pushed off the goddamn cliff.'

'Eh?'

'I'll give you till five Mississippi.'

'Whit?' Charlie spluttered, slowly rising to his feet, struggling to focus on the death in every direction.

'One Mississippi, two Mississippi . . .'

The next Mississippi went missing. Charlie turned to see Eugene gripping his chest, but he didn't hang about to play Florence Nightingale and fled through the forest towards nowhere.

AFTER DEATH:
AN AGENT OF KARMA, PART 2

I've spent much of my time making online enemies and beating my dick as if it owes me drug money. Sometimes I forget I decided to become an agent of karma, and hours and days pass on my phone when I should be doing solid reconnaissance. Solid reconnaissance? That's a laugh. I'm not even doing solid shites since I plunged more into social media and my diet deteriorated. My BO and rogue farting suggest I may not be altogether well, but who is and who wants to be? In this world, the well are clearly insane and my aftershave can help mask the suspect choices.

It was only through doing a deep dive on the internet and friending Mary Sue on Facebook through my alias profile that I learned Eugene, that maniac, that cunt, isn't just alive, but a multi-millionaire. Karma is ripping the pish here. A lottery win? Seriously? Do you need to be a cunt to win the lottery? There must be some good, deserving people who've won it, but all I ever hear about are the fannies, louts and reprobates who tell you they're still going to keep working some forelock-tugging job because they've no fucking imagination.

I can't stop googling this bastard. I can't stop wanting to take all my anger out on him. I've definitely got angrier since death. It erased my financial problems but left me a ghost. I don't know if I'm happy now, but who needs to dwell on fulfilment and the big questions when you've got the world in your pocket to stop critical thinking?

The internet makes everything better. It stops me from too much introspection. It keeps me occupied and feeling connected. I don't care if it's not the real world. Have you seen the real world? At least I can tell people to fuck off on here without any real consequences.

Thirty-nine million dollars for that psycho. No-one needs that money, especially him. I expected him to have built some armed compound and a fallout shelter filled with burgers and torture victims, but he's bought a mansion in L.A. instead and is active on social media. That fucking hypocrite. Who knew it was all about envy and fuck all about reclaiming his daughter? The man of the soil, small-town cop, is just an act, a hustle. Give someone like him the keys to the kingdom, and he's just as vain as the next person.

I've learned through a bit of cyberstalking that my prey doesn't sleep well and hits the gym in the graveyard hours. That heart attack seems to have made him resort to fitness. Either that or he got it all sucked out of his fat arse, and then decided to join a gym to sit in a spa. The latter seems more Eugene. Not that I know him that well, except for the fact he tried to hunt me.

@DeadNLovinIt
@RealDonald You're shit at golf. And you smell like an anchovy. Prick

@DeadNLovinIt
@HeartsFC Albert Kidd Albert Kidd Albert Kidd Albert Kidd Albert Kidd

@jamborambo21
Fuck you ya cunt

@DeadNLovinIt
Albert Kidd Albert Kidd Albert Kidd

@jamborambo21
Away n play tig with buses

@DeadNLovinIt
Albert Kidd Albert Kidd

@GorgieShore
Wanker

And now it's time to tweet my own pearls of wisdom:

@DeadNLovinIt
I have a growth at the end of my cock. I tried
draining it, but I just made it angry. Can't afford to
see the doctor. #cockpride #freehealthcare
#NYEBEVAN

@DeadNLovinIt
Bought a butt plug for my bday. Didn't think I'd
like it, but I wear it everywhere: the church, football
games, theatre, funerals #dildopride #plugthejug
#pluglife

@DeadNLovinIt
Quote of the day - I love making lamps out of
human skin and bukkake porn – L.Ron Hubbard
#scientology #cult

I sip my strong coffee, releasing nervous farts that could wilt the tree of life, and watch a pear-shaped Eugene with a bad combover leave the gym to go to a deli. Fuck knows what he buys from there, but it must be counterproductive to exercising at the gym. Someone like him should be more discerning with his time, especially when he's a scumbag with many potential reprisals in the post.

@DeadNLovinIt
@PhilCasanova00 You've represented more criminals than celebrities #devilsadvocate #moralvaccum #himtoo #patriarchy

DM from **@PhilCasanova00**
Nice try. I'll see you later

'Hey you!' shouts some redneck. Shit! Shit! Shit! I see Eugene coming towards me. 'Yeah, you!' I flood the fucking engine. 'Why are you following me? I see you.' He steps towards my window and tries to place me. I bend my head, hit the accelerator, and drive away. Derailed by social media, and now he knows he's getting stalked. That's just fucking brilliant.

AFTER DEATH:
AN AGENT OF KARMA, PART 2, TAKE 2

@DeadNLovinIt
@godiseverything The book of revelations reads
like it's written by a 12-year-old boy with too much
sugar in him and a bad cell connection to his brain
#fiction #scamartists

Take 2. I didn't half fuck it up the last time. In my
defence, I'm still a beginner at taking people out.
Shackler went like a dream, but that was very much a
happy accident. I just helped induce a heart attack itching
to get out in that deranged blob of perversion.

This time, I'm going to get cold and clinical. In and
out like a premature ejaculator with social anxiety. No
more agonising over the precise time to strike with
minimal fuss. What do I have to lose, except a life that
most people think I've already lost?

I will have my revenge before the walls come crashing
down and I get locked away. Of course, I don't plan on
exiting stage left just yet. What's the point in being dead
if you can't have fun and make it work for you? No-one
knows my connection to Eugene except Mary Sue and
being dead is pretty much the perfect alibi. A random
shooting of a rich cunt who deserved it. That's the kinda
shit that makes America. If I have to live in a harsh,
unforgiving consumer capitalism economy without a
decent safety net, I won't watch utter cunts fail to get any
semblance of justice. Eugene tried to kill me, then he

thrived, and I lost my career and mind and turned my colon into a semi-colon.

Eugene might've placed me by now. Something in his eyes and my paranoia said he'd figure out who I was. I may have changed a lot in the intervening years since he tried to hunt me but fuck me if these piercing baby blue eyes and their accompanying thousand-yard stare aren't one in a million.

My hand keeps going for my phone as I wait. I feel surgically attached to the Apple logo but comfortable with my dependence. I've even started eating three apples a day. What the fuck's that all about? Last night, I had an apple after a Pizza Hut. It's probably better for me than crack, smack or Pringles, but it still seems strange. Apples were never part of my diet until I got an iPhone. I was a banana and grape man, but it's been days since my last banana. I had to remind myself to buy them by writing them down in the notes section of my iPhone, and I still came out of the supermarket with just apples, crisps, Jack Daniel's and lube. That shopping haul is not conducive to a healthy diet, but neither was smoking crack and eating a Happy Meal at six in the morning after being awake for two days. It's a balancing act. Maybe I should take up yoga and give up trying to make any kinda sense of anything.

People probably think yoga is healthier than creating a hitlist and murdering people while trolling dickheads on Twitter. But what worked for me six months ago doesn't work now. Yoga won't settle scores or satisfy my insatiable lust for killing a few deserving cunts. It might make me appreciate a sunset more or write whimsical haikus now and then, but will my shitey poetry about the sun going down like it does every fucking day help the world rid itself of the Eugene Harrison types?

Eugene is an anomaly in this area of L.A. Sure, he's white and trying desperately to fit in lest he give the game away, but you can tell there's a man out of time in there wondering when he gets to unleash his unique brand of torture. I'd bet my left ball that he's still up to something behind closed doors. It wouldn't surprise me if he has a whole Mexican family chained up in the basement with Mike Pence speeches on a loop. Some people can't shock you after you've studied them for a while, and they've hunted you through the backwoods of Arkansas. He might have slightly different hair, a tan, a mansion and be trying to shed pounds, but he's still the same old cunt he always was. You don't go from a psychological blackspot to that L.A. waving-at-strangers dullard type without it being a high percentage of bullshit.

I guess the incident outside the gym spooked him a bit, but he is still attempting this fitness charade. Normally I'd think fair play to people trying to get themselves fitter, but this cunt must be getting fit in preparation for some trip to a dark corner of Europe, like Bathgate, to hunt the homeless and help local statistics. Well, he doesn't get to hunt or hurt anybody anymore. Time's up, dickhead.

Not having a grotesque gate between himself and incursions from real civilisation seems like a bit of an own goal for Eugene. Maybe he's trying to cultivate the illusion of being welcoming. Or maybe he thinks he's still in solitude in Arkansas and can leave his collection of Apple products in an unlocked house, and no cunt will even fart near them.

I stop the freshly painted black Prius down the quiet, clean street behind a line of palm trees and walk the rest of the way with my Covid mask on and a skip hat.

Luckily, the rise of deadly viruses has made this a much more acceptable way for non-muggers to take a stroll. No-one pays me any mind. I'm old, overweight and have a skin colour that doesn't arouse suspicion among the local rich bigots. More fool you, ya shower of bastards.

Phil sorted me out with coke. I didn't tell him I needed it to help me shoot an ex's father, but sometimes it's better to be economical with the details. As much as I'd love to make Phil an accessory after the fact and take him down with me, I can't trust him. I'm still surprised the world doesn't know I'm alive yet. Once Phil's finished milking my death dry, I suspect I'll be front and centre as the new Lazarus. I will say one thing for him, though: this coke is top-notch. He might be useless and a hindrance in other areas, but he's always been a great source of drugs, and in Hollywood, that can take you very fucking far.

My bowels are in a vice, but I still feel ready, capable and focused. One or two shots and that's all she wrote. It'll just be another doorstep delivery from Amazon, but one that would have Jessica Fletcher all over it. I need to get out more and stop watching daytime telly. It wasn't good when I was an out-of-work actor back in Glasgow and London, and it certainly isn't any better just because I'm dead. Dick Van Dyke's white moustachioed coupon flashes in my mind's eye. *Diagnosis Murder She Wrote*, the porn version, with a few choice images makes me poke a finger in that mind's eye. This is serious. This is real murder. Treat it like the time you lost your virginity. You can't enjoy it. You just need to focus on not making an arse of yourself and failing to get a shot away or doing it too quickly and missing the target – clinical precision is the order of the day.

I dip into my bag and stick my finger under my mask for one last bump, the last bump before I pistol-whip a psycho and become the angel of death. No pressure.

'Lovely day, isn't it?' says some pensioner covered in exposed varicose veins. Shame is in short supply about here. Not that I'm ageist, but there's a limit to what my stomach and eyes can put with, and her legs and arms are beyond it.

'Yes,' I say in a generic American accent without slowing down to listen to her genuine affability.

'You got anything for me?' she says, nodding at the small, empty Amazon box in my hand. I lower my skip hat a bit and keep walking.

I see Eugene's house across the road and stop to psyche myself up again. The time is now. There is no turning back. Well, there is. I could easily stop this entire thing, but the coke and a sense of destiny keep me going. Eugene has killed, tortured and maimed. Lawful shooting after lawful shooting despite reports that contradicted the police versions. Numerous allegations of torture and brutality. If the police force didn't take him, he'd have been a serial killer. Having a badge just gave him a licence to do it and get away with it. This depraved lunatic wasn't just doing his duty; he was perverting those duties and behaving like the rules and laws didn't apply to him.

The Mormons used to teach about blood atonement. I don't much care for the whole polygamy thing the fundamentalists do. That sounds like a nightmare. Marriage can be bad enough, but multiple marriages? That's just begging for a straitjacket and premature death. But blood atonement is something I can support for Eugene. Sometimes, the only way to save a murderer is to kill that murderer. Karma, Old Testament, blood atonement, above us only a sky, who the fuck cares? Call it what you will. Eugene is going to fucking die as soon as he answers the door.

The old woman who said hello has disappeared, and the street is empty. I cross the road with my box and keep walking calmly but with purpose until I'm up Eugene's driveway and past his perfectly maintained, lush front garden.

Ding-dong.

He even has a doorbell now.

Ding-dong.

'I'm coming, goddamn it!' he shouts. 'Who is it?' There's that charmer I remember. I try to clear my dry throat and ignore my pounding heart.

'Amazon, sir.' *Ya fuckin cunt, ye.* I look at the ground and dust off my plain black polo-shirt and cargo shorts.

The door swings open, and he stands in a silk robe and white slippers like a Walmart Hugh Hefner. 'That'll be my new earbuds,' he says, reaching for the box. I take a step back, feel the Ruger in my pocket and wonder why it's not coming out. 'Are you giving me the box or what?' My mouth is sandpaper. 'Wait, you're . . .' I step back, drop the box and pull out the gun. My hand is shaking. He looks into my eyes, smiles and laughs. 'I thought you looked familiar. Did you not die?' I'm stalling, doubting my nerve to do this, wondering if I should've parked closer. 'What's the matter, cat got your tongue? What you gonna do with that?' The psycho's actually goading me now. Come on to fuck, Charlie. He's ID'd you.

'This ain't goddamn make-believe.' I squeeze the trigger and shoot past his ear.

'Jesus fuck!' He retreats, cowering into the long, wide hallway, and I follow, firing three shots into his back. He lies motionless, blood oozing from his body. I punch the

151

air and repress the urge to shout until my ears prick at the sounds of light, peculiar footsteps. I see his pug and exhale a sigh of relief, bringing me back to earth and giving me the wherewithal to pick up my Amazon box.

No-one follows me or is watching, but I'm not taking any more chances. I keep my head down and don't engage with anything other than the pavement. My arse is screaming for me to fart, but I don't trust it now. I wait until I'm in the car and have taken several turns towards the freeway before I pull out my phone with one hand and connect it to the car. This may be the longest I've gone without it since I got it, but it's back where it belongs. I rub the remains of the coke over my gums with my other hand and smile, feeling like I could produce lasers from my eyes and jet streams from my cock.

'Siri, play 'Psycho Killer'.'

'*Playing 'Psycho Killer*',' Siri says.

'Cheers, ya mad, creepy boot.'

LONG BEFORE KARMA AND DEATH: THE CHURCH OF HEAVEN'S WITNESS

Desperate people do desperate things – Charlie remembered his mum or his gran or someone saying this. His memory wasn't stellar after all his drug binges, and if he were a betting man, which he was, he'd stick the money on his mum saying it as it had none of the words like fuck, cunt, and shite that his gran preferred.

'Desperate people dae desperate things,' Charlie told his teenage son David, thinking this would connect them and stop them from ignoring each other in one of L.A.'s best French restaurants. David said nothing and kept looking at his phone. 'Ground control to David.' David only showed a sign of life to flick his black fringe out of his mascaraed right eye.

'Give me that,' Charlie said, trying to grab the phone.

'Like, how high are you?' David asked, pulling his phone into his chest. 'Seriously.'

'Ah'm no high at all,' Charlie said, lying and looking again at a waitress who'd caught his eye.

'Please,' David said, like every word was a prisoner. 'You like literally stink of weed. And you should've got a room with that burger you just devoured.'

'Thanks very much,' Charlie said, thinking he was overdue another line.

'You're welcome.'

'Are you still smoking weed?' Charlie tried to play the dutiful, concerned parent, but it felt alien.

'Why?' David said, stone-faced. 'You're hardly in a position to judge, are you?'

'You're 17.'

'And what age were you when you started?'

'26,' Charlie lied again.

'That's total bullshit,' David said, with something that resembled a smile.

Charlie laughed. 'It's not total bullshit.'

'I know you've got awards for acting, but you don't lie as well as you think.'

'Well,' Charlie said, looking for that waitress to get another drink and flirt with her. 'You don't want tae end up addicted.'

'To weed?' David rolled his eyes, and Charlie pondered how much of his money David was spending on mascara and eyeliner.

'Ah don't know,' Charlie said, trying to reach for wisdom to impart. 'It's a slippery slope. And wae your genetic makeup . . .'

'Can you spare me the third degree?' Despite the impertinence, Charlie was glad his son was showing a bit of backbone and not just listening to his lines.

'Right, fine,' Charlie said, abandoning the platitudes. 'How's your sister?'

'She didn't want to come,' David said, fiddling about with his phone again. Charlie wanted to launch that thing into space, but he'd only bought him it a few weeks ago, and he was fucked if he was paying for another so soon. 'She read about you in the trash mags.'

'Don't believe everything you read, especially in that crap,' Charlie said, thinking about all the hacks he'd love to see crossing a road so he could get a chance to speed towards them. William Smith was first over the bonnet. 'Ah wouldn't wipe my arse wae that crap.'

'Well, it would be stupid to wipe your ass with crap.' David smiled before he remembered he was mad at Charlie and that smiling too much or at all wasn't good for his goth credentials.

Charlie looked again at David's Cure T-shirt with a disconsolate-looking Robert Smith seeming positively light-hearted compared to his son. 'What's your favourite Cure album then?'

'I don't know,' David said, putting down his phone dramatically. 'Do you have a favourite child?'

'Eh?'

'We don't have to put everything in order, do we?' David said, picking his phone up again and burying his face in it. 'It's totally tedious.'

'Your wee sister is my favourite right now,' Charlie said, finishing his beer. 'Ah can tell you that much.'

'Ha-fucking-ha. At least I literally turned up for this.' Charlie was getting more annoyed and homesick with every use of literally and totally.

'You phoned me.'

'I know I did. But I didn't call you to get like a laughable *don't do drugs* speech or talk about The Cure.'

'Ah know you didn't. It's just . . .' Charlie got distracted by the waitress bending over at a table at the other side of the restaurant.

'Can we talk about Mum now?' David said, clicking his fingers. Charlie grinned, breathing in the aroma of French onion soup from the table behind, and weed from himself.

'Oh, your phone is out your hands. Speak away, senator. The floor is yours.' David rolled his eyes again, and Charlie's smile vanished.

155

'She's totally living with that church now.' Carly had fallen on hard times and was now a member of a cult masquerading as a church group.

'That cult, you mean.'

'Cult, church. What's the difference?'

Charlie sighed and had to think about it for a second. 'Well, the church doesn't require you tae pay thousands just tae know their daft story, and they generally don't want you staying in the church and daein manual labour for no wages.'

'Whatever,' David said, back on his phone. 'I'm not here to like study religion or whatever. The point is she's literally gone off the deep end. She hasn't spoken to anyone in weeks, and that guru, leader guy that talks about their bodies being like vessels to shed totally has sex with all the women.' Charlie stopped taking satisfaction at Carly's expense and was disturbed.

'Fuckin hell,' he said, looking at his empty beer glass and for any service staff. '. . . Ah never thought your mum would end up in something like this. Ah thought she was a bit ae a hippie wae the scented candles and dreamcatcher garbage, but this is dark.'

'Did you see the documentary about it?'

Charlie didn't watch TV unless it was sport or the news. He didn't even watch his own on-screen performances. 'Was your mum in it?'

'Yeah,' David said, looking up from his phone. 'She was like in the background totally freaking out like she was on Molly. They all were. They all dance about like total whackjobs.' Charlie stifled a laugh. David didn't look amused. Then again, he never did.

'Were they playing Prince?' Charlie asked, remembering them dancing at their wedding to 'Kiss'.

'Prince?' David said, confused.

'Aye, 'Purple Rain', 'Raspberry Beret', 'When Doves Cry'?'

'Yeah, I know who Prince is. Why would they be playing Prince?'

'Because your mum was dancing.'

'No, it was all like out-of-tune sitars and music that totally sounded like hyenas in an orgy.'

Charlie chortled. 'Shit,' he said. 'Your mum didnae even like my Irish folk tunes, never mind out-of-tune sitars.'

'Well, she totally loved this music, if you can call it that. She's obviously been like literally brainwashed.'

'Obviously . . .' Charlie nearly made a joke, but David struck a sombre tone, so it didn't seem appropriate. Being the more normal, less embarrassing parent, however briefly, was reward enough. 'Is she not even speaking tae you?'

'No-one has like seen or heard from her. I only know she's still alive because I saw them exercising in that, like, prison yard they have at the back of the warehouse they call a church.' David recoiled and appeared something more human to Charlie instead of just a zombie. 'Even their exercises are totally creepy.'

'They still dressing in the white uniforms?'

'Yeah, they look total ghosts.' Charlie could sense David's frustration, but he couldn't resist trying to bring levity to a grave predicament.

'You'd think they would've chosen something a bit less KKK,' Charlie said, smiling.

'Very good,' David said, sullen and emotionless again. 'They're literally whiter than the KKK. Not a black person among them.'

'Ah don't think the KKK have any black people either,' Charlie said, looking through the drinks menu.

'That kinda thing is frowned upon wae the racist scumbags.'

'We need to get her out of there and like totally deprogram her,' David said, leaving his phone on the table.

Charlie scratched his nose, shaking his head slightly as he avoided eye contact. 'How am I meant tae . . .'

'Don't say you're not gonna help me.'

'Ah . . .'

'You need to, like, totally step up,' David said, staring intensely. 'God knows it's time you stepped up.'

Charlie sat back in his chair and stuck his hands in front of him like he was under arrest. 'Look, Ah always provide for you and Lilly. You're only living in that nice house because of me.'

'Everything is totally material with you,' David dismissed, picking up his phone.

'You're lucky you've got material possessions,' Charlie said, pointing at David's phone.

'Oh, here we go again,' David snapped. 'Tales of the chimney sweep. You're literally like full of total bullshit.'

Charlie had heard enough. 'Stop saying totally and literally all the time. You sound . . .'

'What?'

'Like a dumb American.'

'Fuck you,' David said, peering at Charlie like he was thinking of pulling a mass shooting but with the phone still there as a barrier. 'I am American.'

'Don't remind me, fir fuck's sake,' Charlie said, deciding he'd have a Long Island Iced Tea and a line of coke.

'You're, like, Scottish. They totally colonised the south and brought over all those rednecks you badmouth, so don't have a go at me for being American. You literally sound like a wasted pirate most of the time.'

Charlie felt a strange surge of national pride and didn't care for anyone denigrating his country when he could do it better himself. 'When did you become such an arrogant wee gimp?'

'Gimp?' David frowned, keeping his eyes on his phone.

'Aye, gimp.' Charlie doubled down and realised he shouldn't have. His son could give it out but never take it. He was just like him in that respect. David got up from the table, stormed off and ordered two of the most expensive meals on the menu for his father to deal with.

It was difficult to reconcile the Carly Charlie had known with this new odalisque version that was uninhibited and dressed in white at all times. Carly never believed in uniformity and was more inclined to look like Morticia Addams than Jesus Christ. Whatever this George Pickford guru prick was teaching had melted a vulnerable woman's brain and reduced her to a gibbering, glorified slave. And your messiah can't be called George Pickford, Charlie maintained. There were school pictures of him as a pot-bellied, snotty kid and records showing he'd spent time in jail after two failed marriages. The man was nothing exceptional. And he was a man. He was not a prophet, a vessel or a messenger. He was a non-descript Midwesterner conning the gullible, lonely and ill.

☆

Charlie hated resorting to such extreme measures as asking Phil for help, but he had no option other than storming the place. Phil sat forward in his dingy, weed-reeking office that was dangerously close to Skid Row and blew smoke from a joint. 'I can get her kidnapped and get her out if that's what you want,' he said, like it was nothing.

'How dae you even know these people?' Charlie asked.

'I'm a Hollywood agent, Charlie,' Phil said, baring his recently whitened teeth. 'It comes with the territory.'

'Ah doubt Spielberg's agent knows how tae stage an abduction.'

'You're not seriously comparing yourself to Spielberg, are you? Besides, Spielberg knows a lot about alien abductions, at least. I doubt he'd need to get his agent involved in abduction. He could probably do it himself.'

Charlie naturally assumed Phil had reached his verbal incontinence stage of the afternoon thanks to too much weed, coke and lunchtime libations. 'Just get her kidnapped, fir fuck's sake,' he said, turning to leave and get high himself. 'And take it easy oan the coke.'

☆

Phil had vouched for the kidnappers even if they both looked like sketchy yokels to Charlie.

'Don't worry bout nuttin,' one of the kidnappers said in a southern drawl as his corpulent face chowed on a chicken nugget and looked around the McDonald's they'd decided to meet for business. 'Your wife's in safe hands.'

'The less y'all know, the better,' said the other, who had a mullet and a wispy catfish moustache on a face that reminded Charlie of horrific historical famines.

Charlie waited until they left before he voiced concerns to Phil. 'Where did you find these inbred cunts?'

Phil dropped a chicken nugget that was just about to enter his mouth. 'Show some respect,' he said with a serious expression 'These guys are veterans.'

'Oh, well. Ah'll thank them for their service after they kidnap my ex-wife.'

'What service?' Phil put the nugget in his mouth and closed his eyes like he was feasting on the finest cuisine.

'You said they were veterans.' Charlie grimaced at Phil's chewing and a bit of nugget falling from his mouth.

'Yeah, veteran kidnappers, thieves. Cletus—'

'Cletus, fir fuck's sake!' Charlie screeched. A family at a table across from them looked over.

'Yeah, Cletus,' Phil said, simply, focusing on which nugget was next. 'What's wrong with that?'

'Is the other cunt called inbred?' Charlie said, trying to suck thick milkshake through his straw, his face turning pink, conceding after managing only a couple of mils of the sugary sludge.

'Why would he be called that?'

'Start as you mean to go on,' Charlie said, pushing the milkshake away from him.

'I don't know what that means,' Phil said, drinking from his large Diet Coke.

Charlie shook his head and sighed. 'Aye, you don't know what a lot of things mean.'

'I'm not rising to that. Besides, Cletus tried to join the military but failed the psych test.' Phil chuckled to himself, but Charlie wasn't seeing the funny side.

'Oh, how reassuring,' Charlie scoffed, pacing up and down. 'You might have mentioned this state of affairs before Ah hired them tae kidnap ma wife and help deprogram her!'

'Relax, Charlie. Stop judging books by their covers. Rednecks have their uses, even in Hollywood. They do this kinda thing all the time.'

'Fuckin hell. Just get things movin and get her out.'

☆

Carly noticed George's sermons had become full of apocalyptic rants about Bill Clinton being a socialist fascist with links to a race of lizard people. Carly wasn't a political scientist, but she was sure socialist fascist was a bit of an oxymoron, and she began to suspect she might be in a cult. George appeared ordinary and desperate, like he was pausing and repeating himself because he was improvising and waiting for the bullshit part of his brain to buffer. The truth was George was getting more strung out on speed and then Valium for when he crashed. Carly didn't air her doubts for fear of solitary confinement by the group – a measure she now realised was barbaric, but inside, she knew she had to escape right away.

The main issue with Carly's escape plan was the compound had become more like a jail than a church. Everything was hindsight now with Carly, but the fences should've been more of a warning sign than they were at the time. George had justified the barbed wire with his spiel about insidious forces in the media seeking to destroy them. But George also said aliens in Area 51 were getting primed to mate with them, and that seemed a wee bit far-fetched even for a Californian cult.

☆

Cletus and Bobby Joe cased the place for nearly 20 minutes and grew more restless thanks to the cocaine they'd just snorted in their dilapidated pickup truck. 'Let's fucking get it done,' Cletus said, with bugging eyeballs behind his red, bloated cheeks.

'Fuck yeah!' Bobby Joe shouted before Cletus smacked Bobby Joe's skinny arm to be quiet.

Cletus looked out the window again at the barbed wire fence around what seemed like an isolated old warehouse. 'Goddamn place is in the middle of nothing but old, empty buildings,' he said. 'It's perfect.'

☆

Carly picked the best time to scarper. She knew everyone, even the thugs, were whipped into a frenzy during one of George's sermons that were now just paranoid rants designed to spread madness. She didn't know if escaping from a bathroom window would work and still feared the repercussions, but she had to try something before becoming just another cult victim.

☆

Cletus and Bobby Joe pulled ski masks over their low collective brain power and had a few last snorts of their cheap and nasty coke.

'This fence is a bit of a problem,' Bobby Joe said, looking at the barbed wire.

'Can't believe we don't have no wire cutters!' Cletus snapped.

'Place is in the goddamn middle of nowhere,' Bobby Joe said, running his hands down his bony face. 'Not even a Walmart to go get us some.'

'Fuck it!' Cletus spat, reversing the pickup down the street to build momentum. 'I ain't waiting no more.'

☆

Carly pushed her prison-style blanket out of the window before pulling her skeletal frame out next. She landed on the ground and was never so glad to be malnourished. Without losing two stones in weight, thanks to the church's strict nothing much to eat diet, she would've been wedged in a window and nailing a part in a mass suicide.

'Fuck,' she said, just as doors opened behind her and one of George's criminal henchmen sparked a cigarette. They made eye contact, and it took a second for him to grasp what he was looking at. He ran towards her just as headlights blasted them and tyres screeched.

'Yee-hah!' Bobby Joe shouted as they smashed through the fence. Carly dived out of the way and watched the car clip George's goon. She didn't stick about to find out what was happening and ran until she could run no more.

Cletus and Bobby Joe went in guns blazing to kidnap Carly. They studied her photo and all the haunted faces of the cult drones and the fuller, more contented faces of the select few in charge. A long haired, bearded, hippie-looking guard in sandals and a tie-dye T-shirt reached for his handgun, and Bobby Joe fired a bullet from his six-shooter into the guy's big toe. Those who weren't completely mentally gone yelped and trembled, thinking they were next and that the sermons were coming true.

'Where the fuck is she, Cletus?' Bobby Joe yelled. Cletus pinched Bobby Joe's arm. 'Ow!'

'Name,' Cletus said, thinking he needed a new accomplice for his next job, which would be a jailbreak at this rate. 'Fuck it. Let's get outta here. I need more coke to get my head straight.'

☆

The storming of the church by masked rednecks brought the day of reckoning forward on the church's calendar. George scrubbed the words 'eternal life' from April 15th, wrote them on March the 2nd and the congregation gathered for one last sermon.

'It is the day of purification!' George boomed, completely unhinged. 'Let us go on into the future!' With promises of some kind of future, the most trusted confidants in the cult dished out the Phenobarbital cocktails.

☆

'Shit,' George said, standing at the clogged, malodorous urinal in the gent's toilet of the ex-warehouse for sex toys and pornos. He failed to piss after watching his followers perish one by one until only him and two of his most loyal minders/thugs were left to kill themselves. 'What have I done? I can't do this.' He was so ensconced in his agonising that he thought he was alone.

'Are you alright, your eminence?' asked his physically imposing bodyguard, Clarence, creeping up behind him.

'Yes, yes, of course,' George said, hefting one drop of piss from his desiccated cock.

'Steve just took his,' Clarence said, casually. 'It's only us two left.'

'Great!' George zipped his fly and hammed it up one more time. 'Let's shed these bodies and bask in eternity! We'll drink our cocktails at the same time,' he lied while throwing water on his face from the sink.

AFTER DEATH:
AN AGENT OF KARMA, PART 3

Panic eventually took over after I killed old Eugene, but part of me is relieved I'm not a complete psycho. I didn't just kill and sit down with a bowl of cornflakes like I'd bought a newspaper and was ruminating on the plight of the Palestinians. I even considered handing myself in and confessing to everything. But how does a dead man surrender? And if I've come this far, why not go a little further? You know and I know that some people deserve it.

I'm only righting a few wrongs, and I'm not wholesale enjoying it. I suppose that's better than collecting trophies and keeping bits of my victims in the fridge beside low-fat Greek yoghurt. I may be mentally unsound, but I'm not elite true crime fodder quite yet. I'm never going to be a dismembered cock in the fridge kinda cunt, but I still have a wee list to work through, and next up is George Pickford.

Old George is the type of conman you have to have a grudging respect for. He knows humans have a desperate need to belong and feel a part of something bigger, and he's spent a shitty lifetime exploiting that. I get on my chair in Phil's apartment, open Twitter and keep tabs on the bastard. He spent a few years in jail and, predictably, nauseatingly, found a God that would allow him to keep scamming. Now, people are actually queuing to buy this sociopath's books and help rehabilitate him. You'd think a low profile would be in order for a guy ultimately responsible for dozens of deaths, but George is the grifting shite that won't flush.

@DeadNLovinIt
@ Gerald Cutler Keep on trucking, Gerry boy. The media is forever spreading lies about autofellatio #effallwrong #thetruthwillout

@DeadNLovinIt
@CNNShackler deserved worse than a heart attack, but you can only waddle so long before God cuts you down and you go straight to hell #sexpest #cholesterolbad

@DeadNLovinIt
@LADailyRecord Wasn't Eugene Harrison some mega corrupt redneck cop? Don't make him out to be some holier than thou upstanding citizen #karmabeabitch

@DeadNLovinIt
@SuckerCarlson It's time to finish cleaning your closet and come on out to the party. #overcompensate #saynotobigots #dontsue

@DeadNLovinIt
@georgeApickford You really are inspiring George! You killed so many and got so little jail time and now you have a bestseller despite not being able to write very well at all! That's so impressive #winning

I'm about to take another bite of my chicken sub and shape a line when Phil comes into the living room wearing just a silk house gown, slimy with sweat, singing

'Maneater' under the illusion he's the blonde cunt from Hall and Oates.

'It's great to see you back on coke and enjoying life again,' Phil says, making me long for solitude. 'You really had me worried with all the fitness and healthy diet stuff.'

'Aye, well, your perspective changes when you're dead.' We both hear Phil's last sex worker conquest vomiting in the toilet. It sounds like she didn't even make the bowl.

'That's why you've got to live for today and not worry about anything,' Phil says, sitting on his chair with his legs open. Luckily, my chair is side-on. 'You never know when you'll die.' She retches again.

'Oh fuck,' she says. 'Fuck, fuck, fuck!' I try to ignore it and draw another discreet veil. Twenty minutes ago, I had to use my over-the-ear headphones and listen to The Pogues on full tilt to block out Phil's loud moans, grunts and horrendous dirty talk.

'Well, it'll be sooner rather than later if ye snort this gear every day,' I say, leaning forward to take a line beside my sandwich from the TV dinner tray.

'Christ, don't bring me down, man. I'm riding the crest of a wave.' Phil has a big smile on his face. The man must be immune to post-coital shame.

'You're riding a spewing skank,' I remind him while moving to the edge of my seat and watching a video of a Brazilian woman with arse cheeks that looks like two lovely planets bumping against each other in slow motion every time she walks.

'That's not very nice, Charlie.' Phil waves his index finger at me, closing his eyes with an infuriatingly smug expression. 'It's actually *very* misogynistic.'

I'm not having him calling me misogynistic and jumping to the defence of that vomiting cretin. 'She called me a gay boy because Ah asked her tae get out ma room. Then she told me she hates Irishmen. Pointing out Ah'm Scottish only made her even mair charming.'

'That skank is costing me a thousand for the night,' Phil says, inspecting his fingernails.

'Buyer's remorse, eh?' Phil gives me the finger. Christ knows where that thing's been. 'Well, make sure you don't ask her for a hug. You'd have tae thaw yourself after it.'

'Hug?' Phil says, guffawing. 'Are you aware of the job description of a prostitute?'

'Sex worker.'

'What?' Phil says, like I'm speaking another language.

'Let me know next time so Ah can make maself scarce. Ah'm meant tae be dead.'

'Relax, Charlie,' Phil says, bringing his bong between his legs. 'Not everybody knows who you are, were. And besides, she's from Colombia.'

'Ah thought this was Peruvian.'

Phil lights his bong and inhales long and hard on the delightful smoke. 'What are you, a fucking . . . geographer now?' he says, among a medley of coughing.

'You don't need tae be a geographer tae distinguish one country fae another. Apparently, you just need tae be fae anywhere other than America.'

'That's some racist shit,' Phil says, pointing at me.

'Nah, that woman in there is some racist shit,' I say, pointing, preparing my next line. 'She doesn't like Jews with the "cut dicks", Irishmen, Scottish people or "black men with emoji dick". She's a weapons-grade cunt.'

'Come on, Charlie. Is skank and cunt not derogatory towards women or some shit?'

'Nah, any cunt can be a skank, including men.' I hear the toilet flushing and the sex worker shouting in what sounds like Spanish.

'Well, I'm sticking my cock in her. I'm not starting a liberal arts theatre with her.' I snort another huge line of coke, pick up my phone and stand up. 'Your problem is you have too many morals, beliefs,' Phil continues, as if he knows anything about having morals. 'That shit will ruin you. Are you eating that sandwich or what?'

'No, you take it,' I say, going cross-eyed, looking at the tip of my nose. This coke may become a problem later, but that's the future Charlie's problem. Right now, I need a wee jolt to see me through my plans. 'Ah'm away a drive.'

☆

I used to romanticise road trips through America. You know, Kerouac and all that beat shite. The truth is it's boring, sweaty and uncomfortable. Sure, there's some beautiful scenery along the way and the occasional pang of reverence for this amazing, batshit country, but all the rampant commercialism and malls can deflate even an artificially happy coked-up cunt like me. Who needs a McDonald's, Denny's or Starbucks every few miles? You could throw a fucking cat and hit one of these identical shitholes.

I stop at a McDonald's drive-through not far from L.A. to stop my stomach rumbling and trying to eject from my body.

'Could you repeat that, sir?' says the guy in the speaker.

'French fries and an ice cream, please.' Sometimes I forget a Scottish accent spooks people or any kinda

171

accent that deviates slightly from their brand of butchering the English language.

My heart is going like the clappers, the clappers with a coke problem. Emperor palpitations. You're 25 times more likely to have a heart attack on coke. Or is it 250 times? Throw in a Starbucks and a McDonald's and this must be it. I tell myself to stop the car, but I'm already stationary between the payment and collection windows in the drive-through. This is not ideal. People take stopping here very seriously, even if your heart might be about to explode. That cacophony of noise around me is the car horns of sugar-addicted fat arses.

Just one last tweet before I die. Just one last fuck you to the world. My phone vibrates with a call from Phil and ruins my last tweet. 'Did you take all my coke?' he shouts.

'Ah think Ah'm having a cardiac arrest,' I say, forcing the words from my mouth.

'What?'

'Stoap shouting! Ma heart is thumping.'

'Of course it is. What the fuck is that noise?'

What's with the questions? Has the cunt become Jeremy Paxman? 'It's ma fuckin heart!'

'It sounds like car horns beeping.'

Is he coming the cunt? 'Ah stopped at a drive through.'

'You'll be fine, Charlie,' he says, laughing. 'Your heart's just getting used to the abuse again. What else have you had?'

'A coffee earlier and a few French fries.' Three big handfuls of salty French fries. All I can smell is McDonald's.

'No booze?'

'You know I don't drink and drive.'

172

'It's fine, man.' He's way too relaxed about this. I see someone approaching my car window. It's an angry soccer mom type. 'Just put your foot on the gas and drive out of there before the cops come. You don't wanna get caught dead at a McDonald's. That would be really embarrassing.' I also have a gun and a disguise in a makeshift compartment in the boot. Embarrassment is the least of my concerns. The soccer mom's chapping on my window, and I try to step on the accelerator.

'Ah'm in some fuckin fugue state.' I tell Phil, staring at my feet, willing them to listen to my brain. 'Ma foot feels dead. Ah cannae fuckin move.'

'You own that foot, Charlie! Now, get it moving. Get the car in drive.'

Phil's words make a weird kinda sense. It is my foot. I should be in control of it. Maybe I'm just hungover and hit the coke a bit too much. Maybe I'm just being melodramatic again.

Some raging, heavyset, goatee cunt is chapping on my other window, leaving his sweaty knuckles on it. I squeeze my left arm and can feel it. Would that not be numb? I need to read more about anatomy or binge-watch *ER*. Fucking Starbucks cappuccinos. Fuck knows how much sugar and caffeine was in that thing. It tasted like shite as well.

I delve into my pocket and rub coke over my gums like Popeye with his spinach. Thank fuck! Another wee jolt!

'You still there?' I hear a voice say.

'Aye, Ah'm still here, God.'

'Did you just call me God?' My right foot suddenly twitches into life and my left is back online too. I press down on the accelerator, and the car horns die away – that corpulent, bearded serenity vacuum and the soccer mom are gone. My car is moving, and my heart is thundering towards another freeway. 'Charlie, are you there?' Phil squawks. 'What the fuck's happening?'

'Ah'm fine, Phil.'

He sighs. 'Okay, man. You had me worried there for a second. Where are you going?'

'Nowhere. Ah'll be back in a day.'

'A day!'

I end the call. I can't be driving while talking on the phone. That's way too unsafe.

☆

Back at Phil's apartment, I see George Pickford has a whole host of new photos on Twitter, including some with his new boat. No-one starves who understands the stupidity and desperation of the American people. Or people in general. But cunts who think they can strike it rich and believe in dreams while still awake can be mined for money more than those who get taught never to dream in the first place.

Pickford gets how to sell a story and drain bank accounts. He also gets that it's better to turn off the comments on a lot of posts and block my Twitter account. Sometimes, I think I'm getting in too deep here, but I am on my way to killing the bastard.

@DeadNLovinIt
@herballife Tell us where the nukes are now!!

@DeadNLovinIt
@thomascruiser Tell us where Xenu is now!!

@DeadNLovinIt
@catholicreal Hail Satan, bitches

@DeadNLovinIt
@metallica First heard you on Napster. Have downloaded all your songs since. Skipped in to see u in concert too. Sook ma plums.

@DeadNLovinIt
@noelgallagher Liam made all those songs worth listening to.

@DeadNLovinIt
@communist4eva You're all a bunch of bourgeois middle-class pussies. Stalin would've purged the lot of you before you even reached Leningrad.

I'm bored, dangerously so. Even the trolling is half-hearted. Maybe I need to take a wee break from it and just read, like and retweet. What is it they say about Twitter? Fuck it before it fucks you? I don't remember. I may have coke and Twitter and, a lot of times, that's all you need in life, but sometimes a wee sprinkling of human connection helps. I miss my kids. I miss my career. Sure, it was in the shitter, and I was in lots of debt, but a comeback could've still happened. Mel Gibson got a triumphant return, and he made *The Patriot* and starred in *What Women Want*. And all that antisemitism was way out of order too. If I had made *Passion of the Christ*, deportation would've happened before the thing hit the cinema. The bastard didn't even give me the time of day when I auditioned for Judas Iscariot. Like I couldn't play a treacherous cunt just because I was doing a wee bit of smack at the time. I had

175

the look, the presence and the experience to fuck over the son of God. And for 30 pieces of silver, no less. I was starring in glorified softcore pornos and adverts after Shackler ruined me. I had the primo experience of doing anything for money.

@DeadNLovinIt
@melgibsonfan Mel Gibson was the worst thing to happen to Scotland since the Darien scheme. Daft Australian tart.

@DeadNLovinIt
@melgibsonnumba2 Mel Gibson is Satan incarnate.

I get out of the Mel Gibson trench and Phil's apartment before I go too far. It's never easy doing a deep dive into a man who is Teflon while you've become a paper plate getting ripped up by a fat bastard of a dog that has no business at a buffet. I realise I'm crying as I start the car. I immediately stop the engine to bump some coke and go on Twitter. That's better. Now I can drive to Vegas and get my murder on. I find it easier to justify my actions if I trivialise it and give it cute names. *Get my murder on. Killsies! Totally murds that guy!* If ever I feel anything for Shackler and Harrison, I take a happy selfie or shout 'whoopsie' to push all the panic and regret down into an imminent heart attack.

People bullshit and wank themselves all the time just to get out of bed in the morning. I am now one of those people. I am evolving, becoming more ruthless and unapologetically uncaring again. Getting back on drugs and allowing myself a wee drink has definitely helped. I mean, who the fuck wants to live in reality all the time?

It's not healthy to eat sensibly every day and have hobbies just to distract yourself from death. I tried all that shit for a year. I tried being good. I tried for karma and amassed more debt, no jobs and still had two kids who were only interested in money I didn't have to give them anymore. Sure, I had regular bowel movements and felt happier helping bums and even more desperate freaks than myself, but at what cost? I'd lost sight of fun and indulgence. Christ, I was even scared to pull myself off in case it wasn't karmic enough for the universe.

Karma wasn't working. I was living a lie, and nothing good was happening. I was still skint. I was still scrambling around for auditions. Cunts like Shackler were on top of the world while I was sneaking food at soup kitchens I was working at because I had to choose between paying the electricity or eating a couple of meals a day. Karma was taking the piss. And then I died and saw the light. I learned about Twitter and realised that if I'm dead, who will suspect me if my enemies and scourges on humanity were to disappear? If karma can't come to me, I can bring karma to others. And if I have to shape karma to what I understand it to be or hoped it would be, then so be it.

☆

Las Vegas

I haven't been in Vegas since I took ether and acid in a misguided tribute to Hunter Thompson. I probably would've attracted a stint in a jail cell anywhere else in the world, but Vegas tolerate those with deep pockets, and that's when I had money. Of course, this was a time before sophisticated camera phones and when you could deny your shitty behaviour without too much blowback. I wasn't Tom Cruise or Brad Pitt. My star was a lot dimmer, and my behaviour was the norm for a lot of fucked up character actors. Besides, I didn't harm anyone except for a few slot machines and that redneck arsehole I punched, or tried to punch and missed.

☆

I snort one last time in the car before I reach Pickford's mansion on another one of these soulless, if affluent, streets that gets a deep clean every time a cunt farts. Vegas is a strange place for a born-again bullshitter and at odds with his holier-than-thou act. But it is only an act. I know Pickford is probably still fucking, snorting, gambling and doing all the things he did when he ran a cult. Much of the world is blind to Pickford's sociopathy. That's a lucrative convenience for him, but it also means he has passed his expiration date. Karma has its agent, and it's sitting outside, down the street, lingering, just waiting for its moment.

Pickford is another who puts his hikes and ridiculous power walk exercises on social media. Decades of getting away with all manner of fucked up shite, except for a laughable stint in jail that's made him even richer, have made hubris inevitable. And now the inevitable is coming to meet him. The tension is rising in me, but I push it down with The Cramps playing 'Psychotic Reaction' on YouTube. Then I tweet the Dalai Lama and the Archbishop of Canterbury about the benefits of militant atheism.

☆

I get so sucked into a YouTube hole about JFK's assassination that I miss Pickford leaving his gates wearing his way too tight fluorescent jogging attire. I only notice him when his fat arse power walks past my car. The old, shapeless arse is mesmerising. For a man who isn't too overweight, his arse has its own neighbourhood watch. It's like all the sins of his life have gone straight to his arse. He really should get surgery on it. Maybe he's tried to, but there are structural problems that prevent it.

I need to focus on the task at hand and not his fucked-up arse. I wanted to kidnap him, take him out to the desert and add another hole to the place, but I think that's just a pipe dream. Sure, I'd be emulating the golden age of mobsters, but it would be a helluva lot messier and fraught with trying to avoid gang raping in some hellhole prison. I can't go there. No gang would have me, except for a gangbang, and there's nothing glamorous about prison gangbangs, or gangbangs in general.

Pickford's power walking reminds me that I need new pillows and a duvet for my bed. I'm sure his arse is the connective tissue here, but who really knows how your brain makes these links? Don't give me a smart-arse answer here, I'm trying to kill some cunt and get away with it. If you'd appeared on an episode of *CSI* like I have, you'd know evading these do-gooder cops and racist sociopaths who have a compulsion to lock people up isn't always simple. It takes due diligence, attention to detail and staying calm under pressure.

I roll down the window and drive up beside him. He gives me a wee glance with his icy blue eyes and returns to walking about like a fanny. I'm insignificant, a nobody.

'Here, Pickford.' I draw my pistol as he turns, then I shoot him in the balls. He collapses. I was aiming for his gut, but I'm no Rambo. I know I've been to gun ranges and took out old Eugene, but that doesn't make me Lee Harvey Oswald or whoever took out that mad shagger president. Pickford is making all sorts of noise and that will not do. I still have a list I'm adding to and I can't stop now. I'm just getting started. I fire another bullet into his head and drive away without speeding, but not exactly cruising.

I hit a stretch of barren road, pull off it and quickly change the plates again. I don't know if this is wise or overkill, but I did it in a film, and it was something I noted that could come in handy if I decided to start murdering people. Of course, at that time, I thought I was a born-again pacifist and could never graduate above a fistfight. But time can make monsters of even the reasonable among us in this spinning asylum. All you need are cunts like Shackler reducing you to boner pill commercials and people thinking you're dead and still giving you abuse on Twitter. But it's not Twitter's fault people are cunts. The world was full of cunts long before social media. It's just more obvious now.

LONG BEFORE KARMA AND DEATH:
A SISTER ACT

Charlie was a heathen, a subversive, a heretic, and above all, damned to an eternity of fire and brimstone. At least that's how his wee sister Paula perceived him after she stayed on the pious path to become a nun. It hurt Charlie to see his sister become his antithesis, but Charlie could use drugs to mask all his problems while Paula had to commit to a life of soul-crushing religiosity as he saw it.

Charlie kept expecting to hear Paula had abandoned her life of poverty to drive about in a Mercedes, but she gradually faded in his memory and barely figured in his thoughts. The only thing that could reunite and reconcile them was also the thing neither of them ever wanted to happen: the death of their mother.

'Sister,' Charlie said, swaying from drink and pills as he got ready for the torture of the priest and people arriving for the mass in the house. He hadn't yet relapsed to smack and crack again, but the day was young, and his mother wasn't getting any older.

'Hello, Charles,' Paula said, with a strange, world-weary affectation as she studied the living room where she'd grown up and wanted to leave for a convent as soon as possible. 'Ah see you're living down to your billing.'

'For a nun, you know how tae stick the knife in, don't ye?'

She almost smiled but caught herself and frowned – going against instinct to preserve the facade always creates pitfalls for the skin. 'You stuck it in yourself a long time ago,' she said, sitting on the couch and looking up at Jesus nailed to a cross. 'Don't blame me.'

'If only,' Charlie said, lighting a cigarette and sitting down on his da's old chair. He only smoked cigarettes when he was stressed, he told himself, but stress was omnipresent these days. 'If Ah was a snake, Ah'd be a lot happier.'

'What?' she asked, waving smoke from her direction.

Charlie thought it was better not to make a self-fucking joke, especially with his mum dead in the bedroom down the hall and a nun in front of him. 'Nuttin,' he said, taking a seat beside her. 'How's life treating you, sis?'

'It treats me the way it's supposed to treat me,' she said, thinking her brother looked about as rough as she'd heard.

'But how are you actually doing?' Charlie asked, hoping she'd confess to despising her life of religious duty.

'Fine, apart from this.'

Paula's knees were still sore from all the praying for her mother's mortal soul. She was a murderer, even if she had good reason, and Paula did have doubts whether such a nice, gentle woman was capable of the required violence.

'How's nunning?' Charlie asked, still in the mood for goading, despite Paula batting him away with ease. 'You speak tae God yet?'

'Every single day,' Paula said, smiling. Charlie scoffed.

'That must be a one-way conversation,' he said cynically, sipping a Jack and Coke.

'Ah don't expect conversation,' Paula said calmly, using her unperturbed face. 'Expecting things from life leads tae disappointment.'

'Aye, you just expect an eternity of bliss after you've died wae nothing doon here,' Charlie said, sounding bitter and just like their da to Paula. 'In eternity stakes, Ah expect a lot less than you.'

'Ah'm not doing this.'

'Whit?'

'All this rancour. Our mother's dead. Let's have some perspective. And decorum.'

'Ah'd sooner have a drink than perspective or decorum,' Charlie said, finishing his Jack Daniel's.

Paula shook her head again. All that acting success and an Oscar nomination, and he was still twisted, miserable and alone. 'You need tae sort yourself out, Charlie,' she said, giving him a look of frustration.

Charlie seemed reflective for a brief moment as if he was taking Paula's advice on board, and then he grinned. 'Whit did ye think ae *Sister Act?*' he said, smiling like a mischievous, immature child.

'*Sister Act?*'

'It's a film.'

'Ah don't really watch films.'

Charlie got up from his seat to get a refill from the kitchen. 'You must be useless at pub quizzes,' he said, shaking the glass with melting ice cubes not far from Paula's impassive face.

AFTER DEATH:
AN AGENT OF KARMA, PART 4

I sit on my chair in Phil's living room and look at the next name on the old list: William Smith. In any decent world, what he does would not be called journalism. Cunts like Smith are why journalism is in the shitter, waiting to be flushed. I suppose there are great journalists and fantastic, vital journalism, but shitey papers, gossip crap and gutter blogs featuring excerpts from your life tend to sour you on an entire industry. I never got the hang of playing these cunts to my advantage and milking them for access. I wasn't savvy enough for that, and my agent was a drug-addled disaster zone. He still is, and I'm eternally grateful for that.

'This is the best shit yet,' Phil says to me as he kneels on the floor and unwraps the coke on the coffee table like it'll cure cancer. 'I swear my entire face went numb when I took some in Olive Garden.'

'You were in Olive Garden?'

'Yeah, I had to meet a potential client there,' he says, dipping his finger and tasting the coke. Cunt still behaves like a novice. 'One that isn't worth wining and dining.'

'Still sparing no expense, ya cheap bastard,' I tell him.

Phil doesn't even bother shaping it into a line before snorting. He just sticks a note right in there. 'Oh, fuck!' he shouts as he gets back to his feet. 'He's a YouTube star and a pretty unfuckable one at that! All cellulite, dork glasses and spots!' He hands me the note. 'Make sure you give me that back.' It's not like he's screwed me out of plenty of five-dollar bills.

'Why the fuck are you courting him then?' I ask, forming an actual line.

'In this economy, this world, you need to play the game. Hundreds of thousands watch this guy play *Halo* on YouTube.'

I shake my head and take a deep breath. 'Ah don't know whit that means.'

'That's because you're a newbie to all this,' Phil says, stretching his face like a maniac. 'Well, a relative newbie who's gone straight to trolling.'

'Ah'm no trolling,' I say, feeling pain in my knees as I ready the note for my line. 'Ah'm just responding.'

'Whatever, man. Like I care what you do to get your kicks. Just make sure you don't go too far. You're meant to be dead, and Twitter is a deadly serious business.'

I snort a line and feel it hit me right away. 'Fuck me!' I struggle to my feet, stumbling over empty beer bottles that are contributing to the stink of yesterday's bad food and essence of fart.

'Good shit, right?' Phil's all smiles and wide eyes.

'Aye,' I manage to say as I make sure I can still feel my face. 'Good . . . shit.' I can't actually be bothered listening to Phil. 'How does this YouTube prick get people tae watch him?'

'Lots of kids these days don't really play computer games anymore. They watch strangers play them on YouTube channels and TikTok.'

This does not compute for me. 'Absolute saddos,' I say, using my camera phone to check for coke in my beard or on my nose. I wipe until it's all gone while Phil sits there looking like Poppin' Fresh. 'The world's fucked.'

'It certainly is. That's why it's important to go down swinging with bills and plastic bursting out of a fat wallet.'

Phil did have a point. I think Dylan Thomas made the same point in a roundabout way. It's important not to go gently into death. I want to make a mark again. Sure, there was a bounce in interest in me after I died, but I wasn't living at the time. I was just existing and hoping some good deeds would reverse my misfortune and unemployability, save for those jobs where I figuratively sold my arse.

Phil is getting emotional; the coke does that to him sometimes. For a borderline psycho, he doesn't half get sentimental when he's had too much face-numbing ching.

'It's so good to see you back to yourself,' he tells me again, wiping a tear and smiling. Wasted does like company, especially coke wasted. It is a bit of a social drug, even if it causes anti-social behaviour, like shooting cunts from a car. 'All that healthy living shit, tidying and helping people all the time . . . it weirded me out. I thought you were going straight for a loony bin.' Give it time.

'Aye, cos yoga and helping out in a soup kitchen is a sign of madness,' I say, ignoring the cops chasing a Hispanic man on TV like he's robbed time travel and not some Oxycontin for himself. Twitter provides a good distraction.

'It is for you, man,' Phil laughs. 'It's a very worrying sign.'

'Well, people change.' I just about put half my heart into that.

'They don't really. I mean, do serial killers just stop killing without getting caught or dying.'

'Sometimes . . . Ah don't know. You need tae stop watching Netflix.' I need to stop watching it too, but at least Phil's true crime problem is worse than mine. If you watch all that morbid shite, it helps to have someone around who's in deeper. This applies to most addictions. You need that person, that mate, that acquaintance who is pishing themselves before dinner time and telling you their dead wife never returns their phone calls. As long as you show that poor, unfortunate soul empathy, it's good to have them about to heighten your pretensions of normality. Not that I'll ever get close to normality. Not now. Not after all the stories about me, some of them lies peddled by Willie Smith, that exist in the public domain.

☆

Willie Smith has retired to a nice little number in a decent L.A. neighbourhood. Telling lies to morons pays well in this society. I don't expect that to be revelatory. It's just observation and deduction. Acting is professional lying, and I made a living out of it, but that's a minor miracle in L.A. Most people who tell you they're actors are tossing a Mars Bar up a close and claiming it touched the sides. Hardly anyone touches the sides in this country or the world, but the dream persists, and many people live for the fantasy. Just look at the box office. The top films used to take place in something resembling reality; now, they all take place in Asgard, Mordor, Gotham, and some optimistic place called the future. Not that I'm necessarily against lying to yourself. It is a requirement to get through the day.

I've barely had to do any recon. Like many old Scottish hacks, the habits die hard, and this prick is still a pub and greasy food junkie. Willie goes from pub to house and back again with few detours. He lives alone, has no woman and probably hasn't had a hard-on or even seen his dick since Bill Clinton was finding his cigars difficult to light in the Oval Office.

I have a line of coke in a wine bar toilet across the road from Willie. Normally, I'd never choose to drink in a wine bar, but a seat at the window in this place is the perfect vantage point to watch when Willie leaves the pub. The only problem is I've been waiting for hours, and I'm almost two bottles of red deep and sinking even further. The old cunt is usually out of the pub by nine at night; now it's 11. Trust him to change his routine on the night he's meant to get murdered. Selfish bastard. It suits him to be a cunt to the very end.

Good old viruses and unabated pollution give me a licence to walk about like a bank robber. It's the halcyon days for wannabe masked vigilantes and ugly bastards everywhere. It's about time ugly cunts got a break. Let's just hope they don't catch more of this virus too. They've had it hard enough without adding insult and respiratory problems to injury.

I want to shout that I'm that dead actor you vaguely remember playing villains and gangsters with one-liners. I want to tell some cunt, any cunt, that I'm still here, and I faked it. I miss the attention, but I'll have to make do with speaking to Phil and dreaming about having a conversation with anyone else.

Fuck it. You're dead now and dishing out your version of karma to cretins. It's not the time for deep introspection or philosophising. Work to the list, get revenge, simplify, and for fuck's sake, don't get caught alive or dead. Kill and remain a ghost. No-one is onto you. Phil might be able to make something of it if he was

188

compos mentis and not a complete fanny for a few minutes a day, but that won't happen anytime soon. Phil is solipsistic, and God bless him for it. Let him not see beyond his own coke-ravaged nose. He'll never know he's living with a serial killer – my da, Shackler, Eugene and Pickford. Aye, I know Shackler had a heart attack, but I caused it. Without me, the cunt might've lived another few weeks.

I do another line and piss again in this god-awful wine shitehole and see he's left and heading for the corner of the quiet street. My bladder ruins me again, and I'm rushing to kill. Willie turns and seems to be illuminated by every streetlight in America. I feel the weight of the gun in my jacket pocket. It's getting heavier and I'm getting drunker. The fresh air has betrayed me. I knew I was getting there, but I realise I've had way too much.

Willie walks up a lane, begging for a bullet. The gun is ready. I'm ready. He does me a solid by stopping to do a pish. It's all falling into place. I can see myself scoring his name off my list and maybe adding another few names to it. I see the pish running down the lane towards me. Willie turns and looks right into my eyes. His face is half-melted, tired and cadaverous. I put the gun to his head and pull the trigger, but nothing happens.

'Fuck,' Willie says, shuffling with his dick out and his trousers falling down his legs. He trips and falls face-first on the ground. I'm no medical expert, but he looks fucked, so I do the humane thing and shoot him through the head. Aye, he's not getting back up from that. I can tell a corpse from the life and soul of the party, and he's definitely the former.

'Hey!' I look up and see a younger, much fitter guy than me in expensive, skintight jogging gear. 'Hey you!' Fuck me, he starts running towards me like the fucking hero he thinks he is. I'm not in the mood for this boy scout, this cunt citizen. I start to run from where I came and come to my senses. How am I, the flabby, wasted cunt pushing 60 meant to get away from someone who looks like he jogs every time he swallows? 'Stop!'

His loud voice is the end for him. I turn with the gun, and he stops in his tracks, realising he's not holding any cards, and I'm gripping a murder weapon. I didn't want to do this. I didn't plan to do this, but I don't have a choice.

Bang!
Bang!

AFTER DEATH
AND COLLATERAL DAMAGE

Why are cunts even out jogging that late? Most people are in their beds, getting ready for bed or stumbling home pished, and this fucking guardian of the galaxy is out with a Fitbit and getting in the way of a routine murder. Now, he's interfered in my life and thrown the whole thing into disarray. I thought I wouldn't have to figure in collateral damage if I was careful, and this prick is forcing me into anxiety sweats and overthinking my kill list. I hope he's happy with himself. He had to go and get in the way of me shooting an old man, and now he's dead for his trouble.

That's what happens when you try to be a hero: you get killed. This is L.A. Where does he get off trying to be a hero in this city? This place is a zoo filled with self-absorbed cunts. Heroes are for the Hollywood studios. They shouldn't be spilling out to the streets and behaving like vigilantes with their pointy nipples in my face when I'm trying to do the world a favour by killing scumbags.

I meticulously planned everything until Willie got greedy with the drink, and I had one bottle of wine too many. What am I supposed to do in a bar? Order a fucking glass of milk? I was there to blend in, not to draw attention to myself. Besides, cocaine and milk aren't a great mixture, even if you White Russian that milk. And given the current resurrection of strong anti-

Russian fervour in these parts, I won't be ordering anything Russian.

Local community outreach hero . . . Heavily involved in philanthropic causes . . .

I shouldn't have researched this guy. The more I read, the less justification I can apply. All the guilt I've been keeping stymied is now giving me a headache. I kneel in front of the coke on Phil's coffee table. I'm not sure booze and cocaine are the solutions, given the evidence throughout my life, but the clean alternative seems fraught with me breaking down in a police station.

'You should go easy on that coke,' Phil says, watching me from his chair while he turns up a monstrous Richard Ramirez true crime documentary. This should be a red flag. It certainly feels like a red flag moment, but I'm not in the mood for sensible suggestions. I'm on my way to oblivion and taking Concorde to get there.

I finish snorting. Phil gives me a concerned expression. The last time he looked at me like that was when I was shooting smack and supposedly sucking myself off in the fast food toilets of America. He points underneath his nose and draws a circular motion around his face.

'You've still got bits over your face.' I didn't bother cutting and shaping it into neat little lines and rationing it out as a responsible cokehead would. I just buried my face on the table and played it as it lay. Phil looks at me like he's my mother and I'm his favourite child. 'You okay, man?'

'Aye, Ah'm fine,' I say as my ears tell me Keith Moon's using my heart as a bass drum. I touch my face and feel nothing. I grab my left arm and dig the nails in to claw until I draw a bit of blood and feel pain.

Phil rushes over and throws a glass of Jack Daniel's in my face. 'Jesus Christ, Charlie!'

I collapse into my chair and panic at the sight of that horrible serial killer Ramirez's face on the telly. I think I can even smell that disgusting, halitosis-ridden creep, but it's just fusty takeaway cartons and my own howling breath. 'Whit?'

'Don't you dare have a fucking heart attack. You're already dead, remember? I can't have you dying here.'

'Ah'm no having a heart . . . attack.' Everything goes black, then stingy. 'Ah, ma fuckin cheek. Why you slapping me like that?'

'Don't fall asleep,' he says, shaking me by my arms. 'Christ, you're the only person I know who takes that much coke and naps like a newborn baby. Here.' He picks up a glass of clear liquid from the coffee table. I drink some and spit it out.

'Water?' The shock is too much.

'Yeah, water. Drink lots of it. I'm making you something to eat.' I think he's trying to kill me for real now.

'Piss off!' I snap. 'Your cooking will finish me.'

'Well, I'll order takeaway food . . . healthy takeaway food. McDonald's does salads now, doesn't it?'

I pull myself up in the chair, then slump over the armrest with my head propped by my left hand. 'Get me a Big Mac and an ice cream,' I say.

'A Big Mac? You're not mixing that with all that cocaine. I'll get you a salad or . . .'

I suddenly feel energised again, stand up and grab Phil by the throat. 'Ah said a fuckin Big Mac, ya fuckin prick!'

'Okay, then.' Phil squeezes out, and I let him go, coming to some kinda sense. 'Fucking hell! I hated your whole sober do-gooding bullshit. But this? This is grim.

You need to set limits when you're taking cocaine and drinking. You're spiralling.'

I burst out laughing, collapsing back into my chair, then see that dead jogger again when he was alive and saving humanity from the brink. I search 'Murders in L.A.' and read he was a scientist working in a lab developing cancer treatments. I may have killed the cancer cure. I keep hoping to find dirt on him, even a scrap of impropriety and corruptibility, but there's nothing. I wanted him to be a health-conscious murderer, sexual deviant or a Lindsey Graham-loving Republican, but no such luck. I've killed a good man to murder a shitty cunt who wronged me. It doesn't feel good. The coke feels good, but the guilt is still fighting with it, and I can't tell anyone. I can't even tell a priest this. I just have to make sure I don't tell a cop or Phil.

I look at David's Twitter, then Lilly's. David's is mostly retweets of bands wearing black and auditioning for vampire smackhead roles. Married life must be grinding him down now. Lilly's is much more interesting. She's come out as bisexual and is in a polyamorous relationship with an effeminate man. Straight, gay, he, she or they, I don't care. I liked her tweet after I looked up polyamorous. Fair play. It sounds like a nightmare to me, but I'm currently dead and on coke, so who am I to judge what works in life or a relationship? It must work for her as she's at least put on a few pounds before she blew away.

'That's it ordered,' Phil says, looking down at me. 'Are you alright now?'

'Aye,' I tell him, not taking my eyes away from my phone. He leaves the room.

Lilly tells Twitter about every meal she eats and everything she reads. Apparently, she read *Ulysses* in three days. She always was an actor in waiting. I'm just glad she's smart enough to lie about reading, even if she took a photo with a paperback that had come right out of the packaging. Maybe that's my fault. I used to read to her but would often skip a few pages when she was drifting off and improvise my own endings to Roald Dahl, Enid Blyton and *Clifford the Big Red Dog*, especially that arsehole Clifford. It took all my willpower not to euthanise that stupid fucking dog.

The jogger, Gareth Dawson, is smiling at me again. I should never have looked him up and given it a second thought. I should've figured in collateral damage. I should've hugged my kids more. I should've read to them even more than I did. I should've bought fucking Bitcoin. I should've taken responsibility for killing my father instead of letting my mother do the time. I should've battered Harvey Weinstein when I had the chance. I should've done a lot of things, but I shouldn't have killed this man.

I can't even troll those who deserve it because of this. I can only keep liking everything connected to Gareth Dawson. 'Where's ma fuckin Big Mac?' I ask Phil after he returns to the living room.

'I just ordered it,' he says, nonchalantly.

'Aye, but where's the driver?' I know I'm coming off desperate, but I need instant Big Mac gratification.

Phil comes over to the table and starts clearing booze and coke residue from the coffee table. 'They've not collected it. Here,' he says, putting pills on the table. 'Valium for the crash.' The cunt's transforming into Sally fucking sensible.

'Ah don't plan on fuckin crashing.'

'Yeah, good luck with that, Charlie.' He's derisive enough to warrant a slap, but I'm not lowering myself to that.

I go to the bathroom, locking myself away from Phil's negativity and feeble attempt to normalise me. Fuck that. I can't crash yet and deal with the fallout. I put on headphones and blast The Fall's 'Totally Wired' on repeat. There's a loud knock on the door and I have visions of San Quentin. I pull off my headphones and clench them.

'Whit is it?' I shriek from behind the door.

'Your Big Mac's here! No ice cream, though!' No ice cream? I can feel the tears coming. 'Hurry up, man. You need food!'

'Ah'll be down in a few minutes.' I sit on the toilet and contemplate my life, or lack of one.

Listening to Phil becoming an agony aunt and lifestyle guru is a through-the-looking-glass moment. I know the biggest part of him is doing this to stop me hoovering up all his coke. It doesn't matter to Phil that he's the parasite, and I'm the one he's still leeching off as he tries to ride my death into a retirement nest egg he'll never achieve. Phil just doesn't want my life to impinge too much on his. He didn't want me sober. He didn't want me alive if he thought my death would make him more money, and now he doesn't want me too fucked up in case I give the game away or spend too much. Phil does acts of Phil, and that's how he is.

I don't know if the kill list and my attempts to become an agent of karma were the best ideas I've had since agreeing to remain dead. I've always been great at coming up with ideas, but I don't know if these ideas are good, bad or indifferent. I should've filtered them through people and asked social media. Then again, how do you ask people if creating a list of enemies to kill is a good idea? How do you approach it without the police taking an interest in your Twitter? I'm nigh on positive that faking my death came from Phil, but I agreed to go along with it, and bouncing ideas off Phil isn't exactly bulletproof. Phil isn't your typical person, and whatever I am falls short of a sound mind.

I look at my Big Mac surrounded on the coffee table by drug paraphernalia, empty cans and wrappers, then at Gareth on Twitter and know I'm fucked. I remove the list from my pocket and see the names I've scored out, the two I had left from the original list and the four I've added.

'What's that?' Phil asks, pointing at my list. I pull it closer to me and fold it.

'Nuttin,' I sigh, reminding myself to be blasé and act my way out of trouble. 'A shopping list.'

'Leave it there, and I'll get it for you.' Phil raises his eyebrows at me, and I keep staring, never moving an inch. He blinks first and walks around the living room floor, picking up debris to add to the coffee table. 'I mean, you can't go out fucked up all the time is all. People will notice. It's a miracle someone hasn't already.' He tilts his head to the side and looks at me like my mother.

'Ah'm no a prisoner,' I say, clenching my jaw and giving him my best psycho eyes. 'You're no *Fritz-ling* me, ya cunt.'

'Man, you need to chillax a bit,' he mumbles.

'Did you just say chillax?'

There's a shamefaced nod from him as he half-heartedly tidies. I see a pencil on the table, get it and write Phil on the list. I can always rub it out if I change my mind. That's why pencils have rubbers.

'Put vodka on your list,' Phil says, slurping his large milkshake. He can fuck off and get that himself.

'Right,' I say, prying myself off my chair after another bite of my Big Mac.

'Where you going?' He stops, hands on hips, wearing a confused expression.

'Out,' I snarl. 'Away fae fuckin here.'

'Where?' He lowers his head and looks up at me with sorrowful eyes, reminding me of those poor dogs that guilt trip you into lifetime direct debit payments because their previous owner was a vocational bully.

I point at the paper with victims past and future. 'Ah've got things tae dae – things tae accomplish,' I lie, lifting my McDonald's.

'Don't you think you should stay home and take it easy for a while?' he says, forlornly.

'You're no ma fuckin mother, Phil,' I say without looking back, opening the door. 'You're ma agent, bleedin me dry.'

LONG BEFORE KARMA AND DEATH: VISITING

Charlie entered the drab prison visiting room, which stank of bleach, and saw several incarcerated women looking over. He could run amok in here, he thought, even though he knew deep down they'd eat an inexperienced overgrown boy hitting 19 like him alive. Casanova pretensions were fun, but all he had to do was open his mouth to remove any doubt that he was anything but a lothario. Once he was famous, he told himself. Once he was famous, he wouldn't have to talk too much. He could let people come to him. At least, that was his plan.

The weight of responsibility and guilt pulled Charlie down, but he put on the actor's face, and Leanne did the same as they smiled at each other. 'You look well,' she said, eyeing her son's brighter colour, and recent haircut and shave, as he sat across from her.

'So dae you,' Charlie lied, looking at Leanne's pallid complexion, tired eyes and dishevelled greying hair. Prison had put years on her.

'You don't need tae act wae me, son,' she said, forcing a smile. 'Ah'm your mother, Ah'm no a casting agent.'

'Fair enough. You look terrible.'

She laughed, and he did too. 'The honest actor. That's much better.'

'You don't look terrible,' he said, feeling guilty. 'Ah was only kidding.'

199

'And noo you're acting again. You might be getting parts in plays, but Ah watched you learn how tae lie.'

'Well, Ah'll need tae up ma game then, even if . . .'

'Even if whit?'

'Even if . . .' Charlie knew how to build tension after learning how to in acting class.

'Are you having a stroke?'

Charlie had a joke but didn't touch it. Your mother isn't the best audience for wank jokes. 'Even if Ah got a part in a TV programme!'

She lit up and managed a smile that didn't seem forced and tragic. 'That's brilliant!' she said, recalling what it was like to feel joy that didn't involve masturbating, which inevitably came with psychological reprisals thanks to a lifetime of Irish-flavoured Catholicism.

'Well, don't get too excited,' Charlie said, tempering the excitement by remembering it was a fledgling programme no-one had heard of and that he might not make the final cut, such was the size of his role. 'It's in a new Scottish programme.'

'Whit's it aboot?'

'Some polis trying tae solve crimes – murders and that.'

'Well, they'll hiv plenty of inspiration then,' Leanne said, briefly holding Charlie's hands on the table.

'It'll probably sink without a trace.' Charlie said, sitting forward and smiling momentarily before resting back in his chair, trying too hard to exude nonplussed coolness. 'But it's still a good opportunity!' He grinned and was at the edge of his seat again.

'Of course. You should be very proud of yourself!' Leanne said, taking his hands again and beaming. 'Ah certainly am.'

Charlie was ecstatic, but still trying to hide it in these surroundings, given he'd put his mum in there and expressing joy seemed a bit insensitive around women who had to return to cells. He knew his audience already and had seen enough spectacular own goals in Scottish football to want to avoid scoring one himself. There was little more humiliating than an own goal. Making an arse of yourself in front of thousands never dug out the debonair in a person. Charlie was keen to avoid drawing every eye in the room towards him, knowing it'd provoke feelings of resentment, GBH and murder. He remembered why he was there, which brought him back to the floor. It was something he would carry for the rest of his life.

AFTER DEATH:
I DREAM OF TWITTER

You start dreaming and know you must be, yet still convince yourself it's all real. Because a naked Margot Robbie always gives you the time of day, doesn't she? And your head's always been able to rotate like that sick wee bastard's in *The Exorcist*, hasn't it?

I'm deep inside the murky organs of Twitter after getting swallowed by a big blue bird that's nothing but a two-dimensional corporate logo. Where's Pac-Man when you need him? Probably banging that wee slut Ms. Pac-Man. She was really just Pac-Man in drag. But you still would if you were a wee yellow cartoon thingy. You can't be fussy in the circumstances, and you need to take your pleasures where you can find them – that's what my maw always said. I hope she didn't action that mantra in jail. Lesbian sex is for everybody else. How did I get to that? This is how dreams quickly become nightmares.

I know I'm dreaming because I'm melting off a laptop screen and into Elon Musk's cup of coffee on a private jet. From here, you get a really good look at a mental breakdown. The Fleetwood Mac song 'Tusk' plays at full blast, and he cuts about in his pants, shouting Musk instead of Tusk. 'Tusk' will never be the same. A billionaire in their pants shouting their name is peak human achievement. It simply doesn't get any better than spending everybody else's money to continue failing to fill the emptiness inside. He doesn't even know I got birthed from his laptop screen. I'll have Dell and Apple on my birth certificate, but neither will pay child support. Then I'll end up in one of the new iOrphanages dealing with sadists that make the old man, that cunt, seem like Elmo. Stop it, Charlie. You're just catastrophising as per.

'Musk!' Even worse, instead of enjoying this dream and all its riches, I have cystitis, and I'm locked in this lovely toilet, failing to pish the nippiness out of my flaccid dick. My cock needs a makeover – a new hard drive. And Grecian for the old grey pubes. It needs queer-eyed for the serial killer.

Fuck me, a serial killer. How has it come to this? Chronic boredom, too much anger and the convenience of being dead? I suppose that's some justification for it. I'm not sure St. Peter will appreciate that, though. He might be one of those bouncers that doesn't let in any cunt unless they're Margot Robbie in a skirt and bung him bribes.

'Musk!' Check the state of this billionaire. I know it's a dream, but my dreams are usually rooted in reality. No matter how much I try to escape reality, it finds me and puts me in a headlock. But at least I have my phone in here and can get on Twitter. I just got shat from Twitter, but I want to get right back in and escape. This private jet with Elon Musk is way too real. The sink made out of gold is too authentic. Donald Trump knocking on my door to get in is obviously genuine. I am balls-deep in a billionaire nightmare. Or a kid-on billionaire nightmare. How the one per cent lives brings me out in a rash and hyperventilation. I'm having a heart attack. I know I'm dreaming, but I can't wake up to stop the coronary.

'Help!' I shout. But no-one comes. Fleetwood Mac is drowning out everything else. I enjoy *Tusk*, *Rumours* and the Peter Green stuff, but not at the expense of breathing. I'd rather hear The Clash with my dying breath or something more profound like 'Mambo No. 5'.

'MUSK!'

I see the defibrillator on the wall and ask Twitter how to use it. No-one replies. No-one gives a flying fuck, even in the sky. I ask Google and YouTube it, but all the videos have people using it on someone else. Not helpful. Not helpful at all, for fuck's sake. Here I am, having an obvious cardiac situation, and I still can't get off my phone. I'll check the Celtic score. That's right. They're playing tomorrow. Well, I'll just check if there's any update on Callum McGregor's injury. The fact he's injured shows that everything's fucked. Maybe I should let nature take its course. Am I playing God if I defibrillate myself?

Do not use Defibrillator in Airplane Bath!

The bath had been there the entire time, and I didn't even notice it. Or has it just emerged? Either way, I'm not getting in a bath. Baths are not for men like me. You might as well cut it off and call me a woman. I put the shock pad things to my failing heart and zap myself to the floor. Smoke rises from my chest, and I inhale deeply.

Big bud, purple widow, pure skunk.

There's enough smoke in here to keep Willie Nelson for a night. My dear Willie. The last American hero. I just want to smell his hair before I die. We need to leave a nicer planet for Willie.

'Smoke is coming from the bathroom!' Someone shouts. It sounds like Phil with his mouth full of Maltesers. Guy's a born-again greedy cunt. 'Charlie!'

I could go some more coke right about now. There must be some on this plane. I'll ask the pilot once my lungs stop billowing smoke. At least my heart seems better. I can see it beating, and it looks fine. It's a wee bit grotesque with all the flesh melting away, but it's only a dream, right? And dreams are meant to be a load of old shite. There's nothing worse than some cunt harping on about their boring dreams, is there? I don't know how therapists cope. Maybe that's why that one I went to see fell asleep. As if I wasn't going to tipple after he started snoring.

'Charlie! Charlie! Charlie!'

Do you think it's for me? I hope not. Anyone shouting like that is bound to be severely unhinged and lacking self-control.

'Charlie!'

It's definitely Phil. That voice can only be his as it's triggered me into inhaling more smoke into my lungs. Phil is peer pressure personified. Just listening to him through a wall makes me dream of smack. All the downsides of rampant drug abuse evaporate when weighed against another day sober in Phil's company. Addiction, penury, shiteing yourself, and tabloid harassment all pale compared to abstinence in his annoying presence.

'Charlie!'

God, he's annoying – like every missed train in your life, all missed at once. I try to answer him, but I can only speak in tweets and WhatsApp messages. He'll need to wait for the ping to have a conversation with me. I'm trying to dream here, and he's forcing his fat arse in here to induce nightmares and paralysis. He never changes. He never grows.

Bang!

The toilet door crashes and swings towards me. My limbs are lifeless, but my eyes are open, and I can see Phil waving his arms in front of me. The luxury bathroom has disintegrated and left me in a place much more familiar and depressing.

'Charlie!' He slaps me across the face. I guess he's never heard of sleep paralysis. Would you slap any cunt else who was paralysed? Of course, you wouldn't. You're not a psycho like my darling agent. The cunt's only making sure I'm not dead because of the inconvenience it'll land him trying to explain how a dead man is a corpse all over again. History repeating itself and that.

'You alright?' He lets me go, and I fall off the toilet seat with my trousers and boxers around my ankles. My cock looks sad, but Phil looks even sadder. He doesn't know you need to wrench yourself out of sleep paralysis, and falling off the toilet has worked a treat. It takes a few seconds to show that panic merchant I'm still alive. Hippocrates is hardly shiteing himself.

'Ah was daein a shit,' I tell him.

'You've been in here for over an hour, and there ain't no shit in that toilet bowl. I can't even smell shit. In fact, this is best smelling room in the house.' That's because the window's actually been opened in here.

'Ah must've flushed it in ma sleep,' I say, getting to my feet and pulling up my boxers and jeans. Christ, my head is pounding. I'll need to lay off magic mushrooms and the mixers.

'Don't talk crap.' Phil is not amused. Fuck him.

'You brought crap up first,' I say, sitting on the toilet pan again to get myself together. 'Ah was probably sleep-flushing.'

'Sleep-flushing?'

'Aye. You never sleep-walked?'

'No!' he yells before sitting on the edge of the bath and putting his head in his hands. He's really developed a flair for soap opera drama in the last wee while.

'Well, you've heard of it, right?' I say, pulling my phone from my pocket and pressing on the Twitter app.

'Yeah.'

'Well, I sleep-shat and sleep-flushed. End of story. People dae all sorts of shit in their sleep. Ma da used tae sleep-drink and wake up even drunker than when he went tae sleep.'

'Bullshit.'

Musk has tweeted again and appears to be on a similar diet to me. I might have to block him.

'Bull truth, ya cunt. In my family, when you become an alcoholic, you commit. You can half-arse everything else, but no getting wasted. Your art is important.'

'This is nothing but justifying self-destruction,' Phil says, trying to guilt me with his pity expression.

'Piss off, ya mad agony aunt cunt. Your only concern is me fuckin up the fake death routine that's helping pay your hooker tab.'

'I'm worried about you, Charlie. That's all.' He's actually giving me the puppy dog eyes. Fucking agents. The world would be better off if they got stuck in gulags to break rocks all day. Stalin knew what to do with these pricks. Phil doesn't even know I'm murdering people. If that's not high functioning, I don't know what is. So what if I'm taking some drugs while I'm working through a list of scumbags that need to be taken care of.

'Ah'm perfectly fine without you interrupting ma shits,' I say, pretending to read my timeline until Phil fucks off.

'You're really not. You've been doing drugs since you woke up this morning.'

'This is ma cheat day. Jack Daniel's, coke, weed, pills, mushies. Count yourself lucky Ah'm showing admirable self-control and no sitting wae a needle hinging out ma arm.'

'You can't do lots of drink and drugs on a cheat day. A cheat day is for burgers, Coke Zero . . . This is more like a cheat month anyway, not a cheat day!'

'Gies peace, ya prick.'

'You're so hostile when you're on too many drugs,' Phil says, shaking his head and getting up to leave. I hope.

'Hostile? Ah'm no hostile! Fuck off, ya mad fuckin sad sack!'

'I never thought I'd say this, but I'm starting to miss the clean you who was scared to eat a protein bar at the wrong time.' He leaves, and I give two fingers to the door.

Phil wouldn't know good company even if it sucked him happy, so there's no point in arguing. I mean, we all get lonely sometimes, but I'm not that desperate yet. Human relationships can wait when you've got goals. I used to think setting goals was the first step to depression, but this to-do list keeps me motivated, focused and righteous. So what if I'm doing drugs along the way? This is nothing I can't handle.

LONG BEFORE KARMA AND DEATH: EXCERPT OF A PRETENTIOUS REVIEW OF CHARLIE DONNELLY'S GREATEST MOMENT ON SCREEN

The River Knows

by Nicholas Silverton

The River Knows is a movie that aims high and strives for elegiac. It is marinated in dialogue until that dialogue metastasises and becomes incidental and impenetrable. It is a supercilious, Oscar-baiting movie and follows a trend of movies where two-dimensional characters say everything and nothing at breakneck speed. This applies tenfold to Charlie Donnelly, the Scottish character actor, who can still be heard chewing the scenery long after he's departed the screen. Here is a man channelling the very worst exhibitionism of Pacino and Oldman without the charm or goodwill in the bank. It is a performance that fuses the most outlandish theatricality of Nicholas Cage and the morose tragedy of Bozo the Clown. That the director, Paul Kettleman, a man who usually has a lighter touch and respect for naturalism, would persist in filming it without yelling 'Cut!' and getting Charlie Donnelly to rein in everything suggests I was wrong in comparing Kettleman with a young, vibrant Milos Forman.

AFTER DEATH:
WHERE DO WE GO NOW? /
AN AGENT OF KARMA, PART 5?

Drugs, drink and madness are the only things keeping me halfway sane. At least that's what I'm telling myself as I sit in Phil's, chained to my phone, and flick through channel after channel of pish, expertly avoiding the burgeoning cleaning and sweaty odour of abandonment problem. I can only imagine the state I would be in if I went sober again and became a noble, charitable citizen. I'd probably be in a cell quicker than a robot reading books. I need to stop putting on shitey, wonderful movies like *Short Circuit* while scrolling this phone. That can't be helping with my state of mind and trying to justify killing an innocent man who was the second coming of Jesus Christ.

I need a hobby other than killing people. Maybe pottery, drawing or writing a script. I miss acting. Sometimes, I act out bits when watching films between Twitter and YouTube, but it's not the same. I need an audience. I need my kids. Sitting in Phil's house waiting for everything to come crashing down is no life for anyone. I wouldn't wish it on my worst enemy. I'd just kill them instead.

I wouldn't say living with Phil and trying to pretend I'm dead is a fate worse than death, but that's because I don't know what awaits me after death. Maybe it's Hell and spending it with no access to the internet. Fuck knows. It just feels like hope is gone, and all I can do is keep avoiding clean living and doing the necessary mental gymnastics to continue with this list and not turn the gun on myself. Dark, I know, but that's how I feel, if you can call this feeling.

@DeadNLovinIt

@God4NuclearArms God hates nuclear arms and she hates you. God no longer rests on Sunday because hating you is a seven days a week job. Ass.

@DeadNLovinIt

@bannuclear Nuclear weapons stop countries from going to war and ensure peace between all the countries that matter. Get with the programme, idiot.

@DeadNLovinIt

@GeraldCutler Say no to drugs, say yes to sucking your own penis. Loving in this world begins with loving yourself.

@DeadNLovinIt

@ConservativeParty It's time for you all to get in a one way rocket to Venus. It's time for you all to do the only noble thing you will your entire miserable lives. Poo.

The next cunt on my list is a film critic. Nicholas Silverton panned my Oscar-nominated performance as cartoonish and helped send my career into a tailspin. I like to think he was in cahoots with Shackler. That helps, even if I just made it up to make it easier and get me back on track. Do you deserve to die for being a snarky, pretentious bastard who's content to criticise, mock and lambast without ever sticking your neck out and creating anything yourself? Granted, he's not a monster like Pickford, Harrison or Shackler. He hasn't battered people in creative and sadistic ways or created a cult to inflate a dangerous ego and manipulate people into beds and coffins. But I like to think Nicholas has done something awful beyond being a film critic. Maybe he throws luxury Belgian chocolates at his cat every time he has to get a thesaurus out. Maybe he secretly loves Marvel movies yet claims he doesn't and continues giving no more than two stars in his pretentious 6-star maximum rating bar. I do know that he gave *The English Patient* a 6-star rating and panned *Casino, Brazil* and *The Sopranos*. That's more justification right there.

There will be no collateral damage this time. I'll be careful, sober. Well, soberer than the last time. The coke is fine if you don't drink bottles of wine on top of it. And with only one Jack Daniel's and a few lines in me, I'm relatively fresh.

We all know the problem with this critic prick: he's over-educated and undersexed – such a combo always brings out the worst in people. Believe me, I know. I have been undersexed, and I wasn't particularly bright at the time either. Even his name isn't sexy: Nicholas Silverton. Cunt sounds and looks like a fucking accountant. And not one of the fun accountants with a coke problem who siphons off a significant proportion of your wealth until you realise their sniffing problem isn't a sinus issue.

Nicholas Silverton and his loft apartment. Nicholas Silverton and his awards for tearing down movies and careers. Nicholas Silverton: the beta male inadequate who ruined my chance for an Oscar. I know you shouldn't do something for the awards. And I know I shouldn't get all mental about something as artificial as the Academy Awards. But I wanted that stupid-looking gold trophy to put in my bathroom. I wanted to take a shite each day and gaze upon my glory. I wanted that fucking Oscar, and I fucking deserved it too. I was better than whoever the fuck else I was up against. My performance was full-on method and just about fucking killed me. And this critic prick spoke about me like I was struggling to do fucking panto in Millport. Well, there will be no collateral damage. There will be no Gareth.

I've done two days of research and have a postal outfit I got from a bizarre charity shop to access his building. It isn't regulation wear anymore, and it's tight about the arse, but it's enough of a disguise to get me to his door. Then I can get into his art deco apartment that presumably floods with natural light to exhibit his bland, pishy art that he probably doesn't even understand.

I ascend the stairs to his apartment and take a moment to gather my composure. The postman always rings twice because they have a lot to do and want to finish as soon as possible. I ring three times just to get the cunt agitated. I hear the footsteps and feel him looking at me through the spyhole. The parcel in my hand and the uniform are a dead giveaway. I decide to go with a gruff mid-western accent. We'll see who the great actor and the daft critic is now.

'US postal service,' I say like a Wyatt Earp wannabe. I watched Kurt Russell play him in *Tombstone* last week. It's a good film if you don't have any lofty expectations and snort some good coke with four homemade Long Island iced teas.

Nicholas opens the door and is about to speak when I push him backwards and enter his totally undeserved luxury apartment filled with Japanese-style art on the walls and homoerotic sculptures dotted around the spacious, clean lounge. I keep the surgical mask on and point my new Glock 19 semi-automatic pistol at his flabby pigeon tits.

'Don't fuckin scream, or you're dead.' His heavyset cat yawns, closing its eyes. 'Ye should've got a dog,' I add.

He's already pissing himself and making me feel sorry for him. I see Gareth. Get him out. Don't think about that. Kill him quietly and leave. No collateral damage. Efficiency, efficiency, efficiency.

'I have money,' he says, on his knees. 'Not on me. I use cards for everything now. But I can get you money!'

'Keep your voice doon.' Shit, I swerved back into my natural Glaswegian. He looks puzzled.

'Doon?' He screws his face up like I've shaken a shite down my leg onto the floor.

'Fuck's sake,' I say, pulling down the mask a little to breathe. He squints his eyes like I'm a burst of sunlight.

'Do I know you?' he says, trembling.

I pull the mask back over my nose. 'Every cunt knows me. Ah'm the grim fuckin reaper.' My improvising days are never over.

'Please. Take anything you want. Just don't shoot me!' I point the gun at his head and see Gareth again.

'Stop it,' I say, hitting my head with my free hand. 'Why dae you tear people down for a livin, ya fuckin pretentious bastard?'

'What?' he says, every part of his body shaking.

'Your reviews,' I growl, jutting the gun closer to his head.

'My reviews?' he squeaks, flinching. 'Is this what this is about?'

'Yeah, it fuckin well is.'

His hands cover his face. 'It's my job,' he pleads, daring to glance at me.

'Your job is to be a cunt?' I position the gun at his temple. He shields his face like that'll make a difference. 'Some fuckin job that is.'

'I'm . . .' he says, looking at the floor. 'I'm a . . . I'm a writer.'

'You're no a writer,' I laugh, stepping back from him but with the gun still pointing his head. 'You're a fuckin critic. You make a living off other people's imaginations.'

'C-criticism is . . .' He's stuttering, sweating, clasping his hands into a prayer position, and farting. 'It's an art form!'

'So, that makes you an artist? Who knew Ah was actually in the presence of a Vincent Van Gogh, a Frida Kahlo, a fuckin Fellini?'

'In a sense.' I have to itch my nose again, and I need another line. Why am I preserving anonymity here when he won't live to identify me? I remove the mask, and he studies my face before my stare makes him look away. Some things I inherited from my da are beneficial. I bump the coke and watch this confessed atheist (it's on Wikipedia) look to the heavens or the opulent chandelier on his ceiling for divine intervention. Like God has any time for all the Bible bashers, never mind the wishes of atheists. The conviction with which Nicholas claims he's an atheist is another reason to kill him. Not agnostic, sceptic or doubter. The man is a fully-fledged, sneering evangelical atheist. At least that prick Richard Dawkins has some intellectual authority about him. Nicholas? He thinks writing a scathing review of *American Pie* gives him the supreme authority on the meaning of life.

I look at the piss on his beige trousers but smell worse. Now you see the true colours: yellow with a mix of brown. I notice a flicker of recognition on his face.

He knows. Fuck me, he knows. But why do I care? Gareth . . .

'What are you going to do here?' he yelps, crying and staring at the floor. He's robbed all the fun from this and no mistake. But I've had to do many routine, unglamorous jobs.

'Well, you've seen me, so Ah think you can predict what happens next,' I say, coldly, moving closer to him and keeping a steady hand on the gun.

He's shrinking again, begging for a hero or clemency. 'But I don't know you! I really don't.'

I can tell he's lying. He's not the actor here. 'You *do* know me. Don't come the cunt wae me, Nic.'

'I don't. Honestly, I don't!'

That wasn't convincing either. 'Ah'm dead, if that helps,' I say.

'Excuse me?'

I remove my phone and go to the notes section, where I saved every word of his hatchet job. '*The plot meanders and stutters from expository to superfluous, with Donnelly turned up to 11 in every scene burdened by his presence.*'

'But . . .' His mouth is shocked open. '. . . You're dead,' he says, eventually. '. . . Wait . . . you faked your death?' He's incredulous, like I'm the only person in history who's done this.

'Ma agent did. Well, he tried tae deny it, but Ah know. He faked it tae get rid of debts, cash in. Ah just went along with it. It's pulled me oot a hole . . .' – the chiselled marble male arse on a sculpture near the TV catches my eye; it's been a long time since I looked like that – '. . . ironically.'

'But,' he looks me in the eyes, pleading. I avert my gaze back to the arse, which makes me jealous, angry. 'Why are you doing this?'

I think briefly about the best way to articulate it, then plump for honesty. 'Ah'm an agent of karma.'

'An agent of what?'

I knew he wouldn't get it right away. He needs his art spoon-fed to him. 'Karma. You deaf as well as pretentious?'

'I don't understand.'

'Aye, you're no as smart as you think.' I can see his daft fucking brain downgrading to something even more pathetic.

'Of course, of course, I should've recognised how good your performance was! It was fantastic!'

I look away from that statue that's provoking too much feeling and down at Nicholas again. 'You fuckin worm. Ah know bad acting when Ah see it. Even wae your life oan the line, you still cannae ruffle ma pillows.'

'Oh, God.'

'Ah thought you were an atheist,' I say, fixing the gun at his head again.

'Please don't kill me!' He scrunches his eyes shut, ceasing to put his hands over his face, and prays instead. 'Please don't kill me.'

I take a deep breath to control my rising anger. 'Dae you think saying please and asking politely will make a difference?' I say, coldly, channelling my antagonist in a western.

'Please, Ah have . . .' – he's full-on sweating, voice quivering, shuffling on his knees to grovel closer to me – '. . . a cat . . . and two brothers!'

I've murdered a man I've convinced myself would cure cancer. A useless prick with a cat and two brothers? This should be nothing, but this is the most I've stalled so far. I feel like a virgin all over again. Maybe I'm becoming one of those Bond villains who spends too much time laying out his master plan and neglects to swiftly kill the one cunt capable of scuppering all those wonderful, dastardly schemes.

'I'm still young . . .' he continues, 'middle-aged. I can give you money . . . sex?'

Fuck's sake. Nah, I'm not stalling until some cunt fucks this up and ruins all my hard work. I'm going through with this come hell or high water. But Gareth . . . Fuck Gareth. He wasn't discovering anything. He was collateral damage and nothing more. He probably had a secret life as a serial killer, peado or Reddit troll. I can feel vanity getting the better of me. It's always been a weakness.

'Why did you write that crap back then?' I say, putting the gun under his chin and raising his head to meet my best evil glare. 'Did you think Ah was bad?'

'No, no, no, no,' he splutters, tears rolling down his cheeks. 'You were good, great! The best!'

'Why don't Ah believe you?' I step back, assuming my kill position and aiming the gun at his forehead.

'It was all Bob Shackler!' he wails, throwing his hands in front of his face again. 'He had something over me, something that he held over me until he died. He told me to trash you! It's his fault!'

Boom! I knew it was that cunt!

'Ah fuckin knew it,' I say. But it doesn't really matter now. I need to kill him. I need to go all the way, or I'll have another Vietnam. That was such a pointless war. The only good that came out of it was some of the music, the movies and a superpower getting a severe black eye for a change. Fuck me, this coke is magic. I mean, I know coke will hardly keep me level-headed in the long run, but it's working a charm right now.

'Please, please . . . please,' he begs. I'm getting distracted here. I have a job to do. That's all it is. This is my job now. People would've killed for this job under Thatcher. They'd do it now. Stick this in the job centre, and you'd have a bigger queue than in the advert that helped elect that evil Victorian doll that got Pinocchio-ed. Christ knows I'm not getting any acting gigs while I'm corpsing, corpsing, corpsed. I need another bump. I've pussyfooted about for far too long. I got my answer. He conspired with Shackler, and that's justification enough. I take my phone from my pocket, turn on 'Wipe Out' by The Surfaris and wait until the guitar gets going and does its stuff.

Bang!

His head jolts backwards, and he drops in a beautiful straight line to the oak wood floor that's beginning to pool with blood. I'm living every actor's dream and gazing upon the bloody corpse of my worst critic – the one who cost me immortality. Forever a nominee just because of this dead prick.

SISTER SLEUTH

Paula hadn't spoken to Charlie since their mother's funeral, and now his coffin was about to burn in an incinerator – something she wasn't best pleased with, despite the acrimony.

'Ah'm so sorry, Charlie,' she said to a closed casket just before pallbearers came to carry it in for the service next door. 'Your ex-wife and kids were kind enough to pay for me tae come and pay my respects . . .' She stopped herself from shedding a tear by fighting it down and bottling her emotions. 'The animosity between us will haunt me, and Ah'll have this stain on my soul when Ah reach the gates.' She reached out and touched the coffin. 'Ah hope tae see you in Heaven, Charlie . . . after you get there from a long stint in Purgatory, of course. Ah really do hope you get tae Heaven. Ah still think you deserve that in spite of . . . well, everything. But you were horrible at times. A . . .' Sister Paula looked around, saw she was still alone and removed her hand from the wooden top of the coffin. 'A scumbag. A loser who's on the first train straight to . . . What am Ah saying? Ah need tae get a grip. Show forgiveness. You deserve redemption even if you were snide, arrogant and an unrepentant, debauched philanderer.'

'You okay, Auntie Paula?' David asked after seeing her call a coffin a philanderer. His dad always said his auntie was a topping short of a pizza, but that was rich coming from him.

Charlie was dead, and Paula had left so much unresolved with him. It didn't sit well. His sudden death seemed expected, and everybody chalked it up to Charlie being Charlie, but the more Paula heard, the more she became suspicious. No-one had seen the body, and his agent, whom Paula knew fleetingly and detested, was heavily involved in all the arrangements yet missing from the cremation.

Paula heard that Charlie had gone straight and was trying to better himself. She asked questions at Carly's house while in L.A. and got unsatisfying answers.

'He got like totally into karma, kabbalah or one of those like hipster religious kinda things,' David said. 'It was obviously just a fad. He's totally, like, full of bull.'

'Dad was talking about this karma thing all the time,' Lilly said. 'He was like totally into all this charity and philandering stuff.'

'You mean philanthropy?' Paula asked.

'Yeah, what did I say?'

'Charlie's default setting is asshole,' Carly said. 'Don't get me wrong, I loved the guy. I still do. But he was possessed by an asshole with a drinking problem, and a drug problem. And a stick his dick in younger women problem. That's three too many problems for me. Oh yeah, and he had a debt problem. He spent like a yuppie with no arms, bought every lowlife a drink in every pub and still expected to be rich. The guy was a walking disaster. That's when he was actually sober enough to walk.'

☆

Paula returned to the convent in Kirkintilloch and contemplated what had gone wrong with Charlie. She couldn't put her finger on it, but she believed there was more to his death. She even thought he was still alive and had faked the entire thing to clear debts and get more attention.

Charlie had an unhealthy obsession with the conspiracy that Elvis was still alive – ditto Jim Morrison, Lord Lucan, Sid Vicious, Hitler and numerous other dead people. It was like he'd never grown up in housing schemes ravaged by booze, drugs, unemployment and frozen crispy pancakes. Paula could remember these conversations about faking deaths, unlike Charlie, whose memory was missing files after his brain bore the brunt of his personality.

Sometimes Paula thought she unjustly expected the worst of her brother, and then she felt she was giving him too much leeway. Charlie was the type of guy she could envision being a lunatic despot in charge of some totalitarian regime or CEO of a euthanasia charity. Then she read that a tabloid journalist who had haunted him got murdered in L.A. And a cult leader who had brainwashed Carly. And that horrible producer with whom Charlie had a bit of a vendetta.

Paula was not a believer in coincidence. She looked further into murders in the L.A. area and saw a murdered film critic. She searched the guy's name along with Charlie Donnelly and, sure enough, she saw why someone as cavillous as Charlie would take umbrage and seek retribution. Was her brother still alive? And not only that, was he now joining the annals of serial killing? She spoke to God again and felt like she was losing her grip on reality. This worsened with a deeper internet search of Charlie's name.

Gary Busey Versus Charlie Donnelly: Who is more of a Shambles?

When Hellraising Becomes Pathetic: The Curious Case of Charlie Donnelly

Rowdy Charlie Peeper? Can Charlie Donnelly's Bathroom Masturbation ever be Forgiven?

Charlie, Where's Your Troosers?

Hollywood Maestro Kingmaker Shackler is out to get me says Paranoid DRUG NUT Charlie Donnelly

His Mother, the Murderer, A Charlie Donnelly Story

Charlie Donnelly's Career Flatlines. Is it DNR Time?

Panto Fires Charlie Donnelly After Bathroom Masturbation Backlash

Charlie Donnelly Pooped in the sink at Hollywood Party says Source

Paula preferred to give charity, but her vow of poverty would always reduce her to begging, and right now, she wasn't too proud. She knew how to pull on the heartstrings when required, and even though she didn't like to, she got right in there with the heavy hinting on the phone to Carly, and soon she was on a flight to L.A.

☆

A couple of hours into her flight, Paula pitied people who couldn't go eight hours without drinking and making an atrocious exhibition of themselves.

'Whit ye writing?' slurred a bleached blonde Glaswegian teenager in the seat beside her. She was drunk and, if Paula knew much about the world, dressed like a sex worker. Paula didn't really want to speak to this sinner, but she remembered to hate the sin and not the heretic harlot. The girl snatched the notebook to read before Paula grabbed it back.

223

'Nothing,' Paula said, closing the notebook with all kinds of conspiracy theories scribbled over it. 'Stop invading my space and touching my private property.'

The girl chortled. 'Who's Charlie Donnelly?' she said, grinning. 'Is that the actor cunt that wanked in a McDonald's and died no that long ago?' She had a conspiratorial smile, but Paula was not her comrade. 'He wis some bit when he wis younger, win't he?' She nudged Paula and snort-laughed.

'No,' Paula said, looking across the aisle and away from the overpowering stench of spirits and rose floral perfume.

'Are you a nun in disguise? Are ye really some polis detective?' Paula smiled and put in her earbuds to listen to her Catholic Hearts podcast. 'Fuck's sake, man. Whit a cunt.' Paula heard the cunt comment and waited until the young drunk woman went to the toilet before subtly spitting in her gin and tonic. A large part of her thought she should be levitating above such pettiness, but she was taking little pieces of revenge wherever she could.

AFTER DEATH:
HIDE AND SEEK AND DESTROY

Some serial killers do stop and never kill again. They grow old, their cocks stop working (thank fuck), or they set up shop with a family, God forbid. Gar– . . . that nearly destroyed me, and I still feel guilty for it. But this whole serial killer shite? I can see why it's moreish. I'm not quite at the berserker stage yet or ready to create carnage and go out in a blaze of glory, but shooting that pretentious critic felt cathartic. I struggled at first, granted, but after he admitted he was Shackler's bitch, it became a lot easier and more gratifying.

I sit in my comfy chair with the last of the Cherry Garcia ice cream and read tributes to Nicholas on Twitter and Instagram – not that there are a lot. I mean, who gives a fuck about middling critics? Roger Ebert, sure. Even that Mark cunt with the quiff on the BBC gave me a few decent reviews. But Nicholas rose to influence because of Shackler, and his star faded once Shackler had finished using him, as he did with every cunt.

Fuck Nicholas. He's dead, and I have coke, ice cream and Jack Daniel's. What else does a man need? Love, empathy, human connection . . . Ah, fuck that. Don't start bringing yourself down by dwelling on that bullshit. You have Phil here cooking for you.

Phil is obviously so worried about me that I've turned him into Martha Stewart – Martha Stewart with a coke problem. He keeps trying to make me eat healthy shit and drink water like he wants me alive, even after faking my death. The man is a sweaty, tacky, hairy, fat paradox.

He bursts into the living room with some cabbage-pollutant Irish stew-type meal made to conjure childhood memories. Only a cretin like Phil would think me remembering my childhood and getting all nostalgic would make me less crazy. 'There you go,' he says, dumping a knife and fork on the table. I put down my phone. My efforts to cancel Meryl Streep are not getting anywhere. The woman is bombproof. Even I don't have anything against her. I actually think she's supremely gifted, but I'm bored and need to cancel some cunt, to use the shitty parlance of our times.

Phil has decided to have a salad and poison me. 'You no eating this?'

'No, no. I can't eat Irish food.'

'Right.' As if the Irish eat this. They would've turned their nose up at this during the famine, for fuck's sake.

I take another line of coke and see myself on *MasterChef* reviewing Phil's attempts to get a job with the CIA in their interrogation division. *The dumplings belonged at centre court at Wimbledon getting fired by Djokovic, the stew was brown chewing gum, and the potatoes were like a fart from a fever that turns into greenish-brown liquid.*

'Ah don't think you've made this properly,' I say after my third mouthful, and that was three too many. Phil looks hurt. 'It's overcooked or undercooked or something.'

'I got the recipe online,' he says with some lettuce hanging out his fat gub.

'Where? Gary Glitter's dark web?'

'What's wrong with it?' he frowns, hands on his hips again.

I decide to be fully brutal. Sometimes honesty is the best policy for saving your arsehole. 'The dumplings belong at centre court, Wimbledon, for a start, and the stew is like trying tae chew tae the centre of the Earth . . . after you've had aw your teeth removed.'

'Well,' Phil says. 'I'm just trying to make sure you don't die! You know, line your stomach before you drink like there's no more tomorrow and snort all the fucking cocaine!'

I really need to get my own place, but everything's more difficult when you're dead and in hiding.

Phil takes his plate to the kitchen to eat in solitude and probably hide the tears. Pathetic sack of shit. I've banged lots of people who don't take the huff like Phil. Imagine I actually stuck my dick up his arse and started hugging him – the guy would be a full-time bunny boiler trying to Kathy Bates me à la *Misery*. God bless Kathy, what a fucking trooper. Is it just me who finds her wildly sexy in that movie? All that running about she did for Jimmy Caan, and he was still desperate to get shot of her – ungrateful bastard.

Ding-dong.

That fucking doorbell. It always puts me on red alert, especially now I'm dead and killing people. Phil peers from the living room door with wide eyes. He's been snorting in the kitchen again.

'Have you ordered something?' I whisper.

'I didn't order anything,' he mutters. The terror becomes real when your doorbell goes these days, and it's not a delivery driver. For obvious reasons, Phil wasn't in the business of inviting people over, and his looks had caught up to his slimy nature, making him virtually repellent to non-sex workers.

The bell rings again. 'Who could it be?' Phil asks me like I'm the second coming of Nostradamus.

'How the fuck should Ah know?' I mumble, gnashing my teeth. He's making me feel like I'm on bad acid and sinking into an ordeal trip that will fuck me up for weeks, if not years. I scurry into the kitchen and hide under the dinner table because no-one will ever find me under here – not cops, earthquakes, or the nuclear holocaust. A serial killer scared of a chap at the door. If only my deserved victims could see me now. Gareth. Well, if there's one person, it won't be . . . well, unless the zombie apocalypse is here. I think I read he got cremated. That's probably my preference too, but the zombie apocalypse is one reason to get buried. Who wouldn't want to come back as a zombie? The life of a zombie is simple. There's no need to hide under tables because you're meant to be dead and are very much alive and paranoid from excessive boozing, drug use and murdering people.

Ding-dong.

'This is freaking me out,' Phil says, entering the kitchen. 'Who would come here without messaging first?' To make matters even worse, I've left my phone in the living room. I can't even get on Twitter to ease my anxiety and relax me. How could I have left my phone there? It's usually in my pocket or attached to my hand. Aye, aye, so I have a problem. So does every cunt.

'What you doing?' Phil says as I army crawl through bits of pizza, sweeties and empty cans to get my phone. At least it's probably not the polis. They would've broken the door down by now or announced themselves.

I get my phone and hear a knock at the window. 'Phil! Ah know you're in there!' The horror is instant. I know that fucking voice. It's Paula, my insane sister. My elbows are on fire from the carpet when I get to the kitchen. 'Ah know you're in there!' she shouts through the letterbox this time. She's persistent. In fact, she's much worse than that. The demented psycho is a recurring nightmare. 'Phil!'

Ding-dong.

Ding-dong.

Ding-dong.

'Jesus Christ, she's like the fucking Terminator,' Phil says, pacing in the kitchen.

'Your car is here!' she shouts through the letterbox. 'Ah need to speak to you about my brother, Charlie Donnelly!' At least she didn't see me auditioning for *Blackadder Goes Forth* across the living room floor. I once overheard Mr Bean call me an arsehole at a party, I think. He denied it, and I didn't actually hear it, but I'm a great lip reader. Who cares if I was out of my mind on speed and hadn't slept for two days? That doesn't make me the arsehole.

'Ah'll wait out here until you answer. Ah never shirk a challenge. Ah'm a nun!'

'What the fuck is wrong with her?' Phil asks, getting under the kitchen table with me and pulling the tablecloth down over us.

'She's a nun,' I whisper.

'Is your entire family missing a chromosome?' I give him the mugshot eyes. 'What are we supposed to do here?' he says, inching way too close for comfort. His fucking breath's barking of tobacco, coffee and illness too.

'You answer the door,' I mutter, pushing him by the shoulder. 'Get rid of her.'

'I don't want to answer the door,' he sulks, like a petulant child.

'Well, Ah cannae fuckin answer it,' I chunter, balling my fists. 'The whole thing's fucked if Ah answer it.'

'Just ignore her.' He shrugs his shoulders like that's a fucking solution.

'She's no a person you ignore. It'll only make her worse. Nip this in the bud now.' I push him again to force him into action.

'Where are you gonna go?' he says a bit too loudly for my liking.

'Fuckin Barbados,' I whisper.

'What?' he blurts out. His face is vacant, extremely punchable. My eyes explode at him. I think he gets the message.

'Ah'll stay here until she leaves.' I kick out at him to get him moving from the table.

'Under the kitchen table?' Maybe he isn't getting the message with his failure to speak quietly and follow a simple fucking instruction.

'I have coke and my phone. Wait.' I get out and grab a bottle of Jack Daniel's and a glass with ice. My fake death scam might be about to come crashing down, but I'll be fucked if that happens without a drink in one hand and my phone in the other. 'Answer the door and get her out.'

'Fuck's sake, Charlie,' he says, moving his fat arse into the light. 'The things I do for you.'

Phil opens the door and talks to her, but I'm not in the business of straining to hear what's going on, or heaven forfend, getting out from under here. This is my safe space with my coke, Jack Daniel's and access to social media.

'You can't come in!' Phil yells.

Shit, my blood runs colder than Jack Frost's bellend.

'You Americans need tae learn a thing or two about hospitality,' Paula says, clearly now in the living room. 'Leaving a nun outside in this awful sunshine.' Paula always despised the sun. She's the only person I knew who went further north to escape the ration of summer we got in Scotland. 'When was the last time you cleaned this place, opened a window? It reeks of cannabis and neglect!'

'I told you I was busy,' Phil says. He's out of his element already, and I'm failing to think of any possible escape route that doesn't involve me making too much noise for that spooky witch to detect me. I put cut coke on the floor and a rolled-up five-dollar note to it. I know, it's hardly *Scarface* under here but needs must when there's a sniffer-nun in the next room.

'You saw my brother dead, didn't you?' Paula says.

I imagine Phil flapping like a big, sweaty octopus.

'Yes!' he spits out after hesitating.

'Ah don't believe you. Ah know a liar when Ah see one. Ah'm a nun.'

'I don't care if you're Jesus fucking Christ himself.'

'Don't you swear about the Lord!'

Something gets thrown against a wall. If there's one thing guaranteed to rile Paula, it's a Hollywood agent with a drug problem badmouthing the big man. I stay under the table, snort as quietly as possible and prepare my snout for another. Maybe it's time to end this charade. Maybe it's time to end it all and move on to the next life.

'Your brother had a heart attack, okay!' Phil says.

That fucking idiot.

'Ah thought it was a brain haemorrhage?' Paula queries.

Phil says nothing for a few seconds, and then Paula clicks her fingers to prompt an answer.

'That's what I meant,' he mutters.

'Who else is here?' she demands.

'What?'

I hear an uncharacteristic dramatic sigh from Paula. Phil is really pissing her off. He does possess that quality.

'There are two glasses, two plates . . .' Give her a spoonful of that stew, Phil. It's our only hope. 'One with . . . is that meant to be Irish stew?'

'My girl is here,' Phil says, unconvincingly.

'No woman lives in this mephitic mess, eating Irish stew and drinking bourbon wae you. Even hookers wouldn't sink that low.'

Her footsteps grow louder as they edge closer to my safe space.

'I'm calling the cops!' Phil barks. 'No! You can't go in there!'

Do you know that moment when your life flashes before your eyes? Fuck replaying that snuff film. I ignore it by putting my face to the floor and snorting more coke. The tablecloth gets whipped away like there's a magician with a flair for the dramatic, except this one's in a habit with a skirt near enough to her ankles. Her face is older but still stern and unamused.

'Ah knew it!' she yells, leaning down, trying to pull me out from under the table.

'Get away!' I shout back, batting away her strong hand.

She switches on the big light to get a better gander. 'Look at the state of you!' she booms. 'You're an absolute shambles!' I hear Phil sniggering. Paula points at him, her face contorted. 'And you can shut up too! You should be ashamed ae yourself, lying tae a nun!' Phil's face tightens and he throws his hands in the air to protest his innocence.

'How did you know he was here?' Phil says, looking down at me with his hands now on his hips like he was powerless. Fucking gimp.

Paula shakes her head at me while I take a sip of my drink. 'He used tae hide under tables when he was stressed.'

Shows you what she knows. I never stopped doing it. 'Hello, Paula,' I mumble, bracing myself to emerge from my safe space and face her bullshit.

'Hello yourself!' she sneers back. 'Pretending you're dead now.'

Phil has a fake smile on his face that I want to wipe off with a bullet. 'So . . .' he hesitates, struggling for words for a change and opening cupboards to avoid Paula's cold gaze. 'When . . . How did you know he was still alive?' He takes a can of beer from the fridge, keeping his back turned on me and Paula.

I pull myself further into the light and cough. 'She's a witch!' I shout, grinning and stumbling back against the table that's now supporting me instead of providing sanctuary. She looks at the ceiling and shakes her big fucking head again. She definitely got my da's napper. Phil's eyes widen at me as he sips from his beer with his pinky raised before turning again and busying himself brushing crumbs to the floor from the kitchen counter.

'You don't need tae be a witch tae see something was suspect,' she says, smug and self-righteous, her arms folded, standing in front of the fridge freezer you could fit Goliath in with room to spare for David. That's definitely tactical to stop me from getting a beer. Fucking puritan. 'No-one saw the body, and everything was done quickly, rumours of debts, people coming into a bit of money. Ah know Charlie. Ah know him all too well.'

Phil gives me a brief worried expression after I look at him to avoid that witch who cosplays as a nun and my sister. 'Well, you're the only one,' he grumbles, shakily, gulping down his beer like it's a razor blade. I'd kick him if this table weren't currently supporting my verticality.

'Ah know he wanted tae be buried in case there was a zombie apocalypse, and he could come back,' Paula gawks, eyes narrowed, top lip curled. I don't even remember telling her that. Then again, I don't remember much in these troubling times. 'And Ah know he was interested in people who supposedly faked their deaths and were still alive.'

I've heard enough of her theory that assumes the worst of me. 'The faking ma death was all his idea,' I point at Phil, 'even though he tried tae play dumb for a while.' My hand slips on the kitchen table, and I almost deck it before recovering my composure. I'm more wasted than I thought. That under the table drink and line have put me way over the threshold. Paula hangs her head before studying me from the feet up until she fixes on my eyes with a weary stare, looking just the way my mother did after the police brought me home. 'Why are you here?' I snipe.

'Why dae you think Ah'm here?' she spits back, moving closer to me and away from the beer in the fridge. Soon, my cold canned beauties. We're back in Glasgow again, her skipping her teenage years to become an unbearable old cunt and me comfortable and exuding effortless cool in my arrested development.

'Ah don't know. The fuckin sunshine?' I say, catching Phil's head going side to side, like he's at Wimbledon.

'You, leave us!' she barks at Phil, who might as well have a bucket of popcorn. 'We need a bit of privacy.'

Phil walks over to the fridge. 'This is my home,' he mumbles, opening the door of the freezer. He yanks at a drawer and lifts out a lidless tub of ice cream. Avoiding Paula's glare, he moves past her, takes a spoon from the open cutlery drawer and plunges it into his tub of ice cream with great force, like he's making some sort of statement.

'Get me a beer,' I tell him, keeping my right hand on the table.

'Don't you dare,' Paula says through gritted teeth, stepping backwards in front of the fridge again. Phil shrugs his shoulders at me and rests his ice cream on the kitchen counter.

'Okay, just fuck off,' I tell him. He stands there as if I gave my orders in Klingon. 'Now!' He huffs and puffs, shuffling away, looking over his shoulder like a kid ordered to the naughty step.

'Wait,' he says, noticing he's left his ice cream and turning to retrieve it.

'Ah told you tae fuck off!'

'Okay, okay, Jesus Christ,' he mutters. Paula's face is flushing from righteous indignation. 'Sorry,' he says to her. 'For the name in vain . . . snafu.' He has one last longing look at the ice cream and leaves the kitchen to no doubt listen from the living room.

'This is low,' Paula says quietly, glowering at me. 'Ah knew you were a desperate, lost person, but allowing people tae believe you're dead? That's another level. That's basement level.'

'It wisnae some big, Machiavellian plan. It just sorta happened, and Ah went wae it. At that point, Ah was better off being dead. It was the only thing that could gie ma career a resurgence . . . for a few months.'

'Your kids are mourning you.'

I look at the fridge behind Paula, dreaming of beer before those intense, staring eyes give me a blinking fit. 'That's nice.'

'It really isn't. It's diabolical.' She might be right there, but why give her the satisfaction?

'It's character building,' I say, giving her a bit of quickly manufactured defiance.

'Look at you.' She's frowning, triggering me.

'Look at you!' I shout.

'What about me?'

'You're still a nun,' I say, feeling mean, defensive. 'For the catholic church. Dae you have tae help cover up . . . anything?' Paula shakes her head. 'Maybe that's why you cracked the faked ma death case.'

'Ah don't cover up anything.'

'Except your head and everything that makes you a woman.' I can tell she wants to hit me, but I'm enjoying this now. The gloves are off. If she's going to denigrate everything about me, I'll do the same to her. That's the mature course of action. She sighs.

'You need tae confess,' she says, quietly, jaw clenched.

'Confess?' I snort. 'Confess tae whit, fir fuck's sake?'

'That you're not dead for a start.' I can hear Phil breathing and pressing against the door.

'No can do.' I look behind me and see that bottle of Jack Daniel's missing its cork. That's convenient. I turn a little, sliding it closer to me. 'It's only been a few months since Ah died.'

'You better tell your kids and Carly.'

Like that's going to work. 'Why?'

'Are you deranged? . . .What am Ah saying? Of course you are. You've got cocaine in your beard and eyes that belong on a mad bull. And don't even think about drinking fae that bottle!'

'Ah'll take that as a compliment,' I say, smiling and drinking from the bottle. Fuck me, that burned my insides. She puts her right hand over her eyes as if I'm white phosphorus. 'Who wouldn't want tae be a part of the matador scene?' I belch.

'You still think you're so charming and cute, but you're not. You're damned for eternity.' Is she for real, still peddling this shite?

'Aw, fir fuck's sake. Give it a rest wae that shite. You're centuries out of date, sister.'

'Ah'll take that as a compliment.' She pulls out an iPhone. Not so pure, after all.

'You've got an iPhone?'

'Aye, Ah do.'

'Dae the church know you're looking up porn?' She's not for giving me a smile or anything other than looks that could freeze Miami in June.

'Ah don't use it for that. Stop projecting.'

'Well, it's wasted oan you then.'

'Did you know he was murdered?' she says, putting her phone in my face. It's the hack, the one that Gareth
. . .

'Naw,' I lie. Always lie when people ask you about someone you've murdered. That's Crime 101.

'You didn't hear about the journalist who badgered you and our mother for so long?' She thinks she's Columbo. At least Peter Falk showed a bit of hair and neck.

'Naw, Ah didnae hear anything about him. Why would Ah?'

Remain calm and neutral.

'Because you live in the same city.'

'This is L.A., fir fuck's sake.'

'Stop swearing, please. It was in the news. It happened not too far fae you.'

'Why you asking me this shite?'

I can see her turning all this over in her mind. She suspects me of this and has been doing her homework. She always was a wee swot. Fucking weirdo. If there's one person I don't want to investigate me, other than Sherlock Holmes, it's her wearing that creepy habit that never seems to move on that napper.

'What happened wae Dad all those years ago?'

'Eh?'

This is really thorough. This is *Back to the Future* stuff.

'Was it you who killed him?' Paula says, fixing those beady wee detective eyes on me as if I'll crack under her interrogation.

'Whit is this? Have you been binge-watching *Murder She Wrote*?'

'Mum wanted tae tell me something before she died, but then she changed her mind. And now, you fake your death, and people connected tae you – people you didn't like – are turning up dead.'

I look at her like she's nuts. This is when having acting chops comes in handy. 'So, whit, Ah'm a serial killer noo?'

There's a stifled cough from the living room.

'Stop listening at the door!' Paula shouts to Phil. We hear him sigh and retreat. 'Ah just find it funny that you fake your death, and then people you hate start being killed one by one. Being dead is the best alibi, isn't it?'

She's definitely got me there. Not that I'm giving her the win. 'You really dae think the worst ae me, don't ye?'

'That is ma default position, yes – wae good reason.'

'How very Christian ae ye.' I'm trying to pile on guilt, but she's unmoved and a worthy adversary.

'So, did you?' she says calmly, moving closer, arms folded and staring into my eyes.

'Naw, and even if Ah did, you'd be the last person Ah'd tell.'

'Ah notice you didnae ask about the other people that have been killed.'

I yawn and sink more booze from the bottle. 'You've some imagination.'

'When are you planning on telling your kids you're not dead?' she nips. I shrug. I feel like I'm eight again – eight years old and high on cocaine. 'Don't you miss them?'

'Aye, of course, but Ah went longer stretches without seeing them when Ah was still alive.'

She shakes her head. For a Christian, she doesn't half love to judge others and get on the high horse. It's almost like she's a bit of a hypocrite who cherry-picks parts of The Bible to suit her in each situation.

'Tell them now and see about getting into rehab,' she demands like she's the older sibling and knows all about raising kids.

'Ah'll tell them in ma own good time, okay?' I snap back. 'They're better off wae me dead anyway.'

'There's that self-pitying again,' she says, folding her arms.

What a catastrophe. I think I might have to add her to the list. How else am I going to get shot of her and stop her putting me in a federal prison full of vocational rapists?

AFTER GETTING CAUGHT FAKING YOUR DEATH AND SUSPECTED OF BEING A SERIAL KILLER

My sister, the nun. The pain in the arse of all pains in the fucking arse. Trust me to start killing people to keep me occupied in between long stretches on social media and have a priggish nun of a sister be the one who's wise to my shenanigans. She always was a witch in touch with the supernatural. It doesn't help that she doesn't drink or do drugs like a normal person and remembers every single little fucking fibre of every fucking thing.

Paula's haunted me, stood in judgment and resented me for my relationship with our mum. She doesn't get that she just isn't all that likeable. She may be in line for canonisation or a place in Heaven to bore the tits of angels, but she's no good at a party or the go-to person for a relaxing conversation. No cunt wants to hear about all the poverty and misery on the planet while they drink. No cunt actually enjoys hypocrites like Bob Geldof lecturing people all the time. Fair dos if you want to help people. I've helped people too. I'm a citizen of the world. But no cunt wants to watch you fellate or lick yourself all day no matter how beautiful you may be. Mix all that shite in with religion and you have a recipe for crushing boredom and the ugliest sanctimony. And I'd wager there's nothing worse than sanctimony. Maybe genocide. And rape. And the CIA, Wall Street, freemasonry, Bernie Madoff and televangelism. But no cunt should have to deal with Paula poring over their attempts to fake their death and work their way through a kill list. That's beyond the pale. I can't even get shot of her now.

I turn up *The King of Comedy*, arguably one of Scorsese's finest pieces of cinema, sink into my chair and get on Twitter to stop thinking.

'What are you gonna do about her?' Phil asks again after returning from the toilet and parking his arse on his farty chair. 'She's relentless.'

He heard way too much at the door when Paula accused me of all sorts of heinous crimes that I admittedly did commit.

'Ah don't know,' I say, looking at my Twitter timeline. Twitter makes everything better. I can feel Phil wanting to ask me something, but he doesn't seem able to speak for a change. 'What is it? Out wae it.'

'Well, it's just . . .' he says, looking at Robert De Niro talking to himself. Rupert Pupkin knows it's the best way to get an intelligent conversation and live a better life. 'I mean . . .'

'Spit it out, fir fuck's sake,' I snarl as he shuffles in his seat. He's not making eye contact, so I look back at Twitter.

'Well, you haven't . . .' – Phil getting nervous is a turn up for the books – 'been . . . like, killing people, have you?'

I stare at the side of his face. 'Whit makes you think that?' I'm actually enjoying his discomfort.

'Well, I overheard–'

'You were eavesdropping oan oor conversation?' I give him a villainous look that used to help get me movie parts in this city. He quickly looks away at the TV.

'I just heard is all,' he mumbles.

'Don't listen tae what Paula says,' I say, clicking on a video of Scottish people fighting outside a bookies in

Dunfermline. 'She's nuts. She always has been. She resented ma success. She thinks Ah'm a sinner.'

'Well, you are, aren't you?'

Is he being serious? 'And?' I spit. 'Every cunt's a sinner. You included. Ah'm just more honest about it.'

'But now she knows you've faked your death.' He's suddenly getting all moralistic and jittery. This is not what I need to reach the even keel.

'And whit?'

'Well, she knows you faked your death,' he mutters towards the coffee table instead of daring to make eye contact.

'*You* faked it,' I snarl, pointing at him.

'You know what I mean.'

Fuck's sake, can I not just scroll aimlessly on my phone and dip in and out of this magnificent film without this tadger getting on my tits? 'Don't worry,' I say, smiling at De Niro talking to himself again on screen. 'Ah've no intention of coming clean just yet.'

'It is only her that knows, right?' he says, looking down at his phone. 'Everyone else is none the wiser, aren't they?'

I wonder if he's hinting at what I think he is. 'Whit are you suggesting?' I ask.

'Well, if you have killed people, then . . .' He still has his face buried in his phone, ignoring me while asking me to murder my sister. I knew his bout of morals had an ulterior motive. It's always self-preservation with this cunt.

'Are you suggesting Ah kill ma sister?'

'N-no,' he stammers, looking from his phone to the telly. 'Well . . .'

I gawk at the side of his face as he pretends to be engrossed in the film. 'Ah'm no a murderer despite whit

242

she's insinuating,' I say, cutting him off before he makes an even bigger arse of himself. 'That's just her nature. She's always thought the worst of me.'

'Of course not. It's just I had a look at when that journalist was killed.'

Christ, everybody with a fucking Wi-Fi connection is now a detective. 'He wisnae a journalist,' I say, leaning off my chair to pick up a bong from the coffee table. 'He was a scumbag hack.'

'Of course, of course,' he blurts out, a bit too eager. 'But you were out that night. And you were gone when that ex-cult guy . . .' He can't bring himself to look at the man he's accusing of heinous crimes.

'How the fuck would you know? You're oan that many drugs you don't know your arse fae your elbow.' I light and inhale.

'Right. Forget I said anything.'

I scrubbed Phil's name from my list after putting it on there in jest, but I may have to revise that and put it down in pen and capitals.

'Dae you actually think Ah'm capable of murder? Not just murder, but multiple murders?' I ask him.

He hesitates and considers what he's going to say next. This is way out of character for him. He usually takes a constant scattergun approach to speaking. 'No?'

'Was that a question?'

'No, of course not. Of course not. It's just, people were looking for money from you. Your death was quite lucrative.'

I tense my right fist and try to remain calm. 'That doesn't mean Ah'm a murderer.' I take a deep breath. 'Or that Ah'm capable . . .' I look over at him. He glances at me and gets back on his phone, pretending he's doing something important. 'And it disnae mean

Ah'm gonnae kill ma sister. If Ah was a killer . . . in fact, scratch that.' I need to keep some things to myself. Cocaine and weed can lend itself to talking the occasional shite.

'So, if killing her is off the table, so to speak, what do you plan on doing?' Phil always needs answers right away. Even though he's in his sixties and far from being a millennial, he's all about the instant gratification. I'm still a stoner at heart and content to delay lots of major decisions. But this has preyed on my mind. My sister, the nun, has a way of barely entering my mind for years, then taking over.

'Ah'll have tae fake ma death for real this time.'

'Eh . . . what?'

'Every cunt else thinks Ah'm dead, so now she needs tae think it tae.' Then I can go back to killing people and trolling on Twitter without worrying about impending doom from a nun who's a mixer short of a cocktail. I really hope I didn't say that last part out loud. Some part of my brain is determined to shop me and put me in an asylum or death row – if I'm lucky. If I'm not, I might end up as an involuntary gimp in San Quentin.

'You can't just fake your death.'

'We've already done it.'

'But that's different. She'll want proof of your dead body. You're not going to give her a dead body, are you? I mean, I'm game for almost anything, but that's serious jail time . . . like . . . I can't ever do that jail time. Ever.'

'Ah'm no a killer.' Lies make baby Jesus cry. Let him cry then. That's what babies do. How else are they going to communicate? Text? Facebook Messenger? That would be too easy.

'Well, how are you going to pull that off?'

244

He's clearly doubtful. This weed I'm puffing is way too strong. Phil's head appears to be giving off an iridescent glow as the light from the telly hits him. The cunt said this stuff was lowish grade. What the fuck have they been doing to it? This is borderline magic mushies. I'll need a few strong drinks and a bump to combat this and get my head straight.

My lack of sleep is getting the better of me. Insomnia seems a by-product of killing people and getting rumbled by your psycho nun sister. Then there's the coke. At least I have my phone to keep me company at all times. The fear of a dead battery right now is worse than two pissed-off detectives chapping the door with my sister chewing their ears. I'll survive as long as I have Twitter, YouTube and Instagram.

I get a beer from the fridge, return and rub coke residue that was spread across the coffee table over my gums. I ignore Phil's concerned looks and remain in control of my emotions by typing *faking death* and *temporary paralysis* into the search bar. It's time to do some proper research and come up with concrete solutions to major problems.

☆

Where else could I find a way to fake my death and get away with it but the internet? Phil returns from his post-sex worker nap and sits in his chair, wafting the air after farting. This place needs a woman's touch or a tactical airstrike of bleach. Oh well.

'Have you moved in the last 24 hours?' he asks me in that cunty tone.

I had slept in the chair for a few hours, looked for faking death solutions and took the overflowing bin out

245

after a line and a whisky. That's more productive than banging some poor woman with no choice and taking a three-hour nap. He thinks because he slept in a bed and went out for a few hours that he's seized the moral high ground when we're both in the dungeon. At least I'm under no illusions.

'There's this scientist guy on Twitter and YouTube who experiments wae spiders,' I say, not answering his question. I've already contacted said scientist who seems up for taking his theories a bit further – for a cash payment, of course. I see Phil shudder; the cunt's a congenital shitebag.

'I hate spiders,' he wavers. 'Like, I actually hate them worse than the Yankees.'

I roll my eyes and swig my beer. 'And Ah'm sure they love fat Hollywood agents wae size ten shoes trying tae kill them fae above.'

'I'm serious. Spiders are evil.' He says this with actual sincerity. I should've taken a picture of it on my phone as it's a rarity.

'They're insects,' I say, simply. People frightened of spiders when there are humans about makes me chuckle. 'They're no dressing in white hoods, burning crosses and sticking their dicks in their sisters.'

'What?'

'Spiders are no evil. They're spiders. And this cunt oan Twitter and that, this scientist, claims he's discovered or created this spider that can paralyse a person for 12 hours.' I can tell he's sceptical from the expression and shaking of his head.

'I don't know. This sounds like Dr Frankenstein stuff. Who is this guy?'

I hesitate because I know the name will ring alarm bells. It did for me too, but my philosophical, evolved nature helps me look past it. 'Dr Rudolf Göring.'

'Fuck no!' Phil blurts out. 'He sounds like a fucking Nazi!' He does have a Josef Mengele vibe and a creepy smirk every time he says his name, but these kinds of scientists/lunatics who get harder than beating Paul Bunyan at a game of Basketball when meddling with nature are hardly your disarming, charming types.

'You're such a fuckin racist,' I say, half-heartedly.

'Yeah, I'm a racist against Nazis.'

'He's just got a German name. That disnae make him a Nazi.'

'He's creating freak spiders that paralyse people!' he protests.

He's such a fucking drama queen. 'Temporarily paralyse people,' I tell him. 'It wears off after 12 hours or thereabouts.'

'How does he know it temporarily paralyses people? What the fuck's he been up to?'

Phil needs more coke and less weed. I get out of my seat and kneel before the coffee table. The old knees creak and crack.

'Jesus Christ, Phil,' I say, starting to cut a few lines to dull all that critical thinking and improve the poor attitude. 'He's done experiments and tested it in a controlled environment.' I assume. 'Don't be such a wee fuckin baby.' Always attack Phil's masculinity. It's paper-thin.

'A baby? I'm not a baby,' he proclaims, getting all touchy. 'This is crazy. I refuse to be a part of it.'

Like he has a choice. He's drowning in this swamp with me, and I'll be fucked if he's getting out without me already on land getting hosed clean.

'Ma sister will haunt us both till oor dying days.' I summon him by holding out the rolled-up 20. 'Now, take these lines.'

BORIS THE SPIDER
AND THE SCIENTIST CUNT

I'm trying to think of a way of not calling this weirdo science cunt 'the spider man', but it's not happening, and Phil isn't too happy about me bringing humour to this predicament. Don't get me wrong, I understand this is a clusterfuck I wouldn't wish on people I tolerate, but it's only temporary paralysis from a genetically manipulated spider. It's not terminal like sticking your head in an alligator's mouth.

The spider man looks how you would expect him to look – basically, dumpy with messy white hair at the side of a bald patch and a pair of horn-rimmed glasses shielding a pair of wide, fierce eyes and a lot of smiling. This isn't putting Phil at ease. Not even several lines and the swanky, if musty-smelling, villa this scientist creep lives in can soothe his troubled soul. His accurate suspicions that I'm a serial killer may have compounded his misgivings. To me, though, searching online for a possibly insane scientist adept at paralysis with the aid of a spider – and later actually sitting in his house – are sound decisions. He doesn't know my sister like I know her. She hasn't given the game away yet that I'm alive, but that's unlikely to last much longer.

Dr Göring is getting all animated as he puts down some cage with a sheet over it on the huge, mahogany coffee table in front of us. Phil sits back on the couch, looking full-fat-mad from too much coke. He nods behind me, and I turn to see a monochrome painting of a depressed, fat clown on the wall. Phil shakes his head, but I ignore him and get to the edge of my seat in anticipation. 'The spider is able to paralyse through a . . . a . . . well, process that—' I cut Dr Nutjob off with a wave of my hand. I could barely retain an emergency service phone number right now, never mind listen to stuff pertaining to a subject I failed in school and haven't picked up much of since.

'Just show us the spider,' I tell Dr Göring, putting the two grand payment on the table. Phil didn't want to part with it, but I know he has a lot more stashed around the apartment due to his mistrust of banks and hatred of the taxman.

'But it's really quite . . .' – with a mischievous glint in his eye, he grins and takes a deep breath that gives me a weird chill – 'f-f-fascinating.'

'Look,' I tell him, firmly, while getting my phone out to provide a nice shield between me and the freak. 'We're both on a lotta cocaine and alcohol. There's no way two people like us will understand this.'

'W-well-well,' he stammers. 'I have ten more of these . . . rare spiders, and it-it-it really-really is . . . well, m-more of a—'

'Will it work?' I bark, interrupting the droning, stuttering prick. I'm trying to look at photos of Monica Bellucci on Instagram here and this cunt's going all David Attenborough on me. There's a time and a place for *Planet Earth*, and this isn't it. I just want my souped-up spider, and I'll be on my way.

'Well, I'm of the mind that it will work . . . 100 per cent,' he says, somewhat befuddled as he whips the sheet away. We see this ugly, hairy, brown and greyish thing that's the size of Mike Tyson's hand, crawling methodically. Phil's eyes bug out at me, his head jerking about like he's got a vibrator on its highest setting in his open mouth.

'That didn't sound like 100 per cent!' Phil squeaks. 'That sounded more 50 per cent at a push!'

'He's just paranoid,' I say, looking at this magnificent, minging creature in a cage. You really do find yourself in some fucked up situations when you're on a binge in L.A.

'Can I watch it happen?' Dr Göring asks, with a mentally cracked expression and wide eyes behind his glasses. He definitely has a touch of the old sadism about him. That's why I'm not going first here, and he's never getting to watch.

'What the hell's that?' Phil asks, pointing at something on the floor in the corner of the living room. I move over on the sticky leather couch and see another framed painting of a clown. At least this one is smiling and in colour, even if it does look like –

'Oh-oh-oh, that's going back up in my rumpus room!' Göring exclaims with a smile. 'It's Pogo!'

'Was that not John Wayne Gacy's clown act when he wasn't, you know, killing teenage boys?' Phil asks, giving me an expression that suggests it's time to leave.

'It-it was indeed!' Göring brings it over, wearing a cheeser, pointing at the signature. 'Look!

'Oh, aye,' I say, ignoring Phil glaring at the side of my face like that spider has just mounted it. 'Ah never knew John Wayne Gacy painted.'

☆

The transparent plastic spider box sits beside empty bottles of booze and Taco Bell boxes on Phil's coffee table. Phil's eyes finally go together, and not even the

251

coke can save him now. In fairness to him, we have been awake for two days and just ate Taco Bell to add to the stink of anal gasses, body odour and spilt beer. Normally, I would've crashed long ago, but I have a plan and determination to see it through. The toilet will be a mess on the next rounds, but that's another delayed problem. Right now, it's all about trying out this spider and getting paralysis on the go.

I keep thinking about Paula. She assumes I'll throw my hands in the air, repent, and stop living life like it's the only one we get. The absolute fucking cheek of it. If I have a soul, it's mine to hawk or surrender to whoever I want. The zeal with which she thinks there are no lost causes, and that every cunt can deny their basic programming like her, is the stuff that padded walls should surround. Yet, in her world, she's more normal than me. I'm the crazy cunt just because I acted in movies, faked my death, took/take lots of drugs and sought ways of paralysing myself to fool people into thinking I'm dead. Say what you want about me, but I'm the cunt actually living instead of lying to myself that I'll get another life to shoot smack to some early Brian Eno or snort ching from a pair of beautiful arse cheeks.

Heaven, for fuck's sake. Well, Paula's not going to expose me as the charlatan and clearly alive cunt I am. I'd rather set this spider loose and take my chances. That's an easier choice now that I've decided to use Phil as my guinea pig. Aye, that's right. It's easier to test this spider shite when you're not the test subject. Of course, Phil doesn't know this yet. He doesn't know much right now, given he's comatose from trying to compete with me in the drug Olympics.

My bigger size and nothing to lose or gain attitude make me odds-on to win any competition with a spoiled

Hollywood agent from a nice middle-class background. It's not fair to expect a level playing field with me. I've crossed over, and nothing short of a heart attack will stop me – not my sister, not collateral damage and not even a part in Scorsese movie.

Phil was on and off the list anyway. He may be a lifeline and a source of money that ultimately came from my efforts and talent, but Phil is a prime candidate to crack under interrogation. One minute of questions, and he'd give up his name, soul, arse and anything else attached to him. In this town, there is no loyalty. Hollywood is a business. It is without sentiment and always about money – and harebrained schemes to fake your death and get left alone by psycho family members.

I cover myself in makeshift PPE – a parka jacket, surgical mask and two pairs of garden gloves. Phil looks like he could be dead already if it weren't for the slight fluctuations in his stomach and chest. If only he knew what I was about to do, he wouldn't look so relaxed.

I jailbreak Boris and let him out into Phil's hovel. This toxic little guy will be right at home about here. This is the best-looking sewer on Earth. Do spiders like sewers? Fuck knows. This spider is an interference job by a mad scientist. You could fire this wee cunt into outer space, and he'd probably return in a spaceship.

I let Boris loose on Phil's midriff, but this isn't as simple as I thought. Nothing is cinematic in this town when there are no cameras.

·'Hurry up and bite him, ya wee ugly shite.' I fetch him with a newspaper and stick him on Phil's left cheek. 'Turn the other cheek.' I crack myself up and no-one else. Talking to myself is becoming more of a problem. Maybe I'm lonely. Maybe it's the drugs talking, or maybe they're not mutually exclusive.

After a minute or so of fucking around, Boris bites, and I feel a wee charge of excitement. I look for a pen to note the time, then try to take a screenshot on my phone right as my battery dies. I take a potent joint from Phil's pocket that I sniff out like a golden retriever and spark it off the gas ring.

☆

I crashed a few hours after smoking that joint and having a wank, but at least I had the presence of mind to note when the spider bit Phil. I battle through the smell of weed, sweat and rotting food to look down at the coke I shaped into the time on the coffee table. Aye, I know, but my phone was dead and charging, and I couldn't find a pen anywhere. Pens will be obsolete soon anyway. They're already a kitsch novelty. We might as well embrace the inevitable.

My phone tells me I've had 12 hours of broken sleep. Sometimes, you just need your 12 hours. It's healthy. Phil should be up by now, but he's still in the same position. I check for a pulse and begin to panic. This kinda thing allied to a 12-hour sleep can take its toll and set in motion the cunt of all hangovers, comedowns and meltdowns. I immediately snort part of the time away. My heart beats like a jackhammer. Ah, shit! Oh fuck! I am Donald fucking Ducked! Phil was my lifeline, and I've killed my lifeline. Getting the spider to bite him seemed a good idea then. Lots of things seem like great ideas when you're off your tits and desperate to keep the bar open.

Phil's dead, and I'm shedding tears for the first time since last week when I had diarrhoea and thought it was the end. Phil was a cunt, but he was my cunt, and now he's another dead cunt I'm responsible for. And the worst of it is, I'll have to dispose of him or flee in a hurry.

I put 'Always Look on the Bright Side of Life' on YouTube. What else am I going to do at a time like this but get on the internet to take the edge off? That lying scientist prick is on Twitter retweeting Elon Musk's shite. His love of Elon should've been an instant red flag. Fucking spiders that paralyse. What the fuck was I thinking? I don't suppose much thinking entered into it. Thinking is overrated, to be fair. Look what happens to people who overthink. A lot of them end up in the gutter or sexless agoraphobes.

I don't want to come over all creationist, backwards and yokel, but this scientist is next for karma. Sometimes, you need to consider the greater good when pondering potential victims. He assured me this would work. He made me feel lower than the layman I am, and now I need to find a way of covering up a corpse like I'm some minder for a royal family. Sure, I've killed, but dismemberment and body disposal are a couple of activities I'm not pissing my knickers with excitement to add to my hobbies list for a potential dating profile.

Part of me wants to leave Phil here and file this whole incident away, but Paula is the wild card here – the world's most boring wild card, but a wild card, nonetheless. I must jettison this corpse to allow me to keep going. It's better to let Paula think we've both done a runner and see what her next play is than for her to find Phil a picture of decomposition. Don't get me wrong, I abhor manual labour as much as the next actor, but I need to get Phil in the boot of the car and take him on a trip. Luckily, I still have enough of a dwindling coke supply to help me get the strength I need to lift my dead agent.

EVEN WEIRDER SCIENCE

Boris is on the loose somewhere, and that's enough to ensure I never return to Phil's. I've got everything I need anyway. Phil wasn't big on banks and savings, especially after the financial meltdown, so he kept stashes around the house and in safe deposit boxes, even with sex workers around. I turned the place upside down and found 28 grand. Not bad for an over-the-hill agent who's always pleading poverty. His holding out makes me feel a bit less guilty about him dying because of me, but I'm sure that won't last long.

The streets are dark, and it's the time of night when perverts, whores and killers really come into their own. I'll include myself in that esteemed company. Aye, I know me struggling and dragging a rolled-up rug with a body is a bit suspect, but a man desperately jamming a rug into the boot at two in the morning isn't too weird in L.A. Seeing nothing untoward or strange would be much weirder. I don't think anyone saw me anyway, apart from a fellow ageing drug casualty, and he probably thought I was packing my magic carpet for Camelot.

I have a plan, and the coke tells me it's the best and most exciting option. The scientist must die, and Phil will sit beside him. I listen to the *Goodfellas* soundtrack on my drive to kill the spider fondler – another obvious choice given the contents of my boot and the backseat. Let's just hope Phil doesn't do a Billy Batts and reanimate while I stop at this KFC drive-through. The

KFC drone on the other side of this intercom thing has a bit of an attitude. I want to pop open the boot and show him what'll happen if he continues getting wide with me, but you know me – I'm calm and collected, to a fault.

☆

I rip into the chicken wings and drive with one hand, letting go of some sulphuric farts that could herald a new leap forward in biological warfare. You usually hear them before you see them about here, and the cops are nearby with their sirens blaring. When you've got coke on you and a body in the boot, a siren tightens your arse like a snare drum and adds another Gordon Ramsay crease to your forehead.

The cops pull up beside me on my right with me in the middle lane, and one with a pasty-white complexion and lantern jaw makes eye contact. A chicken wing falls from my mouth while I pick a lump of coke from my nose. He signals for me to pull over and I sense I may be fucked. I look over at the car on my left and notice two black men in it minding their own business. I'm completely against racial profiling. Of course I am. And I totally abhor racism. Of course I do. But God bless L.A. Some cops here will look past a coked-up white man with a corpse in the boot to pull over two black men driving as if they live in mortal fear of breaching the speed limit.

☆

I reach Göring's house and he lets me in through an intercom to drive past the gate and park right outside his front door under the cover of darkness. For a demented

258

prick, he's way too trusting. I guess I'll need to remedy that.

'So, it worked?' he asks me, keeping me on the doorstep like I'm delivering the sad cunt a pizza.

'It did,' I say with my hands in my jacket, ready.

'Excellent.'

'Can you let me in?' If he allows me in, he's culpable for anything that may happen. I am the vampire of these parts.

'Yes-yes, of course.' He looks behind me and over towards my car. 'Did you bring Boris?' I step to the side and lift up the empty cage with the sheet over it. 'Good. Bring him in.' He turns, and I smack him over the head with my pistol. And again, until he hits the floor.

☆

I finish my KFC and do a few lines. It's always best to line your stomach before getting too high. I've dragged Phil's corpse in and stuck it beside Göring on the wooden floor for dramatic effect and practical purposes. I'll be fucked if I'm digging two graves or cutting up bodies. I don't have the stomach for that, lined or not. I barely have a stomach at all after the abuse I've put it through. Göring begins to stir and his eyes shoot open, muffled nonsense coming from behind his gag.

'Ahh!' he yelps.

Looks like I left that gag too loose. I get sloppy when I do coke and eat too much KFC. I get off my mark and return him to a monosyllabic mess by kneeling and shoving the sock back in before reapplying the tape over it.

'You fuckin lied,' I say. He's trying to speak, but it's unintelligible. I don't know how these sadomasochists persist with all the pageantry and logistics. I prefer to bang and enjoy it without needing safe words and worrying about permanently cutting people's air off. But it suits this cunt. You can tell he's a dark character.

'I-I-I didn't lie,' he lies, after I take the sock from his mouth. 'You just—'

'The spider bit Phil and he died,' I say, looking down at him lying on the floor. Of course, it might've been the drugs and the fact Phil was 61, now that I think about it. Göring slowly sits up and smiles at me. This cunt's a certified nutbag.

'But—'

'Just admit it!'

He blinks at me and remains unusually placid, considering I'm pacing above him with a gun. 'Okay.' He rolls his eyes and shrugs his shoulders. 'I wasn't sure.'

'You seemed fuckin sure!'

'I . . .' He stops, looking all wistful. 'I wanted to see what would happen. It was still . . . hypothetical.'

'Dae you know who Ah am?' I say, and he actually fucking scoffs at me.

'No-no, I don't,' he replies, looking at that painting of the sad, rotund clown that belongs in an incinerator.

Well, that wasn't convincing at all, and he seems like he doesn't even care that it wasn't. 'Ah can tell you're lying.'

'How?' He nods away with a broad smile. I don't think he's appreciating the gravity of this situation. I move closer and bend my knees, looking into his eyes with a blank expression before pointing the gun at the top of his head and leaning over to his right ear.

'Cos Ah'm an actor, and you know Ah'm an actor,' I whisper. 'Every cunt knows that.' I move back around and stand before him, expecting to see the colour drained from his face, but the bastard yawns.

'Wh-what-what are you going to do to me?' he asks, breezily. Fuck me. He's a grade-A creep. 'I never meant for things to . . . go awry with your friend.' He smirks at me. 'Paralysis–'

'Stoap speakin, eh? Ah feel like Ah need a paracetamol wae every fuckin sentence.'

All this talking and grinning makes it justifiable, and there's no time like the present.

Bang!

Blood flies from his chest. He's trying to say something.

'Out wae it!' I boom. I really am a callous bastard. Maybe it's the coke. Maybe it's fucking Maybelline.

'B-b-basement,' he says. 'Base-ment.' He has a crazed look and cracks another fucking smile before closing his eyes.

I can sense there's something fucked in his basement. You get a sixth sense for these things when you're in the house of a weirdo Mengele-type scientist with a genuine John Wayne Gacy and pictures of other less notable, but still horrifying, clowns on his walls.

After walking through his rumpus den with the Pogo painting on the wall, I find the basement and get goosebumps. I sigh and open the hatch door, lighting the stairs with the torch from my phone. There's a switch on the right and I bathe the place in piercing white light as I descend the narrow, creaking, wooden steps, almost gagging on an odour of pish, shit and decay as I go. I hear shuffling and suppressed screams before I see a man of no more than mid-20s, naked and hogtied on the limited floor space, surrounded by stacks of newspapers, journals, magazines and cardboard boxes. Despite my knack for killing cunts myself, I recoil. I slowly make my way over, trying to reassure him with my hands in front of me like I'm an alien coming in peace. I take the gag from his mouth and leave the rest of his ties. He says nothing, only looking up at me with sunken eyes and emaciated cheeks. It's then that I notice another skinny shell of a naked young man lying deathly still in the corner behind a pile of old Playboy and Penthouse magazines.

'He's dead,' splutters a voice from behind me. I swing around with the gun, expecting to see that sicko scientist, but it's the poor naked bastard I just took the gag from. 'He choked him this morning.'

'Jesus,' I mumble, looking down at the corpse of a kid who's all of 20.

'Who are you?' he asks, coughing.

'*His* murderer.' I point above me. 'That freakshow scientist cunt upstairs.'

Göring's would-be next murder victim keeps looking at me, and I don't blame him. He'll make a psychiatrist much richer and heavier with ideas for a harrowing bestselling novel. I know he's kinda seen my face, but that doesn't matter. I have no plans to give a fuck about anything anymore.

'Wait there,' I tell him, as if he has a choice.

'Don't you dare fucking leave!'

'Relax,' I say, walking up the basement stairs without turning back. 'Ah'll untie you when Ah get back.'

'Relax!' he mocks, attempting to mimic my accent. I should've gagged him again. He's exhibiting quite a bad attitude, considering I just saved his skinny arse. I stick to the plan before this wee diversion and go to the boot of my car to get the jerrycan of petrol and a mask.

I stand above Phil's body, blessing myself for reasons probably still unknown even to the best therapist in history. I shake my head and pour petrol over Göring's corpse, the floor and the spider cage. I breathe in the lovely petrol, bringing my lighter out of my pocket to set the fire, when I hear shouting from below.

'Aw, fuck,' I say, remembering that poor cunt in the basement. Maybe I need to cut down on the drugs a bit, get back on the protein bars and make an effort to get a sleep routine again. I sigh, knowing this is more exercise than I need right now. If I weren't such a bleeding heart, I'd save my legs and lungs the trouble, but I guess I must still have empathy.

I open the door to a room that has a neon light illuminating a sex swing, a smell of stale cum and a bed with latex covers. Whatever happened here is best left for anyone other than me to speculate about. I go and open the next door along. It's more of a normal-looking, less semeny bedroom with a glass mirrored wardrobe. On closer inspection, it does have a drawing of Charles Manson with John Wayne Gacy's signature above the unmade king-size bed adorned with Marvel bedsheets. Fuck it. I fish past the plentiful lab coats in the wardrobe, a couple with blood stains, and find a pair of black trousers, a pink T-shirt and a black turtleneck for the captive in the basement. I pass the rumpus room again and ignore Pogo on the wall as best I can.

'You asshole!' comes a muffled shout from the basement. 'Fucking untie me!'

I guess my appreciation must be in the post from this cunt. 'Stop fuckin shouting like that,' I say, entering the basement. 'There's nae need for it.' The stench engulfs me and I remember my wee Covid mask. I pull it over my face, but the thing might melt with this smell.

'What are you doing?' he cries. 'Hurry the fuck up!'

'Don't rush me.' I throw the clothes down in front of him.

'What are those?' he grimaces.

'What?'

'They're hideous! And they look too small.' Is this guy for real? I'm saving what's left of his life and he's calling the fashion police on me. I ignore him, looking around this hellscape for something to cut the knots in the rope tying him. 'Well, what are you waiting for? Get me out of here!' I keep my eyes away from the corpse in the corner, circumvent a shite bucket and look around past the abundant piles of Wall Street Journals and boxes filled with Tupperware, costume jewellery and old McDonald's Happy Meal toys. I pull out Ronald McDonald in a car and drop it. I think I've seen enough clowns for this month. 'What are you, the cleaner? Unite me already!' I move around to face him, eyeballing this mouthy bastard.

'Look! Ah'm getting something tae cut through the fuckin intricate knots he's put you in, so shut the fuck up or Ah'll leave you here tae cook like a fuckin barbecue wing, ya prick, okay?' He looks away from me, muttering something indecipherable. 'What was that?'

'Nothing,' he murmurs, looking at the black turtleneck and shaking his head. I knock over a couple of boxes and find fuck all useful. I stop, sigh and look at the basement stairs and the gun in my hand. I can't kill him just because I can't be bothered doing mild cardio, can I? 'What are you doing?' I could kill him. Easily. But the collateral damage . . . I better not.

'Ah'll be back in a minute,'

'Are you shitting me?'

I struggle back upstairs and go to the spacious, surprisingly upscale kitchen, where I pour and neck a generous shot of Macallan 18-year-old double cask single malt whisky and examine the knife block. I'm not exactly a rope cutting kinda guy, so I just bring the entire block and bottle.

'Ah-ah-ah-aahh,' I hear coming from the living room. What the fuck? I peek my head around the door and see Göring groaning and coughing. Fuck me stone dead. Why can't people just fucking die? Blood is spilling from his mouth, but he's smiling. Is he still baiting me? Fuck this. I sit down the knife block and aim between his crazed eyes.

Bang! His head gets a new hole, and I wipe the sweat from my napper.

'Hey! What's happening up there?' shouts my basement nightmare.

What a night. This is the worst I've sweated since I died.

I head back down, panting, and sit down on the bottom step to catch my breath.

'What the hell was that?' he yells at me. I put my finger in the air to tell him to shut the fuck up and give me a minute, pulling my mask down to swig some whisky. 'Well?' he says, nodding at the knives. Christ, more manual labour without an hourly rate. What have I done to deserve this?

I take a serrated blade and get behind him. 'Be careful now!' he tells me. I start ripping into the rope, clenching my teeth, biceps aching their way out of retirement again. He's still speaking, moaning, but it's white noise. I cut and tear, thinking about my life flashing before my eyes but not seeing much other than me wasted at various movie premieres and parties. I have a wheezing attack and stop. 'Are you alright?' he says. 'You sound like a constipated pig.'

I should've killed this cunt.

I release him, take my mask down and vomit over the already disgusting basement floor. 'Gad,' he mumbles. Don't believe what you see in the movies – the life of a killer is not all glamour. He lays there in the foetal position. All that complaining he did for me to emancipate him from this torture and he doesn't know what to do with himself.

'Well, hurry up and get dressed,' I say, pointing my gun at him just in case. He huffs, turning his nose up at the clothes again like I've left an upsettingly big and stubborn jobby in his previously pristine toilet.

'These are a 36 waist,' he complains. 'I'm a 30 at most.'

'Right!' I snap. 'Put them on upstairs. Ah cannae stand another second in this reeking shithole.' I follow his skinny, bare arse upstairs, trying to ignore his bruises and cuts. Poor cunt. Poor, very annoying, cunt.

In the rumpus room, he throws on the trousers, which are way too small in length and far too big at the waist.

'He must've had some belts,' he snipes at me. 'He's a sadist, for Christ's sake.'

I rub my head with the same hand gripping my gun. 'Just put the rest oan before Ah decorate the ceiling wae your brain.'

'Okay, okay, there's no need to speak to me that way.' He pulls them up more and folds the waist over before dashing over to the bar and lifting a bottle of water from a small fridge. It spills down his chin as he gulps and grunts, like he's auditioning for a blowjob scene.

'Apparently, there *is* a need.'

'That's a thick accent . . . Irish, yeah?' The accent is not as thick as you, son.

'Aye, Irish.' At least if he goes to the cops, they can maybe arrest Bob Geldof for this shitshow.

'What's your name?' he asks, opening a bag of peanuts and putting it to straight to his mouth.

Pfff, like I'm going to start divulging that to the basement hostage when I'm killing his captor to clean up loose ends and fight boredom. 'Dae you want ma national insurance number tae?' I say.

'National what?' he mumbles, nuts avalanching from his gub.

'Just get dressed. This isnae a speed date, fir fuck's sake.'

He snarls at his reflection in a mirror beside the bar in the rumpus room. No wonder. He looks like a below-average-height, out-of-shape man went to sleep under a giant rolling pin, leaving only the clothes intact.

'I want to punch myself,' he says to his reflection.

'You're no the only one,' I retort. 'Come on, let's go.'

'Oh, Pogo!' He goes over to the wall, bringing down that painting. 'This is what I came here to buy before that bastard drugged me.'

'You want that shit?'

'This is a John Wayne Gacy!' he proclaims, like it's a Picasso and not the demented scribblings of an untalented monster. 'I collect murderabilia!' Murderabilia? Good Lord, this cunt might end up owning my fillings one day.

'Right,' I say, pointing to the door for him to exit the rumpus room and, hopefully, my life permanently.

We walk down the hall to the front door and the stink of petrol focuses me. 'Wait here,' I say, locking the door and taking the key.

'I don't have a ride, by the way. That sick fuck brought me here.' Aye, as if I'll be chauffeuring him about to add to the list of what I've done for him. 'I don't even have shoes.' He points to his feet like there's any ambiguity about where he puts his shoes.

'Neither you do.' I give him a smile before walking down the hall to the living room.

'What are you doing?' the insufferable prick shouts from behind me. 'Is that gas I smell?' I get to the living room door, open it and take a few steps inside to light the trail of petrol. I quickly get out of there and down the hall to put the key in the front door. 'Did you just light a fire?'

'Aye!' I yell at him.

'Well, hurry up and open the door!'

'Ah'm trying, ya daft cunt ye!

'Out of the way!' he howls at me, pushing me aside and unlocking the door with one swift flick of the wrist.

'Right,' I say, remembering the porch of a burning house of corpses is the last resort for a loiter. 'Nice knowing you.' I point the gun at him and shoosh him along with it. He looks down at his feet and back at me, shaking his head, Pogo in his hands. But I'm all out of sympathy for him. My only sympathy right now is for the firefighters.

FIRE DOWN

The fire spread to the nearby wooded area, and Charlie, in a perilous mental state, began ascribing great meaning to coincidence and saw synchronicities everywhere. A misguided understanding of karma had set him on a path, and now, he was dead and burning down parts of California with it. His brain was mush, and insomnia fuelled by cocaine and Twitter turned him into a coiled spring. He'd sunk to downtown L.A. after setting the fire with the intention of only staying for one night in a cheap, seedy hotel before fleeing California and starting anew, but he'd become stuck there for two weeks and ditched hopes of anything better.

Lying to himself, intensified with his coke use, he was delusional most of the day. He made lists and threw them away. *Quit while you're ahead*, he told himself. *You'll get caught eventually*. Every cunt did these days. The heyday of serial killing went out with DNA, surveillance cameras and the internet. He knew he was getting sloppy and complacent. It wasn't sustainable. The faces were haunting him: Phil, the collateral damage, his da, his mum, his kids, Maggie Thatcher. It was enough to send any sane person catatonic, never mind Charlie.

All his victims filtered into the room. He told himself it was all fiction. They were only ancillary characters in an epic movie, but even in L.A., he knew this was a bullshit coping mechanism. He was a presumed dead actor who had spent his leisure time killing people he had a grudge against.

A loaded gun sat in front of him in his dingy hotel room with the abandoned, lawless Skid Row just beyond its walls, but blowing his brains out seemed way too theatrical for a movie actor. That sort of thing was alright when it was fake, but disfiguring a handsome, legendary face of the silver screen would be an affront to creation. It was too grand a statement.

SHOULD'VE WON AN OSCAR

I know I will survive as long as I have drugs to take. It might not be pretty, but it's life. People in other countries have to walk miles for contaminated water. People in other countries are exploding in front of their loved one's eyes. Where's their fucking karma?

All things considered, I'm not too bad. Sure, this tiny, crumbling hotel room is a shitehole. Sure, everyone on this floor is jailbait, on junk or another Richard Ramirez in waiting, but home is what you make it. Skid Row is out there, and I'm in here with half-decent Wi-Fi.

Some sex worker on smack told me that evil bastard Richard Ramirez kipped here from time to time when he had to crash after killing, raping, and breaking and entering. It's always nice when your room has a backstory, even if it is horrific. I guess some people will see me as a monster fit for a horror movie, especially if I add more victims to pad out my true crime series and make Netflix an offer they can't refuse.

I don't have the desire to keep doing all this killing. Well, not at the minute anyway. Right now, I'm checking in on my kids online again. I want to reach out to them, but not in this state, not like this. I don't know what I'd say anyway. How does a person announce they're back from the dead? Only Hollywood has any frame of reference for that, and Hollywood is long overdue a colonic.

There's a Bible in here, but I'm not opening that Pandora's box. It's better as a little reminder of the paradoxical nature of everything. Down on the street, people are fighting, spewing and scratching their arms until they bleed, but in my damp and BO-smelling room, they're selling me salvation and eternity in paradise. If there is a heaven, I'm not a hot candidate for it, am I? Even before the murders, I could feel the heat of somewhere else.

My new profile on Twitter – sorry, Musk's dick X-tender – now says feel the heat under my photo of a tree. I have nine followers and follow twelve. It was a shame to lose my last handle, but I got nervous after I posted abuse about the Pentagon and Elon Musk's endowment.

@zombiefuckredux
> @DalaiLama Chairman Mao can stir ma porridge any day. He knew what was good for Tibet.

I have to deal with the reality that I was once someone, and now I'm no-one. A non-person living in squalor with coke, crack and smackheads everywhere. But it's better to live in ignorance and misery than to contemplate too much. You know how I feel about too much reality.

I expect the drugs and the stress of my current deprivation will finish me off, and I'll be just another dead punter in one of the biggest toilets in the world. My new list has my name on the bottom of it. I was so high and drunk when I wrote it that I misspelt my surname. That's quite a feat for a man who still fantasises about his name in lights and on movie posters. Sad, I know. But life is a sad joke when you're on Skid Row watching yourself in a film you nearly won an Oscar for on an antique telly.

I'm running low on cash, but I've never been much of a saver or sensible planner. I'm more of a live for today and potentially die today kinda guy. We can't all live until we're 100, having barely lived a day. Some of us need to keep you motivated to turn up at proper jobs and hit that CrossFit like you can outrun time and the reaper. You're welcome.

I watch myself on the telly, heaving the body of my dead bank robber accomplice into the river.

'Ah should've fuckin won that Oscar,' I say as I enjoy watching the tear running down the cheek of a man who I need to remind myself was me.

Bang!

Someone's at the door with the fist of Goliath. I turn my crowning moment up to full volume.

Bang!

Nicholas fucking Silverton and Shackler.

Bang!

My door is booted open and serious, snarling faces burst into my shitey room, armed with guns and badges. I wish I could say it was The Village People, but it's not.

'Ah should've won that Oscar, ya bastards!'

ACKNOWLEDGMENTS

To my family and friends, may you live long, enjoy it and see any enemies off to the cemetery.

To my editor, the great Dickson Telfer, for the excellent attention to detail and advice.

To Derek and the rest of the fantastic people at *Razur Cuts*.

To my daughter, Erin. Thank you for being everything you are and gifting me the sleep deprivation that helped me come up with this novel.

John Tinney got wrenched from the womb in Rottenrow Hospital, Glasgow, which he thought was called Rock 'n' Roll Hospital before better cotton bud technique. This momentous event for him occurred on Friday the 13th, a date picked specifically for the challenge. He grew up in the tranquil, always sunny Gorbals and Govanhill, and still lives in Glasgow's southside.

BOOKS

razurcuts.com

@razurcutsmag
@johntinney888